"So you think Ellen Williams is the one?"

"Eleanor," Luke corrected automatically. "And I won't know till I've had a chance to talk to her a bit more."

"I don't know, Luke. Marrying's a serious business." The laughter died out of Daniel's eyes, which were the same clear gray as his brother's. "Maybe this ain't such a good idea after all. Maybe we ought to just forget the whole idea and try another housekeeper."

Luke opened his mouth to agree that it had been a dumb idea from the start and that they should put it behind them. And found himself remembering Eleanor's big brown eyes, the shy smile in them, and heard her voice saying that she'd lived in Black Dog six years, four months and twelve days.

"I said I was going to find a wife and that's what I'm going to do," he heard himself say stubbornly. For some reason, the idea of having a wife just didn't seem as bad as it once had.

Dear Reader,

This month, we are very pleased with the long-awaited return of Dallas Schulze to Harlequin Historicals with her terrific new Western, *Short Straw Bride*. This award-winning author, who has written numerous contemporary novels for Silhouette and Harlequin, will make her MIRA debut in early 1997. Meanwhile, don't miss this heartwarming tale of two people who marry for practical reasons, and wind up falling head over heels in love.

Reader's Choice Award winner Laurie Grant is also back with her new medieval novel *My Lady Midnight*. This intriguing story features a Norman widow who becomes a political pawn when she is forced to go undercover as a governess in the home of the baron she believes responsible for the death of her best friend.

Miranda Jarrett's new Sparhawk book, *Gift of the Heart*, is a touching story set in the wilds of the New York frontier where a woman, abandoned by her no-good husband, discovers happiness in the arms of a fugitive haunted by his past. And *Beauty and the Beast*, by Taylor Ryan, is a Regency tale about a troubled nobleman who is badgered into health by an interfering young neighbor.

We hope you'll keep a lookout for all four titles wherever Harlequin Historicals are sold.

Sincerely,

Tracy Farrell
Senior Editor

Please address questions and book requests to:
Harlequin Reader Service
U.S.: 3010 Walden Ave., P.O. Box 1325, Buffalo, NY 14269
Canadian: P.O. Box 609, Fort Erie, Ont. L2A 5X3

DALLAS SCHULZE

SHORT STRAW BRIDE

Harlequin Books

TORONTO • NEW YORK • LONDON
AMSTERDAM • PARIS • SYDNEY • HAMBURG
STOCKHOLM • ATHENS • TOKYO • MILAN
MADRID • WARSAW • BUDAPEST • AUCKLAND

ISBN 0-373-28939-1

SHORT STRAW BRIDE

This edition published by arrangement with Harlequin Books S.A.

® and TM are trademarks of the publisher. Trademarks indicated with
® are registered in the United States Patent and Trademark Office, the
Canadian Trade Marks Office and in other countries.

Printed in U.S.A.

Books by Dallas Schulze

DALLAS SCHULZE

loves books, old movies, her husband and her cat, not necessarily in that order. A sucker for a happy ending, she finds that her writing gives her an outlet for her imagination. Dallas hopes that readers have half as much fun with her books as she does! She has more hobbies than there is space to list them, but is currently working on a doll collection. Dallas loves to hear from her readers, and you can write to her at P.O. Box 241, Verdugo City, CA 91046.

Chapter One

"There's just no getting around it, Luke. We need a wife."

Daniel McLain's tone was grim, befitting the serious nature of his pronouncement.

"There's got to be some other way." Luke's expression was even bleaker than his brother's.

"None that I can see." Daniel splashed a goodly measure of whiskey into his glass and then did the same for Luke. "We've put a lot of work into this place. If something happens to us, the ranch'll be sold to some stranger. Neither of us wants to see that."

Luke could have pointed out that, under those circumstances, they wouldn't actually *see* the ranch fall into someone else's hands, but he didn't. Daniel's logic might be slightly skewed but there was a basic truth in what he was saying.

"A son. That's what we gotta have, Luke. One of us has to have a son to take over when we're gone."

"It isn't like either one of us has a foot in the grave," Luke said with some annoyance. At thirty, he didn't consider himself yet on a nodding acquaintance with eternity. "We've got plenty of time to think about wives and sons and who's going to take over when we're gone."

"Maybe." Daniel's expression was solemn. "But Heck Sloane was younger than both of us and Bill Parley wasn't even thirty-five. Look at them."

In point of fact, no one could actually *look* at either man. They'd both met their demise in the past six months.

"Heck was a fool to take on that shootist. Him and those damned pearl-handled Colts of his were just looking for an excuse to die young."

"Bill didn't have pearl-handled Colts," Daniel noted gloomily. He was well into his third glass of whiskey and clearly feeling the fell hand of fate on his shoulder.

"No, but he had that hammerhead roan. Meanest horse this side of Julesburg. It's a wonder he didn't throw Bill into a wall years ago."

"It could have happened to either one of us," Daniel said, reaching for the whiskey bottle.

"Not unless one of us is stupid enough to get on a horse that's half rattler and the other half just plain mean," Luke said. But the words lacked conviction.

The fact was that it didn't take a mean horse or overestimating your talent with a gun to get a man killed, and they both knew it. Even a good horse could step in a prairie dog hole or get spooked by a rattlesnake. A man left alone on the prairie, without a horse and far from home, stood a fair chance of dying of thirst or exposure. Hell, it didn't even take anything dramatic to end a life. Their own father, as tough a man as Luke had ever known, had torn open his hand on a nail and died of blood poisoning a week later.

Luke frowned at the scarred surface of the kitchen table. He reached for the makings and rolled himself a cigarette, scraping a match across the tabletop. He frowned at the mark it left behind. If their mother were alive she'd have skinned him alive for leaving a mark on her clean table and then she'd have done it again for daring to smoke in her kitchen. But she'd been dead for three years now and the once-immaculate room bore evidence of its neglect since then.

The thin lamplight revealed that neglect with merciless clarity. The big iron stove was covered with a thick layer of baked-on grease, bits of food and soot. The muslin curtains that had once hung in crisp white panels in front of the windows were gray with dirt. Not that it mattered much, since the window behind them hadn't been washed in three years. The wooden floor his mother had been so proud of, that had been brought in from Denver, was obscured by the same layer of filth that covered everything else.

Luke stirred uneasily and reached out to rub his thumb over the black streak the match had left. Erasing it left a slightly cleaner spot on the dirty tabletop. He could almost see his mother's accusing eyes, feel her disapproval. Though the whole house would just about have fit into the ballroom of her father's home in Virginia, Lucinda McLain had been proud of this house, proud of the work her husband and sons had put into building it for her.

The McLains might have lost almost every material possession in the War Between the States but they hadn't lost the most important things—their pride and determination. At the war's end they'd sold what they could, abandoned what couldn't be sold or brought with them and moved west, chasing the dream of a new life, just as it seemed half the country was doing.

They'd lived in a soddy at first, literally building their home from the land around them.

He and Daniel had broken wild horses to sell to the army and used the money to buy cattle. Those first years had been hard. All four of them had worked from sunrise to sunset—can see to can't see.

Before the war Lucinda McLain had never had to dirty her hands on anything outside the home, and even there, she'd had servants to help her. But she'd learned to milk a cow and use a hammer. Her hands had grown callused and her pale skin had burned in the hot sun but she'd never forgotten that she was a lady and she'd never let her sons forget that they were gentlemen. They might have been eating day-old bread and beans but there was always a linen tablecloth, even if the table was a wooden crate. And no matter how many hours she'd put in working outside, she'd still made sure her husband and sons had clean clothes, even if they were mended.

Luke frowned and picked at a three-corner tear just above the knee of his jeans. When had they last been washed? he wondered uneasily.

"Thinking about Mother?" Daniel asked, reading his older brother's mind.

"Place doesn't look the way it did when she was alive," Luke said.

Daniel followed his gaze around the kitchen, taking in the dirt that covered every exposed surface. The rest of the house was in slightly better shape, but only because they didn't spend much time in any of the other rooms.

"She'd box both our ears," Daniel admitted, looking uneasily over his shoulder as if expecting to see his mother's shade bearing down on them.

"We could hire a housekeeper," Luke suggested.

"We tried that. Twice. The first one drank every drop of liquor in the house and damn near burned the place down. The second was more interested in finding a husband than in cooking a meal."

"As I recall, you were the husband she had in mind. She might have caught you, too, if you'd been a mite slower." Luke grinned at the memory of his brother's panicked reaction to the housekeeper's blatant pursuit.

"You didn't think it was so funny when she turned her sights on you," Daniel observed. "Besides, a housekeeper isn't going to solve the problem of having a son to leave the ranch to."

"I wish you'd stop talking like we both had one foot in the grave," Luke said irritably.

"We aren't getting any younger, and having a son isn't like ordering a new saddle. It can take a little time."

"Nine months, last I'd heard." Luke ground the end of his cigarette out in a plate left over from breakfast. Or was it supper the night before?

"First you've got to find a wife. And then you've got to go about the business of making babies. It took Dick Billings and his wife almost five years to have their first."

"If I had a wife as pretty as Almira Billings, I don't think I'd mind five years of trying," Luke said with a grin. "Besides, all that practice must have paid off, since they're working on their third in six years."

"All we need to do is find you a pretty girl, then," Daniel said cheerfully.

Luke choked on a mouthful of whiskey. During the ensuing fit of coughing, his brother pounded him on the back with helpful force, nearly dislocating a shoulder in the process.

"Find *me* a pretty girl?" Luke wheezed when he regained enough breath for speech. "Since when am I in the market for a wife?"

"I thought you agreed that we need a wife." Daniel's dark eyes widened in surprise.

"If *we* need a wife, why am *I* the one getting one?"

"You're the oldest. It's only fitting that you get to marry first."

"Get to marry first?" Luke raised one dark eyebrow, questioning the privilege his brother had just offered him. "I'm not a consumptive old maid and you're not a snake oil salesman, so there's no sense in you trying to weasel me into getting hitched. Seems to me that *you* should be the one to find a wife. You're younger, less set in your ways."

"I'm only three years younger," Daniel protested. "Besides, I don't want to get married." The thought was enough to make him reach for his glass and down a healthy shot of whiskey.

"I don't want to get married, either," Luke noted.

There was a lengthy silence while they considered the problem. Outside, a cricket scratched plaintively, the sound swallowed by the vast emptiness of the land.

"We could draw straws," Daniel said. "Whoever gets the short straw has to find a wife."

"Might work." Luke rolled the idea around. It wasn't ideal. Of course, the only thing that would be ideal was to forget the whole thing. But Daniel was right, they did need a wife. And since neither of them *wanted* a wife, it was only fair to let chance decide which of them had to be sacrificed on the matrimonial altar.

He got up and crossed to where the broom leaned in the corner. A thick lacing of cobwebs tied it to the wall and the handle stuck to his fingers. Frowning, he lifted it and broke two dusty straws off the bottom. He brought them back to the table and sat down again. Daniel watched as he measured the two straws and then carefully broke one off halfway down. There'd be no mistaking which of them had drawn the short straw.

"You sure about this?" Luke asked.

Daniel dragged his eyes upward to meet his brother's. "I'm sure."

Without looking at what he was doing, Luke rolled the straws between his fingers, then closed his fist around them. "You first."

Both men looked down. The tops of both straws were visible above the tanned skin of his hand. One straw was higher than the other but there was no telling which was longer overall. Daniel studied the two straws as intently as if his life depended on it, which, Luke guessed, it more or less did. He reached out, his fingers hovering above Luke's hand, and then quickly drew a straw, choosing the one that showed the least.

There was a moment's silence and then Daniel drew a deep, relieved breath. His face expressionless, Luke slowly opened his hand and stared at the short piece of straw lying on his palm.

Damned if he wasn't going to have to find himself a wife.

Eleanor Williams leaned her elbows on the windowsill and looked up at the fat yellow moon. It sat in the middle of the sky, surrounded by twinkling stars like a plump matron with dozens of servants dancing attendance. But Eleanor barely noticed the beauty of the view.

Today had been her birthday. She was now twenty years old and, according to her cousin, Anabel, could consider herself practically an old maid. The catty remark was the only acknowledgment there'd been of Eleanor's birthday and Anabel had only mentioned it because it gave her an opportunity to say something unpleasant. Unfortunately, in this case, Anabel's nastiness was nothing more than the truth. She *was* practically an old maid, Eleanor admitted with a sigh. And likely to remain that way as long as she was so completely overshadowed by her younger cousin.

Anabel had just turned sixteen and had every expectation of being a wife before her next birthday. How could she not be, pretty as she was? Her hair was the color of just-ripened wheat, all soft and golden, and when it was tied up in rags, it turned into perfect ringlets that set off Anabel's pink-and-white complexion like a gilded frame.

Unlike Anabel's obedient golden locks, Eleanor's waist-length hair was a mass of thick, soft curls that refused to be completely tamed. Even now, when she'd just braided it for bed, tiny curls had already sprung loose to lie against her forehead. And instead of being rich gold, it was a plain brown—dirt brown Anabel had told her when Eleanor first came to live with her aunt and uncle six years ago.

With a sigh, Eleanor released the heavy braid, letting it fall back over her shoulder. It wasn't just Anabel's golden hair that made her so lovely. Her eyes were a beautiful clear blue, the color of a summer sky, as one smitten swain had told her. No one was going to wax poetic about plain brown eyes. And Anabel was tall. Not too tall, Aunt Dorinda would have quickly pointed out. Just tall enough to display the elegant slenderness of her figure.

Thank heavens her Anabel wasn't a little dab of a thing, Eleanor had once heard Aunt Dorinda say, with a pointed glance in her niece's direction. At barely five feet tall and with a figure that was neither elegant nor slender, Eleanor couldn't even attribute the remark to Dorinda Williams's acid tongue. She *was* a little dab of a thing, and there was just no getting around it.

His little chicken, her father had called her. Always fussing over him like a mother hen with only one chick, he'd tease. Every night he'd come to her room wherever they were staying and she'd solemnly inspect his person. Always, there'd been some small flaw for her childish fingers to adjust—a tie not quite properly tied, a lock of hair slightly out of place, a loose button to be quickly stitched onto the crisp white linen of his shirt.

The memory made Eleanor smile. It was only after he was gone that it had occurred to her that those little flaws had been deliberate. Nathan Williams had understood his daughter's need to be needed. If they'd had a settled home, she could have fussed with the cooking and cleaning. But he was a gambler and they rarely stayed in one place more than a few weeks at a time. Since he couldn't give her a house to fuss over, he'd given her himself.

Eleanor's mother had died when Eleanor was six, and for the next eight years she'd traveled with her father. Nathan Williams had been a gambler by profession. He'd started out gambling on the Mississippi riverboats before the war. When he married Emmeline St. Jacques, he'd purchased a store in St. Louis and settled down to try his hand at being a tradesman. Eleanor had vague memories of a high-ceilinged room, with sawdust on the floor and goods piled high on every side.

But after Emmeline's death Nathan hadn't been able to stay in one place, and he'd gone back to his old profession. He'd brought his young daughter west and they'd traveled from town to town, staying in each only a short while, until he judged it time to take his skill with the cards and move on. It hadn't been a conventional upbringing and Eleanor knew there were those who'd say that he'd had no business dragging a child all over the country the way he had. But she'd never minded the travel as long as she could stay with her father.

It had been six years since he was killed by a stray bullet in a barroom quarrel between two cowpunchers, and she still missed him. Eleanor's eyes grew wistful, remembering her father's quiet smile and the gentle warmth of his laugh. There was rarely any laughter in her Uncle Zebediah's house. When she'd first come here, newly orphaned and almost paralyzed with grief, one of the first things she'd noticed was how seldom her aunt and uncle smiled.

At first she'd thought it was because they were sorry about her father's death, but it hadn't taken long for her to realize that Zebediah had sternly disapproved of his older brother's profession. Gambling was an activity steeped in sin and, as far as they were concerned, Nathan's death in a common barroom brawl was confirmation that God punished all sinners, even if it did occasionally take Him a little longer than Zeb would have liked.

Eleanor might have been offended on her father's behalf if she hadn't already begun to realize that there wasn't much that Zeb and Dorinda Williams *didn't* disapprove of. Where her father had always made it a point to find pleasure, even in small things, his younger brother and his wife seemed to try to do just the opposite. They could find fault with anyone and anything, no matter how small. Over the past six years Eleanor could almost count the number of times she'd seen a real smile from either of them, and she couldn't ever remember hearing them laugh.

Anabel smiled and laughed, but her smiles were well practiced in front of her mirror and her laughter was generally at someone else's expense. Her parents doted on her, and they'd spoiled her terribly. Anabel had only to express an interest in something for them to leap to get it for her, whether it was a new pink ribbon for her golden curls or watercolor lessons to show off her refined sensitivity to the finer things in life.

It was no wonder she was so bone-deep selfish.

Anabel had been only ten when Eleanor came to stay, but she'd already been well versed in getting her own way. At the suggestion that she might share her big, sunny bedroom with her cousin, Anabel's pretty pink complexion had flushed an ugly shade of red and she'd begun screaming. Eleanor could still remember her cousin standing in the middle of the parlor, her hands clenched into fists at her sides, her body rigid with anger as shriek after shriek issued from her perfect Cupid's-bow mouth.

Eleanor, dazed by the abrupt changes in her life, had waited in vain to see one of Anabel's parents slap her to stop her hysteria. Dorinda's pale blue eyes had filled with tears and she'd quickly promised her daughter that ''Mommy's precious'' wouldn't have to share her room with her cousin. After all, Dorinda had told her husband, without regard for Eleanor's presence, there was no telling what kind of manners they could expect from a child raised in saloons. Best not to risk Anabel's delicate sensibilities by subjecting her to bad influences.

Eleanor could have told them that she'd never been in a saloon in her life and that she certainly had better manners than her young cousin, but it hadn't seemed worth the effort. She'd been grateful for the privacy afforded by the boxy little room at the rear of the house—the maid's room, Anabel had pointed out with a smug smile the first time they were alone together—and the more she got to know her cousin, the stronger her gratitude had become.

When she'd first come here her aunt had explained that she undoubtedly had a great deal to learn about proper living. Raised as she had been, she'd no doubt picked up many improper notions, and such notions wouldn't be tolerated in the Williams household. Six years later, Eleanor still didn't know what 'improper notions' she might have had, but she did know that if this was "proper living," she was not impressed. Zebediah and Dorinda Williams might be proper but they were also small-minded, parsimonious people who took no pleasure in life.

She sighed again and rested her chin on the hands she'd propped on the windowsill. She could leave, of course, but she had no money and no way to earn a living. Though her father had done his best to shield her from the more sordid realities of life, she'd seen enough to know just how difficult the world could be for a woman on her own.

She might be able to wangle a job as a school-teacher in some remote area. There was always a crying need for such. Or she could marry Andrew Webb and become a mother to his four small children. She could do worse. Andrew was pleasant enough and, as owner of the general store, considered a good catch, particularly for a young woman of no real beauty or expectations, as her aunt Dorinda had pointed out when Mr. Webb began making his interest in her niece obvious. *It isn't as if Eleanor can simply have her pick of beaux, after all. Not like dear Anabel.* This last had been said with a fond look at her daughter, who'd managed to blush and look modest, no mean feat for a girl who spent nearly every waking moment in front of a mirror.

Aunt Dorinda was right, of course. She could do worse than to encourage Mr. Webb. It was just that... The thought trailed off as a cloud drifted across the face of the moon. A light breeze blew through the open window, its chill cutting through the light cotton of her nightgown. Shivering, Eleanor rose from the trunk where she'd been sitting and lowered the window.

It was just that she was a silly, romantic fool, she told herself as she climbed into her narrow bed and pulled the covers up around her shoulders. She was still clinging to the childish idea of a handsome knight who'd ride into her life and fall instantly under the spell of her negligible charms.

It was past time to put away such foolish notions, she told herself briskly. She was twenty now, no longer a girl. Unless she wanted to prove that little cat Anabel right and end up an old maid, it was time to stop looking for a handsome knight and start thinking of marrying a good man with whom to build a solid, dependable foundation for the future.

An image of Andrew Webb's thin face and watery blue eyes rose in her mind's eye and she felt her determination falter. She wasn't clear on just what intimacies being married entailed, but whatever they were, it was difficult to imagine sharing them with Mr. Webb. Still, his first wife had clearly had no difficulty doing so, as witness the four children she'd given him before falling victim to consumption.

Eleanor set her chin with determination. Tomorrow was Sunday and she was sure to see Mr. Webb at church, since he attended the services as regularly as the Williams family. When she saw him, she'd do her best to discreetly indicate that his attentions were not unwelcome. If she was not mistaken in the strength of his feelings, she could find herself Mrs. Andrew Webb before the summer was out.

She used the edge of the sheet to dry a tear from her cheek. It was the sensible, mature thing to do. If it wasn't the love match of her childish dreams, it would certainly be better than spending the rest of her life as Aunt Dorinda's unpaid housekeeper.

Closing her eyes, Eleanor forced back tears that threatened to spill over. Despite the turmoil of her thoughts, she was soon asleep. Through her dreams drifted images of a dark-haired man with a dazzling smile who swept her up onto the back of his horse and carried her off to a castle that sat incongruously in the middle of the prairie.

Chapter Two

The last time anyone could remember the Mc-Lain brothers setting foot inside a church was three years past when their mother had been laid to rest beside her husband. So their arrival on this fine spring morning created a buzz of talk as people wondered what had caused their sudden attack of piety.

The speculation was already well advanced by the time Eleanor's family arrived. Zeb Williams had a firm, if unspoken, belief that God rewarded not merely godliness but punctuality. But this morning Anabel had been unable to find a particular hair ribbon and their departure had been delayed while the house was searched for the missing item. Though the pink ribbon was found in Anabel's reticule, exactly where she'd apparently put it, the blame for their lateness had somehow fallen on

Eleanor and she'd been treated to a telling silence on the carriage ride.

She was actually grateful for the opportunity to review the decision she'd made the night before. Though she tried desperately to find some flaw in the plan, none presented itself. No matter how she looked at it, marrying Andrew Webb seemed the best option available to her. He was a respectable man, a kind man, even. She'd be a very foolish girl indeed to turn him away.

So, when Mr. Webb greeted the Williams family today, she'd put on her very best smile for him and try to look as if the prospect of wedding a man with cold, damp hands and four small children filled her with something other than dread.

But the whispered buzz that hummed through the small church pushed all thoughts of Andrew Webb momentarily aside. Of course, even without the whispers running through the pews, Eleanor would have noticed the McLains. They sat in the front pew, next to the aisle. Broad shoulders beneath neat black coats, dark hair worn just a little too long for complete respectability—even from the back, they drew a woman's eyes.

Though she'd attended church there every Sunday for six years, it seemed to Eleanor as if the building was suddenly much smaller than it had been, as if the McLains' presence filled up the available space in some way that mere mortal men had no business doing.

It was doubtful that anyone paid much attention to the Reverend Sean Mulligan's sermon that day. Eleanor certainly couldn't have repeated a word of it. When the sermon ended, the murmured amens were perfunctory, everyone's mind occupied with things of more immediate interest than the hereafter.

It was the normal practice for people to linger in front of the church, exchanging greetings with each other, complimenting the minister on his sermon. On this particular Sunday there was only one topic of conversation among the womenfolk—what had brought the McLains to church after all this time. And though the men pretended to be above such common speculation, it didn't stop their eyes from sliding to where the McLains stood talking with Reverend Mulligan.

Cora Danvers suggested that they'd come to repent their sins in the eyes of the Lord. But no one who looked at either McLain—and *everyone* was looking at them—could give much credence to that theory. Neither of them looked as if they felt the need for repentance. There was too much confidence in the way they moved, too much arrogance in the way they carried themselves.

Perhaps they were lonely, Millie Peters said. After all, they were orphans, alone and without family. Her soft blue eyes teared up at the thought, her plump face crumpling in sympathy, and Eleanor had no doubt that Millie would try to take the McLains under her wing. But they didn't look as though they needed Millie's wing, nor anyone else's, for that matter.

She'd never actually seen either Luke or Daniel McLain but, like most people in Black Dog, she knew who they were. They owned the largest ranch in the area, a ranch their father had begun and that they'd continued to build after his death. Their patronage kept half the businesses in town in the black. She knew Mr. Webb's store depended in large part on orders from the Bar-M-Bar.

But she wasn't thinking about Andrew Webb as she watched the brothers talk to Reverend Mulligan. Though there was a strong resemblance between them, it was the taller of the two who drew her eyes. He looked dangerous, she thought, studying his profile. A strong chin, an almost hawkish nose, his hair brushing the collar of his conservatively cut black coat—there was something just a little untamed about him. And the gun that rested so snugly on his hip completed the image. Not that he was the only man wearing a gun—this was still a wild land in many ways, after all, and most men went armed. It wasn't the presence of the gun but the ease with which he wore it that was just a little shocking.

As if sensing her gaze, he turned his head abruptly and their eyes met across the packed dirt of the churchyard. He was too far away for her to see the color of his eyes but she felt the impact of that look all the way to her toes. She knew she should look away, that it wasn't ladylike to stare, but she couldn't drag her gaze from his.

"Stop staring like a cheap tart. Try to at least pretend you're a lady," Dorinda Williams hissed in her ear. Eleanor gasped as her aunt's fingers found the tender flesh on the back of her arm in a vicious pinch. She lowered her lashes to conceal quick tears of pain. Out of the corner of her eye she saw Anabel smile with pleasure and had to restrain a most unladylike urge to slap her smug pink-and-white face.

"What I've got in mind is a gentle girl, one who won't be too demanding," Luke said. "I've got enough on my hands with the ranch work. I don't want a wife who expects me to dance attendance on her."

Sean Mulligan had known Luke and Daniel since the family had first moved to Black Dog after the war. He'd been a friend of their father's, and he'd often thought that Robert McLain would have been proud of the way his sons had kept the ranch going after his death, fulfilling his dream. He was fond of both boys—men, he corrected himself, looking up at the two of them. He'd been pleased to see them in his church this morning, but his pleasure had rapidly changed to dismay as he'd listened to Luke coolly outline his plan to find a wife.

"I don't want to waste a lot of time," Luke was saying now. "Spring's a busy time, what with calving and all."

"Finding a wife isn't like buying a horse, Luke," Sean protested.

"Buying a horse would be a damn sight easier," Daniel put in, grinning at his older brother. "Just check the bloodlines, look at the teeth, take it for a ride and you know what you're getting. Too bad you can't do the same with a woman."

"Well, you can't," Sean snapped. He dabbed at the beads of sweat on his forehead. The mild spring sunshine suddenly felt uncomfortably warm.

"It can't be that hard, Sean," Luke said, looking impatient. "People get married all the time."

"Yes, but they generally spend some time getting to know one another. They court. A man doesn't just pick out a bride like . . . like . . ."

"Like picking out a horse?" Daniel supplied helpfully.

"Exactly."

"I don't have time for courting, and we can get to know each other after the wedding. As long as she doesn't have a temper like a wolverine or a face like a mud fence, we'll do fine. I need a wife, not a best friend."

"But . . ." Sean sputtered and dabbed the handkerchief frantically over his forehead. How could he explain the impossibility of what Luke wanted?

"There must be some unmarried females in town," Luke said, his eyes skimming the crowd, unconcerned with the interest he was receiving in return.

"Yes," Sean admitted cautiously.

"What about the redhead in the blue dress?" Luke asked, narrowing his eyes on the statuesque girl.

"Dorcus O'Hara," Sean supplied, following Luke's gaze. Sensing their gaze on her, the girl lifted her chin. "I don't think she's what you have in mind, Luke. Dorcus is a bit, er, high strung," he said delicately.

"Temper like a hungry grizzly?" Daniel asked shrewdly.

"Well, er, yes," Sean admitted, sighing.

"What about the little one with the brown hair? The one wearing the blue dress and the ugly hat?"

"Eleanor Williams." Sean's pale blue eyes widened in surprise.

"She taken?"

"Not that I know of."

"Ain't much to her," Daniel commented. "What about the yellow-haired one next to her?"

"That's her cousin, Anabel."

"Too narrow between the eyes," Luke said critically. "Reminds me of that mule we had in Virginia, the one that'd try to bite anything came within reach."

Sean choked on swallowed laughter, trying to imagine Anabel Williams's reaction to hearing herself compared to a bad-tempered mule.

"Why don't you introduce me to a few possibilities?" Luke asked his father's old friend.

Eleanor watched discreetly as Reverend Mulligan began introducing the McLains around. Her eyes lingered on the taller one and she felt her heart beat a little faster when he smiled at something his brother said. His teeth gleamed white against his tanned features and she thought she'd never seen a man even half as handsome.

"I'd hoped to see you today, Miss Williams." Andrew Webb stepped in front of her, blocking her view of Reverend Mulligan and his companions. She'd been so wrapped up in watching the Mc-Lains that she hadn't even been aware of him greeting her aunt and uncle.

"Mr. Webb." She smiled at him and resisted the urge to try to peer around him to see where the McLains were.

"You look very pretty today, Miss Williams, if you don't mind my saying so." Andrew flushed a little at his boldness.

"Thank you, Mr. Webb." He was lying through his teeth, of course. His crooked teeth, she added when he smiled. The powder blue dress she wore was a remade castoff of Anabel's, and neither the color nor the style suited her. Not to mention the appallingly ugly hat Aunt Dorinda had purchased for her the week before. The brim dripped with ribbon roses and fat bows and made her look like an overdressed mushroom.

"I knew that hat would look a picture on you."

"This hat?" Eleanor lifted her hand to touch the despised headgear, her attention fully on Andrew for the first time. "Aunt Dorinda bought it from *you?*"

"Yes." Andrew smiled happily. "As soon as I saw it, I thought of you."

"You did?"

"Yes." His smile widened. "I'm so glad to see you like it."

"It's...lovely," Eleanor said weakly. It was also the only hat she owned, at least until she could refurbish last year's bonnet. The tattered condition of that item was the only reason she'd forced herself to don the hat at all.

"I've often thought it remarkable how close one can feel to someone with whom one shares one's tastes, even in such small and unimportant things as styles of dress," Andrew said, his watery blue eyes focused intently on her face.

Eleanor stared at him, groping for an appropriate reply. Should she admit, right up front, that she despised the hat in question? If she did, would that end the possibility of Mr. Webb being a suitor for her hand? Did she care? To her relief, she was saved the necessity of a reply by Reverend Mulligan's arrival.

"Zeb, I'd like to introduce you to some friends of mine. This is Luke McLain and his brother, Daniel. Mr. and Mrs. Williams."

Andrew Webb was instantly forgotten. Eleanor felt her pulse suddenly beating much too fast in the base of her throat. Luke McLain. She rolled the name around in her mind and decided that she'd never heard one she liked more.

"We've already met," Uncle Zeb was saying as he shook hands with both men. "Dealings with the bank, of course. Haven't seen either of you in quite a while. How'd your place come through the winter? Did you lose much stock?" He looked ready to settle into a lengthy discussion of ranching but a subtle nudge from his wife reminded him of his duties. "Oh, excuse me. Allow me to introduce my wife, Dorinda. And my daughter, Anabel," he said, pride evident in both voice and expression.

"Miss Williams." Luke smiled at Anabel, and Eleanor felt something close to despair. No doubt he'd be dazzled by Anabel's pale beauty, just as every other man was.

"Mr. McLain. And Mr. McLain." Anabel smiled, revealing the perfect dimples in her cheeks. "I'm very pleased to meet you."

"The feeling is mutual."

Eleanor was unreasonably pleased that it was Daniel and not Luke who gave her cousin that reassurance.

"We haven't seen you at church before, have we?" Anabel asked, widening her blue eyes in a way that drew attention to their pure color.

"We haven't attended much lately," Luke said, and Eleanor felt the deep richness of his voice slide over her skin.

"I hope you mean to change that," Anabel said.

"Now, Anabel, Mr. McLain is going to think you're being bold." Her mother's voice was too indulgent to be called a scold.

"I was just thinking of the importance of tending one's immortal soul, Mama." Anabel thrust her lower lip out ever so slightly in the pretty pout that she'd spent hours perfecting.

"Very admirable of you," Reverend Mulligan said dryly.

"Is this another daughter?" Luke asked, turning to look directly at Eleanor.

"My brother's child." Zeb Williams's tone was flat. "We took her in when he was killed a few years ago."

There was an awkward little pause, and Eleanor felt the color rise in her cheeks. Her uncle couldn't have made it more clear that she was an unwanted burden, hardly worth noticing. Tears of embarrassment burned the backs of her eyes.

"Eleanor, this is Luke McLain. His brother, Daniel." Reverend Mulligan hurried to fill the silence when it became clear that neither her aunt nor her uncle had any interest in introducing her.

"Pleased to meet you, Miss Williams."

Eleanor raised her gaze to Luke McLain's face, oblivious to his brother's equally polite greeting. Up close, he was even more overwhelming than he'd seemed from across the churchyard. His eyes were gray, the same clear color as a lake under a stormy sky. They were like polished steel against his tanned skin.

"Mr. McLain." The whispered acknowledgment. was all she could get out. Her heart was pounding against her breastbone, making her voice breathless. She could barely hear Luke's greeting to Andrew Webb over the sound of her own pulse in her ears. And then he turned back to her and smiled and she felt her knees go weak.

"Have you lived in Black Dog very long, Miss Williams?"

"Six years, four months and twelve days," she answered, without thinking. She saw his brows shoot up and immediately wished she could catch the words back. She'd kept track of the days like a prisoner counting out her sentence, but she'd never intended to reveal as much to anyone, least of all Luke McLain.

There was a moment of shocked silence, and then Anabel giggled. ''You shouldn't tease Mr. McLain, Eleanor. Why, it almost sounds like you haven't been happy with us.''

''I didn't mean that at all,'' Eleanor mumbled, lowering her lashes to conceal the rebellion in her eyes. She'd get an earful from Aunt Dorinda later, she knew. And heaven knew what Luke McLain must think of her.

The awkward moment was interrupted by the arrival of Letty Sinclair. Eleanor felt a twinge of annoyance. Letty was her best friend and, ordinarily, she would have welcomed her presence, but on this occasion Eleanor couldn't help but feel that Anabel's soft blond beauty overshadowed her enough without the addition of Letty's more exotic dark good looks. Guilt over the selfish thought made her smile all the more warmly as she turned to include Letty in their little group.

Reverend Mulligan made the introductions. Eleanor watched in resignation, sure that Luke McLain would be completely smitten by Letty's raven hair and dark eyes. *There's Italian blood there, mark my words,* Aunt Dorinda had said darkly when Letty first moved to Black Dog. But

Italian blood or not, the healthy condition of Letty's bank balance assured her place in the town's small society, even if her charm and generosity hadn't already done so.

Better that Luke be smitten by Letty than Anabel, Eleanor thought. Better almost anyone than Anabel. By the time the minister had finished the introductions, Eleanor was already envisioning the wedding with herself as a heartbroken but noble bridesmaid.

"Pleased to make your acquaintance, Miss Sinclair," Luke said, looking polite but not overly smitten.

"It's Mrs. Sinclair," Letty corrected, smiling in a way that made her eyes sparkle. "I'm a widow these three years past."

"You must have been a child bride," Daniel McLain said, his eyes blatantly admiring Letty's trim figure.

"I'll take that as a compliment, Mr. McLain."

"It was intended as such, Mrs. Sinclair," he responded with a grin that might have put a flutter in Eleanor's heart if it hadn't already been beating double time in response to his brother's proximity.

A glance at Dorinda Williams's face showed that she was less than pleased about this addition to their small group. While she'd rather have eaten nails than acknowledge that anyone could overshadow her precious Anabel, there was no denying Letty Sinclair's charms.

After exchanging a few more pleasantries, Reverend Mulligan and his companions moved on. Instantly three of Dorinda Williams's closest friends descended on them, wanting to hear every word that had been said.

"What charming young men," Dorinda said, her superior look only slightly spoiled by the pleased flush on her cheekbones.

"What did they say?" Millie Peters demanded, her small nose quivering with eagerness.

"We merely exchanged a few pleasantries," Dorinda said, trying to look as if she wasn't enjoying being the center of attention. Letty and Eleanor exchanged an amused look.

"But why did Reverend Mulligan bring them to meet you particularly?" That was Cora Danvers, blunt spoken, as always. If her husband hadn't owned half the bank, she wouldn't have had a friend in the world. Dorinda stiffened at the question, her smile tightening into something more nearly a grimace.

"I'm sure the McLains wanted to meet my Anabel," she said through tight lips. "Isn't it obvious that they've decided to take their rightful positions in our little society? Naturally, they'll be interested in finding wives, and my little Anabel *is* the prettiest girl in town," she admitted with an air of false modesty that clashed with her smug tone. She sighed and put on a regretful look. "Of course, if your Mary hadn't run off with that drummer last fall, she might have given Anabel a run for her money."

Cora flushed an unbecoming shade of purple, and Eleanor found herself almost admiring her aunt's ability to find the most vulnerable place in which to slide the barb. Everyone in town knew about Mary Danvers running off with the corset salesman, but few people would have dared to mention the incident to her face. Since Zebediah Williams owned the other half of the bank, Dorinda felt safe in striking such a blow.

"Anabel is such a pretty girl," Millie Peters said hastily, her soft voice filling the taut silence. "It would hardly be a surprise if one of the McLain boys came courting."

"*I* wouldn't wonder if they both came courting," Dorinda said, forsaking modesty for maternal pride.

Eleanor watched Anabel preen, and ground her teeth together. Just the thought of her spiteful little cousin clinging to Luke McLain's arm made her want to plant her foot firmly in Anabel's fanny.

Chapter Three

"A girl with a gentle temperament—that's what I want." Luke narrowed his eyes against the sun. "One who won't throw fits at a man."

"The woman ain't been born that won't throw a fit." Daniel reached into his pocket for his tobacco pouch and papers.

The brothers were riding back to the Bar-M-Bar, walking their horses in the midafternoon sun. After church they'd had lunch with Reverend Mulligan, who'd done his best to talk Luke out of his determination to find a wife.

What about love? the older man had asked, running his fingers through his thinning hair. Though he'd been loath to admit it, the question had given Luke pause. It had made him think of the bonds between his mother and father, of the way they'd seemed to complete each other. After her husband's death Lucinda McLain had carried on, but there'd been something missing, a light that no longer shone in her eyes.

But love like that was a rare thing, he told himself. And he couldn't afford to spend his life hoping he'd be lucky enough to find such a thing for himself. Besides, he was a little old to be chasing after dreams like that. If he hadn't found a great love by now, he wasn't likely to find it, especially not with the ranch demanding most of his time. Even if he wanted to go off on some wild-goose chase to find a woman he could love, he didn't have the time for it. No, a marriage based on more practical considerations would suit him just fine.

"You see any likely-looking girls?" Daniel's question dragged Luke's thoughts back to the present. Daniel finished rolling his cigarette and flicked his thumbnail over a match to light it. Cupping his hands to shield it, he lit his cigarette, his eyes sliding to his brother as he shook out the match. "There were pretty girls there. If I'd known there were so many pretty churchgoing girls, I might have been more inclined to pay my respects to the Lord on a regular basis."

"Careful. You don't want to find yourself on the wrong end of a father's shotgun." Luke paused and then grinned. "Of course, if you did, there wouldn't be any reason for me to get married."

"I've got no intention of doing anything foolish," Daniel said, dashing any hopes he might have had. "Though, from the looks of some of those girls, I'm not sure it'd be such a hardship to take one to wife. That redhead wasn't hard on the eyes, and a little temper might make life interesting. A little fire can be a good thing."

"In a horse, maybe, but not in a wife. My life is interesting enough." Luke let the reins go slack as he reached for his own makings and began to roll himself a cigarette.

"What about the dark one? The widow. She was easy on the eyes."

Luke considered Letty Sinclair briefly and then shook his head. "Sean says she lives on her own. A woman who's been living on her own is likely to be set in her ways. I want a girl who's willing to get set in *my* ways."

"How about the one with the yellow hair?" Daniel suggested. "I can't say I'd mind looking at that one over the breakfast table."

"Too young." Luke dismissed Anabel Williams out of hand. "Besides, I'd bet my last dime there's a streak of mean in that one that'd make a man's life mighty unpleasant. And a girl that pretty probably spends half her time in front of a looking glass, admiring her own reflection."

Luke lit his cigarette and narrowed his eyes against the drift of smoke. "What I want is a girl who's not so young that she's got her head all full of romantic notions but not old enough to be set in her ways. Pleasant enough looking that it won't be hard to go about the business of having sons with her but not so pretty that she'll expect me to spend all my time admiring her. She's got to be strong and willing to work."

"That's quite a shopping list," Daniel said. He reached up to tilt his hat down a bit, the better to shield his eyes from the afternoon sun. "You see a girl you think might live up to it?"

"Eleanor Williams," Luke said, drawing on the cigarette.

"Don't remember meeting an Eleanor Williams," Daniel said after a moment. He blew out a thin stream of smoke and frowned at the endless vista of prairie ahead of them. "She wasn't the one with the nose like a buzzard, was she?"

"No." Luke shot him an irritated glance, though he couldn't have said just why it annoyed him that Daniel didn't remember the girl.

"She was the one standing next to the girl with the yellow hair. The cousin."

"The one wearing the god-awful hat," Daniel said, making the proper identification.

"Her choice of headgear don't interest me," Luke said shortly. Privately, he promised himself that the first thing he'd do when they got married was burn that hat.

"There ain't much to her," Daniel said, just as he had when Luke had asked Sean Mulligan about her.

"I'm looking for a wife, not a pack mule," Luke said irritably.

"Need some of the same qualities in both," Daniel said. "Strong and steady, even-tempered—" He caught his brother's annoyed look and broke off but there was nothing repentant about his grin. "Course, I've never seen a pack mule I wanted to share a bed with."

"Pack mule's got more sense than to look at the likes of you," Luke said.

"So you think Ellen Williams is the one?"

"Eleanor," Luke corrected automatically. "And I won't know till I've had a chance to talk to her a bit more."

"I don't know, Luke. Marrying's a serious business." The laughter died out of Daniel's eyes, which were the same clear gray as his brother's. "Maybe this ain't such a good idea, after all. Maybe we ought to just forget the whole idea and try another housekeeper."

If he'd thought about it, Luke would have said that he wanted nothing more than to give up the idea of finding himself a wife. And here was Daniel, saying that he *should* give it up. He opened his mouth to agree that it had been a dumb idea from the start and that they should put it behind them. And found himself remembering Eleanor Williams's big brown eyes, the shy smile in them and heard her voice saying that she'd lived in Black Dog six years, four months and twelve days.

"I said I was going to find a wife and that's what I'm going to do," he heard himself say stubbornly.

Out of the corner of his eye he saw Daniel's surprised look. Since he was no less surprised himself, the last thing he wanted to do was talk about his decision. He nudged the gray into a canter, effectively putting an end to the conversation. For some reason, the idea of having a wife just didn't seem as bad as it once had.

The Wednesday after he and Daniel attended church, Luke found himself driving the buckboard into Black Dog to pick up supplies. He hadn't expected to find himself back in town quite so soon and was irritated by the necessity. But since their last cook had decided that California's winters would suit his old bones more than the biting prairie winds, Luke and Daniel had been sharing the duty, and it was Luke's turn to make the trip.

He nodded to Chet Longman, who ran the livery stable and was also the sheriff, when Black Dog had need of such. He heard the tinny sound of a piano from the Gold Dust Saloon as he drove past and decided he'd stop by for a drink before making the long, dusty drive back to the ranch. It wasn't much consolation for a wasted day but it was better than nothing.

They had to find another cook, he thought irritably. Or a wife. His eyes narrowed as his attention was caught by a particularly ugly hat—a familiar hat. The woman wearing it was walking briskly down the boardwalk, the skirts of her mint green dress swaying invitingly. As Luke watched, she pushed open the door of Webb's General Store & Emporium, and Luke allowed himself a grin. Maybe this trip wouldn't be such a waste of time, after all.

When her aunt Dorinda had sent her out to buy a length of linen for new towels, Eleanor had welcomed the chance to get out of the house and enjoy a walk in the spring sunshine. And going to Webb's would give her a chance to make amends to Mr. Webb for her blatant inattention to him after church on Sunday. When Reverend Mulligan had brought the McLain brothers over to be introduced, Andrew Webb had been promptly and somewhat rudely forgotten. She couldn't expect to draw a proposal from Mr. Webb if she ignored him just because she'd been introduced to another man. Even if that other man did happen to be the most attractive—

But that wasn't the point, she reminded herself briskly. Even if Luke McLain was the embodiment of every girlish fantasy she'd ever had, she was no longer a girl. She was twenty now and it was time to put away childish dreams. There was no knight in shining armor to come riding out of the prairie and sweep her off to a better life. She was going to have to build that better life for herself, and Andrew Webb offered her the best hope for a new future.

So she'd put on her favorite dress, a soft green cotton that suited her coloring much better than most of Anabel's castoffs, and she'd put on the ugly hat Mr. Webb had thought suited her. She'd wondered briefly if she could really be contemplating spending the rest of her life with a man who had such dreadful taste in millinery, but then reminded herself that there could be worse things. Like living with her aunt and uncle.

She'd spent a moment batting her eyes at her own reflection and trying to imitate Anabel's way of looking at a man from under her lashes. But the look that was coquettish on Anabel seemed simply foolish on herself. Since Mr. Webb was looking for a mother for four small children, perhaps he'd be more impressed by common sense than coquetry. Common sense she had in abundance.

Drawing a deep breath, Eleanor pushed open the door of Webb's. She immediately had the urge to turn and run, but the little bell over the door had already given away her presence and Andrew Webb was stepping out from behind the counter, his thin face wreathed in a smile.

"Miss Eleanor. What a pleasure to see you again so soon."

"Mr. Webb." Eleanor gave him her warmest smile and was pleased to see him blink and swallow hard.

"What can I help you with today?" he asked, regaining his composure.

"My aunt was hoping you'd have some good linen toweling. We've just finished spring cleaning and she'd like fresh towels to finish things off."

"I have just the thing. Got it from St. Louis not two weeks ago."

Eleanor followed him as he went to find the requested item. Looking at his scarecrow-thin figure and neatly combed sandy hair, she tried not to picture a pair of broad shoulders beneath a plain black coat and a head of deep brown hair in need of a cut.

"Best money can buy," Andrew said proudly as he lifted a bolt of fabric onto the counter. "Your aunt won't find any better, even if she went to Denver."

"It looks like just what she had in mind," Eleanor murmured. Her eyes were drawn to a bolt of royal blue grenadine. The deep, rich color would suit her coloring much better than her cousin's castoff pastels. She reached out to finger the soft fabric, picturing it made up in a simple gown with a minimum of decoration, with perhaps just a touch of lace at the neckline and wrists to soften the severity of the cut.

"That's much too dark a color for a young lady such as yourself, Miss Eleanor." At Webb's comment, she let her hand drop away from the fabric. "Something in a softer shade, perhaps. My late wife favored pinks and the softest of blues," he said reminiscently. He seemed to suddenly realize to whom he was speaking and flushed a deep shade of red. "I hope you don't mind me mentioning my wife."

"Not at all. It's only natural that you think of her."

"Yes. But life goes on and I've put aside my grief and am looking to the future."

The fervent look he gave her left no doubt that he was hoping the future he looked toward included her. Looking into his watery eyes, Eleanor felt her heart sink. Was she really contemplating spending the rest of her life with this man? At most, she felt a mild liking for Andrew Webb. Could a happy marriage be built on so little?

She was saved the necessity of having to answer either him or herself by the jangle of the bell over the door. It rang again almost immediately and the harsh tones of Cora Danvers admonishing her son about something echoed through the store. Andrew jumped and blushed again, like a boy caught smoking his father's cigars behind the privy. He glanced over Eleanor's head toward the front of the store.

"Are you in a hurry, Miss Eleanor?"

"Not at all. Please take care of your other customers, Mr. Webb. I'll find plenty to occupy myself." She was relieved when he hurried back toward the front of the store. Perhaps if she didn't have to look at him she'd be able to bolster her determination a little.

She heard Mr. Webb greet Cora Danvers, heard Cora's son Horace offer some whined complaint, the words indistinguishable. She reached out to finger the blue grenadine again. She had a little money, but it would be wildly foolish to spend it on a bolt of cloth when she already had four dresses hanging in her room. But wouldn't it be wonderful to wear something that suited her, she thought wistfully. In a dress like the one she'd envisioned, she wouldn't feel like such a little dab of a female. She'd feel elegant and almost pretty. Maybe even pretty enough to draw the eye of a man as handsome as Luke McLain.

At the sound of someone approaching, she snatched her hand back from the fabric and turned, annoyed to feel herself flushing as if she were guilty of some crime. Luke McLain stood not three feet from her, and Eleanor felt her breath catch and her cheeks blush fiery red. She pressed one hand to her bosom, as if to physically still the sudden pounding of her heart.

Luke wondered why he'd thought of her as plain. The face beneath that god-awful hat was not beautiful, by any means, but it was certainly not plain. Not with those big brown eyes that made him think of a fawn and that full mouth that seemed just about made for a man to kiss. Her flush deepened and he realized he'd been staring at her without speaking.

"Miss Williams. Reverend Mulligan introduced us at church last Sunday."

"I remember, Mr. McLain." *As if I could forget.*

"A new spring dress?" he asked, gesturing to the bolt of grenadine.

"Oh, no." She glanced guiltily at the beautiful fabric. "I'm here to buy new toweling for my aunt. We just finished spring cleaning and she wanted fresh towels."

"Spring cleaning." Luke remembered his mother's annual frenzy of cleaning when every rug had to be taken out and hung on a line to have the dirt beat from it. Then fresh straw had to be spread on the floor before the rug was tacked back into place. The memory was superseded by an image of the layers of dust and dirt that covered her once tidy home, and he winced.

"If you'll excuse me, Mr. McLain."

Eleanor started to step around him and Luke saw his opportunity to talk to her vanishing.

"I was wondering if I might ask your advice, Miss Williams."

"My advice?" She raised her dark brows in surprise. "I can't imagine a topic on which you could possibly need my advice, Mr. McLain."

Neither could he, but it had been the only thing he could think to say to keep her from leaving. Now she'd actually expect him to ask her something. He shot a quick glance around, looking for inspiration. He found it, more or less, in the bolts of fabric stacked beside them. He could hardly claim to have come in to buy new toweling. The coincidence would be too great.

"Curtains," he said abruptly, remembering the graying rags that hung at the kitchen windows in the ranch house. "I...ah...wanted to buy fabric for curtains. I was hoping you could offer some suggestions."

"Curtains?" She looked surprised. "What kind of curtains?"

"For the kitchen," Luke answered with a promptness that concealed the fact that the idea had just occurred to him. "To tell the truth, since our mother died, my brother and I have sort of let the place go a bit and I was just thinking it was time we put a little work into it."

At the mention of his mother's death, Eleanor's face softened. It wasn't really proper for her to talk to a stranger like this, but she knew how difficult it was to lose a parent. And the idea that he cared enough about his mother's home to buy new curtains for it went straight to her tender heart. She didn't think most men would even have noticed worn curtains.

"How big are the windows?" she asked briskly, deciding that propriety could be pushed aside, just this once.

Luke held out his hands to estimate the size, but Eleanor's attention was drawn to the width of his chest. He was wearing a plain blue shirt tucked into denim pants, and the soft cotton clung to muscles no decent woman should be noticing. She blushed and dragged her eyes away from the broad strength of his body. What on earth had gotten into her? she wondered as she forced her attention to the task at hand and began looking for something suitable to make curtains.

"Do you enjoy living in town, Miss Williams?"

"It's certainly convenient," she said. She frowned at a bolt of blue calico before setting it aside. "But I've no particular fondness for it. When I was a child, I always longed to settle in one place where I could have a garden and a real home." She stopped abruptly, embarrassed at having revealed so much of herself. But when she slid a quick glance

at him, he didn't look as if there was anything un-
usual in what she'd said.

"You traveled a great deal?"

"My father did, and I traveled with him. I tried
to make a home wherever we stopped, but there's
not a great deal one can do with a hotel room." Her
mouth curved in a rueful little smile.

So her father had traveled a lot, Luke thought.
And she'd always longed to settle in one place.
Well, he could certainly offer her a home and room
for the garden she'd said she wanted. From the
sound of it, those might be powerful arguments, if
and when he proposed.

"I think plain muslin might be best, after all,"
she said, drawing Luke's attention to a bolt of the
stuff.

"I'll have to find someone to make the curtains," he said.

Eleanor opened her mouth to offer to do the
work but closed it without speaking. She'd already
been bold enough. If her aunt heard that she'd been
talking with a man in Webb's, particularly a man
like Luke McLain, whom her aunt had already
earmarked as a possible suitor for Anabel, she'd
never hear the end of it.

"Mrs. Larkins does sewing," she said instead.
"She has the little house on the north edge of town

and she does good work for a reasonable price." It had to be her overactive imagination that made her think he looked disappointed.

Behind them, the bell over the door tinkled, announcing the departure of Cora Danvers and her obstreperous son. Though Eleanor couldn't see past Luke McLain's large frame, she could hear Andrew hurrying in their direction and she felt a totally irrational resentment toward him for interrupting. Not that there was really anything to interrupt, she reminded herself.

"Are you finding everything you need, Miss Eleanor?" At Webb's question, Luke reluctantly stepped aside to allow the other man to pass him. Webb moved to stand next to Eleanor, his weak eyes darting from her to Luke with suspicion. There was a certain possessiveness in the way he stood, a look only another man would recognize.

Luke's gaze sharpened on Eleanor's face, but if there was reason for Webb to feel possessive, he couldn't read anything in her expression. Something told him that any feelings of possession were strictly on Webb's side. The thought pleased him.

"If you'll cut some of the linen for me, Mr. Webb, I'll be on my way," she said, giving him a quick, impersonal smile.

"I'll be with you in just a minute, Mr. Mc-Lain," Webb said as he and Eleanor walked past.

"I'm in no rush."

The storekeeper's hand hovered a moment, almost touching the small of Eleanor's back, and Luke was surprised by the annoyance he felt at the idea of the other man touching her. When Webb's hand dropped away without making contact, Luke felt a satisfaction out of proportion to the moment. He followed them to the front of the store.

Eleanor was vividly aware of Luke McLain's gray eyes watching her while Andrew cut the fabric for her aunt. She told herself that she was not so foolish as to read anything into his interest. She'd just happened to be nearby when he'd found himself needing a woman's opinion. He'd probably have been just as happy to ask Cora Danvers, if she'd been handy. But the brisk mental lecture didn't have any effect on her rapid heartbeat.

When the toweling had been cut and wrapped in brown paper, she gave Andrew an absent thank-you without really seeing him. Picking up the package, she turned to leave, her eyes catching Luke's.

"I hope the new curtains are what you wanted, Mr. McLain." She hoped he wouldn't notice the slight breathlessness in her voice.

"Thank you for the help, Miss Williams." He nodded and smiled at her, and Eleanor hurried out before she could make a fool of herself by collapsing at his feet.

Luke let his eyes follow her as she left, watching her walk past the big front window. It wasn't until she'd disappeared from sight that he turned his attention to Andrew Webb. The suspicion in the other man's eyes had deepened but Luke ignored it. Webb had had plenty of time to make his intentions known to the girl. If he hadn't done so, then he had no one to blame but himself if someone moved faster.

Luke gave him the order for the supplies. He loaded a case of canned peaches and sacks of flour, sugar and other staples into the buckboard. It wasn't until they were almost done that he remembered the curtains he was supposedly anxious to have made. He didn't give a damn about curtains but, remembering Eleanor's earnest help, he felt his conscience tug at him. Moving to the bolts of fabric, he picked up the muslin she'd indicated. He started to carry it to the front of the store and then hesitated. Obeying an impulse, he picked up the bolt of blue fabric she'd been fingering. If he married her, he could give it to her. And if he didn't, well, then, he could give it to whomever he *did* marry.

Chapter Four

Luke McLain attended church alone the following Sunday, and his presence incited only a smidgen less speculation than it had the week before.
After the services he exchanged greetings with people he knew but made it a point to intercept the
Williams family before they reached their carriage.
A few minutes' conversation and a smile and he was
the recipient of an invitation to join them for Sunday supper.

It was no wonder Mr. McLain had hinted for an
invitation to dine with them, Dorinda Williams
pointed out on the carriage ride home, what with
Anabel looking particularly pretty today.

"Just be your own sweet self, precious, and Mr.
McLain won't be able to resist you." Dorinda gave
her daughter a fond look. Luke was following on
horseback, giving the family a few moments alone.

"I don't know if I want to marry a rancher, Mama. All that dirt...and those animals." Anabel wrinkled her short, straight little nose.

"The McLains are just about the wealthiest folks hereabouts," her father put in.

"Really?" Anabel straightened and gave her father a calculating look at odds with her delicate pink-and-white image. "How wealthy?"

"Now, you know I can't tell you that, pussycat." Zeb clicked his tongue at the horse that drew the little carriage. "That's confidential information."

"But this is important, Daddy." Anabel thrust her lower lip out in a pout. "I'm not asking for myself, you know. I'm thinking about you and Mama. It's my duty to marry someone who can provide for you in your old age."

"Isn't that just like her?" Dorinda said, to no one in particular.

"Yes, isn't it." Eleanor's muttered comment brought her aunt's attention to her. The sentimental tears that had filled Dorinda's hard blue eyes vanished the moment she looked at her niece.

"You see that you don't push yourself forward the way you did last week. 'Six years, four months and twelve days,'" she mimicked sharply. "I was never so embarrassed in all my life. You just remember where you'd be if your uncle and I hadn't taken you in."

"Yes, Aunt Dorinda." Eleanor kept her eyes lowered, knowing that her resentment must be plain to read, even to someone as insensitive as her aunt.

"Is everything ready for supper?"

"Yes, Aunt Dorinda."

Cora and Hiram Danvers were to join them for Sunday supper, and Dorinda Williams was determined that everything be absolutely perfect. She didn't want to give her "dearest friend" a single flaw to find. Luke McLain's presence was icing on the cake, as far as she was concerned.

As soon as they arrived at the house, Eleanor slipped into the kitchen without waiting to see the arrival of her aunt's guests. She stood in the center of the cramped, airless room for a minute, her hands clenched at her sides. She wasn't sure which she wanted to do more—cry or break something.

She heard the low rumble of Luke McLain's voice from the direction of the parlor and felt her eyes sting with tears. When she'd seen him at church this morning, she'd felt her heart bump. Her stupid heart, she thought savagely. So what if he was the handsomest man she'd ever seen. He was just as foolish as every other man in this town, unable to see past Anabel's big blue eyes and golden curls.

When he'd approached the family after church, for one giddy moment she'd thought that their brief encounter in Andrew's store might have made him want to see her again. But he'd barely acknowledged her presence before turning that devastating smile in her aunt's direction. From the look he threw at Anabel, it wasn't difficult to guess why he had gone to the trouble to charm Aunt Dorinda into inviting him to supper.

Eleanor stalked to the big stove and lifted the lid on the pot she'd left simmering. Picking up a fork, she jabbed a potato hard enough to break it in two. If Luke McLain was stupid enough to fall for Anabel, then he deserved every minute of misery she'd dish out. She herself had better things to think about, like getting supper on the table.

She threw a few sticks of wood into the stove and opened the damper a little wider. The chicken had been floured and left to sit, covered with a clean towel. All she had to do was melt lard in the big iron skillet and start the chicken frying. While it cooked, she'd have time to mash the potatoes and whip up a batch of biscuits. And if her eyes stung while she was doing it, it was purely because of the heat. It certainly had nothing to do with a particular dark-haired cowboy.

Luke sat in the cramped little parlor and struggled to remember all the lessons his mother had drummed into him about making polite conversation. He talked about the weather, the possibility of the town building a new school and the latest government negotiations with the hostile Indian tribes in the Southwest. He didn't give a damn about any of the three. What he really wanted to do was demand to know where Eleanor was, not discuss the possibility of a drought with these two overfed bankers.

The two older women sat on a black horsehair sofa, twin to the one he occupied and probably just as uncomfortable. Dorinda Williams was busy with some sort of needlework, her fingers moving swiftly over a mass of fine cotton. Probably another doily like the ones that covered every available surface in the overcrowded room.

Annalise or Anamae or whatever her name was sat on the piano bench, poking her fingers on the keys in a series of unrelated notes that grated on his nerves. A beam of sunlight had managed to struggle past the layers of draperies that smothered each window and the light fell across her, turning her hair to spun gold, highlighting her pretty features.

Cynically, Luke wondered if she'd chosen that spot for just that reason. It sure as hell couldn't be out of a love for music, he thought, wincing as her fingers descended on the keys again.

"Where is Miss Eleanor?" he asked, waiting only for the smallest of breaks in the conversation. He looked at his hostess, hoping his expression was politely interested, rather than impatient.

Dorinda Williams looked at him blankly for a moment, her niece so far from her thoughts that she seemed to be having a difficult time remembering who she was. Her daughter had no such difficulty.

"She's in the kitchen, earning her keep," she said, throwing him a bright, sharp smile.

"She's employed by you?" Luke asked, knowing full well that wasn't the case.

"Of course not." Dorinda Williams threw her daughter a warning look before smiling at Luke. He didn't find her smile any more appealing than her daughter's had been. "What Anabel should have said was that Eleanor insists on helping around the house. It's her way of thanking us for taking her in when her father was killed."

"Does she always stay in the kitchen when you have guests?" Luke's expression of polite interest drew any sting from the question.

"Can't say I've seen much of her," Cora Danvers said, her harsh voice unnaturally loud in the stuffy little room.

"Eleanor is very shy," Dorinda said in a strained tone. "Her upbringing before she came to us was rather—shall we say, unconventional?"

"*We* aren't saying anything," Cora said, withering her hostess's coy tone. "And if you're hinting that Eleanor's father taught her anything less than perfect manners, I'll say flat out that I don't believe it for a minute. Nathan Williams had manners smooth enough to please the queen of England. So if you're suggesting that Eleanor might be inclined to blow her nose on her sleeve or some such thing, it doesn't seem likely."

Dorinda's face had turned a pale shade of purple during Cora's speech, and Luke hid a smile behind his coffee cup. He thought he could come to like at least one banker's wife.

"Of course, Eleanor's manners are impeccable. *I* certainly wouldn't allow anything less. I merely meant that, with her father having practiced a less than respectable profession, perhaps Eleanor is not as comfortable in polite company as a girl like my sweet Anabel, who was raised in more cultured surroundings."

"What was her father's profession?" Luke asked. "If you don't mind my asking, of course." Not that he really cared whether anyone minded or not. He wanted to find out as much as he could about the girl he was considering marrying. Eleanor had said her father had traveled a lot, but he hadn't given much thought to the man's profession.

"My brother earned his living on the turn of a card," Zeb Williams said in a repressive tone that made his opinion of such a profession quite clear.

"A gambler?" Luke's brows rose.

"Yes. It's not something we talk about a great deal, for obvious reasons." Zeb looked as if he'd just confessed to having a wild Indian in the family.

"Look how serious we've all grown," Anabel cried with forced gaiety, annoyed that everyone's attention had somehow been drawn away from her. "It's much too nice a day to be so serious. Don't you agree, Mr. McLain?"

She widened her pretty blue eyes at him and thrust her lower lip out in the merest hint of a pout. Luke would have bet a good horse on the fact that she'd practiced that look in front of her mirror. He smiled and wondered if maybe her parents shouldn't have spanked her a time or two when she was younger.

"Why don't you play for us, dear?" Dorinda smiled indulgently.

"I'm not very good," Anabel protested prettily, but Luke had the idea that it would have taken a tornado to budge her from her seat on the bench.

"Nonsense, my dear. Miss Brown said you had a natural talent," Zebediah said. "Miss Brown learned to play in Boston," he added proudly, giving the impression that Bostonians had some sort of an edge over the rest of the country when it came to piano playing.

"Miss Brown said the same thing to my Horace," Cora put in. "And he can't carry a tune in a bucket."

There was an awkward little pause and Luke saw Anabel's eyes flash with fury, the first genuine emotion he'd seen from her.

"Well, Anabel doesn't need a bucket to carry a tune," Dorinda said with a tight little smile. "Do play something, precious."

"Only if Mr. McLain promises to make allowances. I feel a little shy. I don't often perform for anyone but the closest family."

"You played two weeks ago at my house with half a dozen people watching," Cora said. "Didn't look shy at all, then."

"I'm sure no one needs to make allowances for your performance, Miss Williams." Luke spoke quickly, staving off the explosion he could see building in his hostess's face. "I'd enjoy hearing you play."

About as much as I'd enjoy having a tooth pulled.

Anabel conjured up a pleased blush before turning to the piano, where her music, by coincidence, of course, just happened to be laid out. It didn't take more than a few measures for Luke to realize that Miss Brown was either completely tone deaf or a terrible liar. Anabel might have a natural talent but it sure as hell wasn't for piano playing.

He was starting to wonder how much of this he'd be expected to suffer through when Eleanor came to the door of the parlor. She didn't speak and no one else seemed to notice her presence but Luke knew the moment she appeared.

As Daniel had said, there wasn't much to her, but what there was was very neatly packaged, Luke thought, admiring the feminine softness of her figure. After all, when it came to women, a man didn't need more than an armful and Eleanor looked as if she'd provide plenty to hold on to on a cold winter's night.

He was grateful to see that she'd left off the ugly hat she'd been wearing both times he'd seen her. Her hair was drawn back from her face, but the severe style was softened by the delicate fringe of soft curls that had escaped to frame her face. He found himself wondering what her hair looked like when it was down. Would it curl over a man's hands, pulling him closer to her? And would she welcome a man's passion or be frightened by it?

He was surprised to realize that he was becoming aroused just looking at her. Irritated with himself, he looked away, turning his eyes to where Anabel sat abusing the piano keys, thereby missing the wistful look Eleanor turned in his direction.

Though he certainly wouldn't choose a wife based solely on her cooking skills, Luke was pleased to find that Eleanor's were more than adequate. He and Daniel had hired a cook but he'd quit almost a month ago and since then, they and the hands had been cooking for themselves. Even when they'd had a cook, the food had been less than inspired. The meal spread out before him was the best he'd had since his mother's death. The biscuits were as close to pure heaven as he'd ever eaten in his life. He said as much, and from the startled look Eleanor shot him, he suspected few compliments came her way.

"Thank you." Her voice was low and soft, just as he remembered it, and Luke added another item to his list of prerequisites for a wife—a pleasant speaking voice. He didn't want to spend the rest of his life with a woman with a voice like a cat who'd got its tail caught under a rocking chair.

Anabel, who'd been seated next to Luke, looked annoyed that someone had noticed her cousin. When Hiram Danvers seconded Luke's comment about the biscuits, her pout became a little less studied and not nearly as pretty as it had been. Eleanor looked uncomfortable with the attention being given her and Luke decided that modesty was a good attribute in a woman.

Though Luke participated in the conversation, his attention was centered on the dark-haired girl across the table from him. He saw nothing to make him think his first assessment had been in error. The more he watched Eleanor Williams, the more convinced he became that she'd make a suitable wife. Her looks were pleasant, her demeanor quiet—she was the very picture of the docile bride he'd described to his brother.

When the meal ended, Eleanor rose and began to clear the table. Luke noticed that neither Anabel nor her mother moved to offer any assistance. Since Eleanor didn't seem to notice the omission, he assumed this must be another example of how she "earned her keep."

As Eleanor disappeared into the kitchen, Anabel caught Luke's eye. Her smile was pure invitation, too old for her sixteen years. Luke was surprised by his own lack of interest. Perhaps Anabel read something of that lack in his expression because her soft, pink Cupid's-bow mouth tightened momentarily and something cold and hard flickered in her baby blue eyes.

Just like that mule Pa owned, Luke thought again. Remembering the mule's tendency to bite when riled, he had to restrain the urge to shift his chair a little farther away from Anabel's. But he underestimated her intelligence. Anabel knew exactly who was to blame for his indifference.

Eleanor carried in a pie and Luke's mouth watered at the pungent, sweet smell of warm cherries. He couldn't remember the last time he'd had cherry pie. And if her pie was anywhere near as good as her biscuits...

"That smells mighty good, Miss Eleanor," he said, enjoying the flush of pleasure that brought a sparkle to her eyes.

"Serve our guest first, Eleanor," Dorinda Williams said, with the air of a queen giving out favors.

Still flushed, Eleanor set the pie down next to her aunt and used a narrow spatula to lift an already cut slice onto one of the small china plates that sat ready to receive it. It had never occurred to Luke that a woman could look graceful doing something as simple as serving a piece of pie, but there was a quick grace about everything she did and he found himself thinking that it wouldn't be a hardship to watch her around the house.

Eleanor moved down the table and reached between him and Anabel to set the plate down in front of him. Luke was looking at the pie but out of the corner of his eye he caught a quick movement from Anabel. Eleanor gasped as her arm was jogged. The plate tilted and Luke's white shirtfront was suddenly decorated with cherry pie.

There was a moment's stunned silence as everyone at the table stared at the bright red cherries splattered across his chest.

"I'm so sorry. I don't know how—"

"Eleanor, you clumsy little idiot!" Dorinda's sharp voice cut off her niece's breathless apology. "Can't you do anything right?"

"It's all right, Mrs. Williams," Luke said.

"It's kind of you to say so," Zeb put in, his long face drawn in tight lines of disapproval. "Naturally, Eleanor will see to the cleaning of your clothing or its replacement. Tell Mr. McLain you're sorry, Eleanor."

"She's already apologized." Luke spoke before Eleanor could say anything. She'd set down the plate and grabbed Luke's napkin and was dabbing at the stain on his shirtfront. He closed his fingers around hers, stopping her futile attempts to repair the damage. "I'm just glad the pie wasn't hot," he said, glancing up at her with a smile.

Her mouth curved, but the lower lip quivered and her eyes were bright with unshed tears. Luke found himself wanting to bang her aunt's and uncle's heads together. He still held Eleanor's hand and he could feel her pulse jumping erratically under his touch.

"If I could have a towel?" he suggested gently.

"Get Mr. McLain a towel, Eleanor," her aunt snapped immediately.

There was an awkward silence when Eleanor had vanished into the kitchen. Luke found himself wondering why his mother's lessons on etiquette had never covered what a man should say when he found himself wearing a slice of pie and knowing that the cause of the disaster was sitting right next to him looking as if butter wouldn't melt in her mouth.

"I can't tell you how sorry I am that this happened, Mr. McLain." Dorinda's voice was heavy with mortification.

"No need to apologize, Mrs. Williams. Accidents can happen." He let his gaze settle on Anabel, who looked back at him without the smallest trace of guilt or remorse in her pretty blue eyes.

Eleanor returned and Luke scraped cherries and pie crust off his chest and into the towel she'd brought. Aside from his shirt, there was no real damage done. Once the towel was disposed of, he fixed Eleanor with his best smile, the one that had generally succeeded in getting him just about anything he wanted from a woman.

"I'd still like a slice of that pie, Miss Eleanor."

She gave him a grateful look and reached for the pie plate, but her aunt spoke before she could touch it. "*I'll* serve the pie. I'd prefer to avoid another scene."

Eleanor flushed and moved around the table to sit down, her hands in her lap.

"Anabel, my dear, please pass this to Mr. McLain."

"Yes, Mama."

Anabel took the plate from her mother and turned to Luke, who eyed her warily. But she set the plate in front of him, giving him a sweet smile in the process. She turned that smile on her cousin. "You see, Eleanor, all it takes is a little care."

Luke saw Eleanor's dark eyes flash with anger. She knew as well as he did just who was to blame for spilling the pie. He waited, wondering if he was about to see a display of temper, but she only drew a deep breath and looked down at the table.

His expression thoughtful, he picked up his fork. She had a temper but kept it under control. That was a good thing in a wife. As he'd told Daniel, he didn't want a wife who was prone to throwing fits. The more he saw of her, the more she seemed a likely candidate for marrying.

Besides, she baked the best darned cherry pie he'd ever sunk a tooth into.

"It was just awful, Letty. It looked like I'd shot him with a shotgun, only it had been loaded with cherries instead of buckshot." Eleanor's face flushed at the memory.

"It doesn't sound like he was upset." Letty Sinclair picked up the teapot and filled both their cups.

"He was nice as could be," Eleanor agreed. "And that little cat, Anabel, sat there with a smug little smile on her face. I just wanted to shove her headfirst into a mud puddle."

"Or a cherry pie," Letty suggested.

"That would have spoiled her mood," Eleanor agreed, smiling at the thought of Anabel with a faceful of cherry pie. Her smile faded. "Luke must think I'm clumsy as a bull at a tea party."

"Luke?" Letty raised her eyebrows at the familiarity.

"Mr. McLain," Eleanor corrected herself with a guilty blush.

"I've seen him and his brother in town a time or two even before I met them at church last week," Letty said. "They're both very attractive men. You could do worse than to set your sights on one of them."

Eleanor choked on a mouthful of tea. "Me? Set my sights on a man like Luke McLain? I'd be making a total fool of myself."

"I don't see why." Letty's pretty chin set stubbornly.

"What would a man like that see in a dab of a girl like me? Ouch!" She cried out more in surprise than pain as Letty rapped the back of her knuckles with the silver spoon she'd picked up to stir her tea. "Why did you do that?"

"Because you sounded just like your aunt Dorinda," Letty said, showing not the least sign of remorse. "You're not a dab of a girl, Eleanor Emmeline Williams."

"I'm hardly statuesque, either."

"Haven't you ever heard that good things come in small packages?" Letty stirred her tea and fixed her friend with a stern look. "You've lived with that harpy of an aunt and that nasty little cousin of yours too long."

"I haven't had much choice," Eleanor muttered. She took a sip of tea, savoring the rich flavor of it. When Aunt Dorinda made tea she always skimped on the tea leaves, turning out a watery brew more reminiscent of dishwater than a beverage.

Good tea was only one of the many pleasures she took in visiting Letty Sinclair. Letty was her dearest friend. She'd moved to Black Dog three years before to take care of an elderly uncle. When her uncle passed away, leaving her a small house and a comfortable inheritance, Letty had stayed on. There were those who were scandalized by the idea of an attractive young woman living alone, but the fact that Letty Sinclair could always be counted on to donate both time and money to any worthy cause kept the whispers to a minimum.

She was a widow, after all, the ladies of the town comforted themselves. Though she was young, it wasn't as if she were a single girl living alone. Letty's husband had drowned when the wagon he was driving overturned in the midst of a river he'd been trying to ford. A widow at twenty, Letty had welcomed the opportunity to leave Ohio and all its painful memories behind and move west to care for her great-uncle Lazarus.

Letty and Eleanor had met at church and become fast friends almost immediately. Letty was the one person in Eleanor's life with whom she felt completely at ease, the one person with whom she could share her dreams and her fears.

"I've decided to marry Andrew Webb," Eleanor announced abruptly.

"What on earth for?" Letty set her teacup down and frowned at her friend.

"Because I don't want to spend the rest of my life as Aunt Dorinda's unpaid housekeeper."

"You don't have to marry Andrew Webb just to avoid that. I've already told you that you could come live with me. We'd have such fun, Ellie. You know we would."

"You know as well as I do that it would never do."

"I don't know any such thing." Letty's fine brows drew together and her soft mouth set in a stubborn line. "I have a spare bedroom just sitting empty. And if it would soothe that annoying pride of yours, I could even hire you as my housekeeper.

Since there's not much house to keep, we'd have plenty of time to enjoy ourselves."

But Eleanor was already shaking her head. "Can you imagine what people would say about two young women living alone together?"

"I'm a widow. How could anyone complain if I choose to hire a companion?"

"A companion even younger than you are?" Eleanor asked, raising her brows.

"I ought to be able to have any companion I want," Letty said stubbornly. She caught Eleanor's eyes and sighed. "Oh, all right. You're right and I'm wrong. But I don't have to like it."

"I thank you for the offer." Eleanor smiled at Letty's disgruntled look.

"Even if you can't come stay with me, I don't want you to marry Andrew Webb just to get away from your aunt and uncle," Letty said after a moment.

"I don't see that I have much choice. I've no skills with which to earn my own living. He seems like a kind man and his children need a mother." Even to her own ears, Eleanor sounded less than excited and she forced a false note of enthusiasm into her voice. "I've always wanted children of my own, you know."

"That's an altogether different thing from gaining a husband and four children all in the same day and not knowing any of them any better than you do some stranger just arrived on the train from St. Louis."

"They're not exactly strangers," Eleanor protested.

"What are the children's names?"

Letty's unexpected demand left Eleanor momentarily speechless. "The oldest girl is Elizabeth, and the boys are—" She hesitated, groping to put a name to the four towheaded children who sat so quietly beside their father in church. "Simon and ... William. And the littlest is Mary—no, it's Margaret." She gave Letty a triumphant look. It was short-lived.

"The oldest girl is Liza and it's not short for Elizabeth. The second boy isn't William, he's Willard, and the baby's name is Minerva." Letty ticked off the names on her fingers before fixing her friend with a stern look. "You can't marry Andrew Webb when you don't even know the names of his children, Eleanor."

"I can learn their names." Eleanor set her chin in a way that would have startled Luke McLain.

"You don't love him," Letty noted.

"Not everyone marries for love. Love can come after marriage." Eleanor tried to sound more confident than she felt. "He's a nice man."

"With terrible taste in hats," Letty observed, nodding to the overdecorated hat that Eleanor had set on the sofa next to her.

"I can learn to live with that," Eleanor said, casting a doubtful look at the item in question.

"I don't think it's possible," Letty said, shaking her head mournfully. "A man who'd choose a hat like that for a woman...there's just no telling what else he might do."

Eleanor laughed, just as Letty had intended. "I've never heard anyone suggest that poor taste in millinery was an indication of serious character flaws."

"Well, it can be, and I forbid you to marry the man until we know something more about him."

"He hasn't asked me yet," Eleanor observed. "But if he does, I'm going to say yes."

"Then I hope he doesn't ask you, because I can't bear to see you marry someone just to get away from your aunt." Letty's hazel eyes reflected her distress. "There must be someone you'd rather marry."

Luke McLain's strong features immediately popped into Eleanor's mind but she pushed the image away. The idea that he'd have interest in marrying her was so farfetched as to be an absurdity. She might as well wish to marry the man in the moon as to dream of marrying Luke McLain.

Chapter Five

It was two weeks before Luke could spare the time for another trip to town. Two weeks during which he realized that if he took the time to get to know every eligible female in Black Dog, the business of finding a wife could drag on for months. And it would cost him time he could ill afford to spend. Trips back and forth to town, Sunday suppers with each girl's family—the prospect filled him with dread.

Of course, he could take Daniel up on his suggestion that they just forget the whole idea. But then they'd have to see about hiring a housekeeper, and that would still leave the problem that had started this whole mess in the first place, which was the need for one of them to have a son. True, that had been more Daniel's concern than his, but the idea had taken hold of him and he couldn't get it out of his head.

A housekeeper might solve the problem of the cooking and cleaning but only a wife could provide him with a son and turn the neglected house back into a home. And he was starting to realize that he wanted one as much as the other. So a wife was what he had to have. But he didn't see any sense in drawing out the process of finding one. As far as he was concerned, his needs were fairly simple—a girl not too old and not too young, one not hard on the eyes but not so pretty that she'd be spending all her time primping and preening, a girl not afraid of hard work. An even temper, biddable and not too skinny.

Luke stared between the gray's ears, his dark brows hooked in a frown as he considered the list of necessary attributes. It didn't seem as if he was asking anything unreasonable. No more than any other man, anyway. In return he was willing to provide for his bride's comfort and safety. He didn't drink to excess—or at least, not very often. Nor did he swear in the presence of females. Women seemed to set store by security and he could offer her as much of that as any man could. His wife would never go hungry and he could afford to clothe her and house her in comfort.

Thinking of the persuasive arguments in his favor, Luke nodded, confidence swelling in him.

There was no reason he could see that Eleanor Williams shouldn't accept his proposal. Unless she was seeing someone else, of course. His frown returning, Luke considered that possibility. But he dismissed it almost immediately. Sean Mulligan had said that Eleanor wasn't being courted. He had a suspicion that Andrew Webb intended to change that, but if the man hadn't done anything by now, it was his loss if someone else married the girl.

Pleased with the results of his reasoning, Luke dug his heels into the gray's sides, clicking his tongue to hurry the gelding along. There was work waiting to be done. The sooner he made his proposal and got an answer, the sooner he could get back to it.

Eleanor was pinning the hem on a dress for Anabel when someone knocked on the front door.

"Now, who could that be?"

Eleanor assumed her aunt's question was rhetorical, since the room's other occupants could not be expected to see through walls and identify the caller.

"Could be someone on bank business," Zeb Williams said, looking up from the paper he'd been reading.

"It's a Sunday afternoon," his wife protested.

"Not everyone observes the Lord's day as they should," he said pompously. The paper crackled as he folded it neatly and set it on the arm of his chair. "Don't worry, my dear, if it's business, I'll send them on their way in a trice."

"I should think you would. Imagine doing business on a Sunday." As Zeb left the room, Dorinda settled deeper into her chair and reached for another chocolate from the box sitting next to her before opening the novel she'd been reading.

"It's probably someone calling for me," Anabel said, craning her neck as if she could see around the corner to the front door. "Rose Ellen Miller said she'd bring over the pattern book her aunt sent her all the way from New York. It would be wonderful to see some really fashionable dresses instead of the dowdy things we get out here."

"You know you look a treat in anything you wear, precious," her mother said, dragging her attention from the heroine of her novel and fixing her daughter with a fond look.

"I just know I'd be a laughingstock in Boston or even San Francisco." Anabel was angling for a new gown and had no intention of being consoled until she had one.

"I didn't know you were planning on going to either of those places." Eleanor's mouth was full of pins, making the muttered comment indistinguishable. Still, the other two glared at her, perhaps sensing sarcasm even though they hadn't actually heard her.

"It's Mr. McLain," Anabel hissed suddenly.

Eleanor hadn't needed Anabel to identify the owner of the deep, masculine voice in the hall. Her fingers were suddenly shaking, making it impossible to slide the pins into place. She was vividly aware that her hair, which had been ruthlessly tamed for church earlier, had begun to escape its bonds and curl about her face. She was wearing a pale pink dress that made her skin look the color of old flour, had a mouthful of pins and was kneeling on the floor at her cousin's feet—probably just where Luke McLain thought she belonged, she thought bitterly.

In the moment before her uncle and his guest appeared in the parlor door, Eleanor spit the pins into her hand. At least she didn't have to look as if she'd swallowed a porcupine. Her aunt was not so lucky. Dorinda had just popped an entire chocolate into her mouth, leaving her with a choice of swallowing it whole or chewing in a most unladylike fashion.

"Mr. McLain has something he wishes to discuss with me," Zeb said in what Eleanor privately labeled his "I'm an important man" tone.

Dorinda smiled, keeping her lips tightly pressed together. Her silence might have seemed odd if Anabel hadn't jumped in to fill it.

"We've missed you in church these past two weeks, Mr. McLain," she said, softening her boldness with a dimpled smile and a coquettish look from under her thick lashes.

Eleanor felt her heart sink as Luke's gaze seemed to linger on her cousin. Standing on a low stool as she was, Anabel must look to him like a porcelain figurine on a stand. As for herself, she might qualify as a dusty brown mouse fit only to kneel at Anabel's dainty feet.

"That's kind of you to say, Miss Anabel," Luke said, and Eleanor knew it had to be wishful thinking that made him sound cool toward the younger girl. No one—no *man*—was ever cool toward Anabel.

"Miss Eleanor." She felt herself flush like a foolish child as those gray eyes settled on her.

"Mr. McLain," she whispered, lowering her eyes to prevent him from seeing the longing she was afraid must be blatantly revealed.

The moment the two men disappeared into Zeb's study, Dorinda opened her mouth wide enough to masticate the half-melted chocolate.

"What do you suppose Mr. McLain needs to talk to Papa about?" Anabel's tone was thoughtful, her pretty blue eyes full of cool speculation.

"I'm sure I have no idea," Dorinda said, annoyed at having been caught in an awkward position. She closed the box of chocolates and pushed it from her.

"Did you see the way he looked at me?" Anabel asked. "Do you think he noticed how pretty I look?"

"You shouldn't say such things, Anabel. Modesty is one of a woman's best virtues."

"But I *am* pretty, Mama. Everyone tells me so. Wouldn't it be false modesty to pretend otherwise?" Her mother was still blinking from the impact of that question when Anabel continued. "Besides, since the Lord must have been the one to make me pretty, then I'm actually praising His work when I say as much."

If Eleanor hadn't been busy trying to choke down a laugh, she might have almost felt sorry for her aunt. The dazed look in her eyes suggested that, this time, even she couldn't ignore Anabel's incredible arrogance. Anabel, of course, was oblivious to the shocked silence she'd created.

"Do hurry up, Eleanor," she snapped peevishly. "I bet Mr. McLain is asking Papa for permission to see me, and I can't go out walking with him with my hem dragging in the dirt."

The probable truth of her words wiped out Eleanor's brief spurt of amusement. She didn't know how she'd stand it if she had to watch Luke McLain come courting Anabel. If that happened, she'd ask Andrew Webb to marry her, she promised herself fiercely.

"Ouch!" Anabel cried out as a pin pricked her ankle.

"Sorry," Eleanor muttered without looking up.

"You did that deliberately," Anabel snapped. She jerked her skirt away, ignoring Eleanor's gasp of pain as a pin tore into her fingertip. Stepping down off the footstool, she glared at her cousin. "You poked me on purpose because you're jealous."

Though she hadn't deliberately stuck Anabel with a pin—at least, she didn't *think* it had been deliberate—Eleanor couldn't deny the accusation that she was jealous. Not when she was all but seething with that emotion. She sucked a droplet of blood from her finger and allowed herself a brief wish that she had jabbed Anabel harder.

Choosing silence as her best defense, she gathered up the packet of pins with trembling fingers and stood. Ignoring Anabel's furious glare, she put the pins away in her sewing basket.

"Mama—" Anabel's whined complaint grated on Eleanor's taut nerves. "Eleanor poked me deliberately."

"I'll deal with her later, precious," Dorinda promised absently. "Why don't you go change into something pretty? Perhaps when Papa and Mr. McLain have finished their business we can persuade Mr. McLain to have some tea with us. You can't entertain him in a dress with a pinned-up hem."

Anabel flew from the room. Eleanor shifted a few items around in the sewing basket, aware that her fingers were trembling. For a brief moment she was tempted to change into another dress, but there wasn't much difference between the powder pink castoff she was wearing and the dusty blue dress that was her other Sunday best garment. Besides, she'd only come out looking like a fool if she tried to outshine Anabel. Like a mud hen trying to best a peacock, she thought.

Sternly controlling the embryonic quiver of her lower lip, Eleanor picked up her embroidery and settled herself in one corner of the uncomfortable sofa. No doubt Anabel was right and Luke had come to ask for permission to call on her. Painful as it might be, she was simply going to have to deal with that reality.

Anabel returned to the parlor so quickly that Eleanor wondered if she'd simply cut her way out of her other dress. She was wearing a pale pink dress with a soft flounce at the hem and a touch of lace at the neckline and wrists. She looked like an angel, her mother told her, and, much as she would have liked to do so, Eleanor couldn't disagree.

It was no wonder if Luke McLain was smitten with Anabel, she thought with a sigh. How could a man be expected to see past all that beauty to the nasty core of her?

The three women waited with varying degrees of patience. Dorinda pretended to read her novel. Eleanor pretended to concentrate on her embroidery. And Anabel posed prettily on the edge of the piano bench and admired the graceful folds of her skirt, not bothering to pretend an interest in anything other than herself.

Though it seemed like forever, it was something less than half an hour before they heard the door to the study open. Dorinda dropped her novel. Eleanor promptly jabbed her finger with a needle. Anabel merely lifted her head, tilting it attractively, a smile wreathing her pretty face as her father entered the parlor.

"What did Mr. McLain want, Papa?" she asked with just the right combination of shy hope and feminine confidence.

Zeb Williams didn't respond immediately. He cleared his throat and looked away from his daughter. His eyes met his wife's, skated over Anabel again and finally settled on his niece with a mixture of dislike and disbelief. "Mr. McLain would like to speak with you, Eleanor," he said slowly.

"With me?" Eleanor's voice rose in a surprised squeak.

"Yes." The single word seemed to take a considerable effort. He cleared his throat again and focused his gaze somewhere past her shoulder. "You may speak with him in my study but you're not to close the door more than halfway, do you hear?"

"Yes, Uncle Zeb." She hesitated, but her uncle didn't seem to have anything more to add. She set aside her embroidery and stood.

A quick glance at Anabel showed her pretty mouth half-open with surprise. Eleanor was pleased to see that she looked a little like a trout. Knowing that it was only a matter of seconds before Anabel regained her breath and demanded an explanation, Eleanor didn't delay her departure.

She paused outside her uncle's study and smoothed her palms over her skirt. She knew from experience that there was no sense in even trying to pat her hair back into place—the curls would just spring right back out again. Drawing a deep breath, she pinned what she hoped was a serene smile on her face and walked into the den. Mindful of her uncle's concern about propriety, she pushed the door half-shut behind her.

Luke had been standing in front of the bookcase, his head tilted to read the titles on the rows of leather-bound books. He turned as she entered the room, and Eleanor was helpless to control the color that rose in her cheeks. Nor could she prevent her heartbeat from accelerating beyond all reason.

"Miss Williams."

"Mr. McLain. Uncle Zeb said you wished to speak to me?" She was pleased to hear the steadiness of her voice.

"Yes." He cleared his throat and gestured to the small sofa that sat against one wall. "Perhaps we could sit down?"

They were barely seated when a piercing shriek issued from the direction of the parlor. "I won't have it! I won't, I won't, I won't!" Anabel's voice rose in a crescendo of rage, peaking in another shriek that ended abruptly in the sound of a slap. Eleanor's eyes widened in shock. In the six years she'd lived here, she'd never once seen anyone raise a hand to Anabel, no matter how uncontrolled her behavior.

"My cousin is, uh, terrified of mice," she murmured in response to Luke's inquiring look. Other than lifting one dark brow, he didn't comment, but something in his eyes suggested that he had his doubts about the outburst having been caused by a mouse.

She folded her hands neatly in her lap in a ladylike pose that served to conceal her trembling fingers. She gave Luke McLain a look of polite inquiry and hoped he couldn't see the way her heart pounded beneath her bodice.

"I, ah, wished to speak with you, Miss Williams." Now that the moment was here, Luke wished himself anywhere but where he was. It had all seemed so straightforward and simple when he'd thought about it. He'd propose. She'd accept because there was no good reason for her not to. They'd set a date, he'd be on his way and it would be settled.

"Yes, Mr. McLain?" She tilted her head, those big brown eyes looking at him inquiringly, and Luke suddenly realized that his collar was too tight. He resisted the urge to run his finger underneath the starched linen. He cleared his throat.

"My mother has been dead these past three years," he began, groping for words.

"I know. You must miss her a great deal."

"Yes." He found his eyes drawn to Eleanor's mouth. He hadn't realized what a soft, kissable mouth she had. Her lower lip was fuller than the upper, giving her mouth a sensual pout that seemed to invite a man to taste it. Had that stick Webb kissed her? The thought was more irritating than it had any business being.

He realized that she was still looking at him, waiting for him to get to the point of his visit. He wanted nothing more than to oblige, but dammit all, he hadn't expected the point to be so hard to get to!

"The fact is, with my brother and I living alone and all the work that's required to run a ranch, we don't have much time to put into taking care of a house. Cooking and cleaning and suchlike." He gestured vaguely to indicate the myriad tasks that went into running a house.

"I can understand that. You must have a great many responsibilities." *Is he going to offer me a job?*

"Yes. And more than just the responsibilities on the ranch. There's the future to think of." *Now where did I come up with a pompous piece like that?* But Eleanor was looking at him with those big brown eyes, seeming to hang on his every word, and Luke found himself continuing. "When a man works to build something up, he has to think toward the future, provide for its care."

"That's very true, Mr. McLain." *Good heavens, he is going to offer me a job!* Eleanor was torn between excitement and uncertainty. She couldn't possibly go to work for him and his brother. The whole town would be scandalized.

"When I saw you at church, you seemed like just what I had in mind," Luke said, starting to feel a little more at ease. "I realize this is kind of sudden and that we don't know each other all that well but there'd be plenty of time for getting to know each other afterward."

After what? Eleanor felt as if she'd lost some vital thread of the conversation. After he hired her?

And what difference did it make if they knew each other? Hiring a housekeeper didn't require an intimate acquaintance.

"I didn't mean to rush things so much but, what with spring being a busy time of year and not wanting to put things off till summer or even fall, and you seeming a sensible girl, I thought you might not be offended by me taking a few short-cuts."

"Shortcuts?" Eleanor blinked in confusion. *What on earth is he talking about?*

"Your uncle said he'd give his permission, so there'd be no problem there."

Uncle Zeb had given his permission for her to live on an isolated ranch with two bachelors?

"He said it was up to you." Luke looked at her expectantly and Eleanor found herself wanting to agree to anything he asked. But if she went to live with the McLain brothers, her reputation would be in shreds before the buggy made it to the edge of town. Was Uncle Zeb so anxious to get rid of her that he'd throw his precious propriety completely to the winds?

"Mr. McLain, I'm afraid I don't know exactly what it is I'm to make a decision about," she said finally.

Luke stared at her in surprise. What did she mean, she didn't know? Hadn't he just asked her to marry him? He went over the conversation in his mind and felt color creep over his cheekbones as he realized that he'd talked around the question without ever once actually saying the words. He cleared his throat, annoyed to find himself nervous.

"I'm asking you to be my wife, Miss Williams."

The words fell like stones into a pool, spreading ripples of silence in their wake. Eleanor stared at him, her dark eyes round with shock, that soft mouth of hers ever so slightly open. The sound of Anabel sobbing could be heard from another room.

"Your wife?" Eleanor's voice rose in a squeak. She lifted one shaking hand and pressed it to her bosom, wondering if it was possible that a heart could beat so hard it actually jumped right out of a body. "You want to marry me?"

"That's the idea."

She was going to turn him down. He could see it in her face, in the stunned look in her eyes. She was going to say no, which was no more than he deserved, rushing into this like a thirsty bull heading for water.

Luke gave in to the urge to tug at his collar. This had been a damn fool idea from the start. When he got back to the ranch he was going to find Daniel and punch him right in the nose. It had been his damn fool notion that one of them had to get married in the first place. If it wasn't just like his little brother to get him into a situation like this. He'd knock him into next Sunday. He'd—

"Yes." Luke was so absorbed in his plans for revenging himself on Daniel that it took a moment for Eleanor's breathless response to penetrate.

"What?"

"I said yes. I'd be most honored to be your wife, Mr. McLain."

"You would?"

"Yes." She flushed and lowered her eyes to stare at the fingers she'd twisted together in her lap. "Of course, if you regret your proposal, I'd not—"

"No. No, of course not." There was more conviction in his voice than in his heart. Now that it had come right down to it and he'd found himself an engaged man, Luke was less sure than ever that this was a good idea. But he'd proposed and she'd accepted and that's all there was to it.

He stared at her downbent head, wondering what he was supposed to do or say now. Should he kiss her? The thought held considerable appeal, but from the way she was all but tying her fingers in a knot, he thought she might jump like a scalded cat if he touched her.

Now what? Eleanor wondered, staring at her fingers. Was he going to kiss her? The thought made her tremble with an emotion somewhere between terror and delight. It was one thing to imagine what it might be like to have Luke McLain kiss her. It was something else altogether to actually contemplate it happening.

"I'm honored, Miss Williams," Luke said as the silence threatened to stretch awkwardly.

"The honor is mine, Mr. McLain." She couldn't bring herself to look at him.

There was another period of silence.

"Maybe we should talk to your aunt and uncle," he said finally. "Make arrangements about dates and such."

Torn between disappointment that he wasn't going to kiss her and relief about the same, Eleanor could only nod, her eyes still on her hands. It was only when he rose and went to the door that she dared to steal a quick look at him. She felt dizzy, her thoughts tumbling wildly. The only one that came clear was that Luke McLain had just asked her to marry him. Incredible, unbelievable as it seemed, she was actually going to marry him.

The idea didn't become much more real, even when Uncle Zeb and Aunt Dorinda joined them in the study. Dorinda's eyes, a faded version of her daughter's, reflected such dazed disbelief that Eleanor wanted to giggle. There was no sign of Anabel. She was probably lying in her room with a damp cloth over her forehead, trying to absorb the reality that, not only was her despised cousin going to make it to the altar before she did, but she was marrying a man Anabel had set her own sights on. The thought made Eleanor smile, the first time she'd done so since Luke's proposal.

Luke didn't know what had made his affianced wife smile, but he was glad to see a little color creep back into her face. She'd been so pale that he'd wondered if she might not just keel over right where she was sitting. Her eyes skittered past his and her cheeks took on a bit more color before she looked back down at her hands. She really was a shy little thing, he thought, feeling almost indulgent.

"I guess you'll be wanting to set a date," Zeb Williams said grudgingly. He'd offered the appropriate good wishes in a flat tone that drained any meaning from them.

"I think I could manage by the end of summer," Dorinda said reluctantly.

"I had in mind two weeks from this next Saturday," Luke said.

"Two weeks!" Her voice rose sharply. "Impossible!"

"I don't see why," Luke said. "Unless the preacher isn't going to be around. Spring calving should be just about over by then. Seems to me like a good time for a wedding."

"It's obvious that you've never been married before, Mr. McLain," Dorinda said with heavy-handed humor. "Weddings take time to arrange. There are things to be done."

"What kind of things?" Luke asked, starting to feel impatient. Dammit, this whole business of finding a wife had already taken enough of his time.

"Since this has been so sudden, I think we should have a small party to announce the engagement and introduce the two of you."

"Introduce us?" Luke raised his brows. "To who? Unless there's been a sudden rush of immigrants, there's not many people in this town that don't already know each other."

"Introduce you as a couple, Mr. McLain," Dorinda said, with just a touch of condescension. "We need people to get used to the idea that you and Eleanor are...seeing one another." The words seemed to stick in her throat. "Then we can announce your engagement. There'll be a few parties. We'll have invitations to write and Eleanor will need a wedding dress. These things may not seem important to you, Mr. McLain,'' Dorinda said, anticipating his objections, ''but this sort of thing is dear to the female heart. God willing, a woman only has one wedding in her life. I'm sure you wouldn't want to deny Eleanor the opportunity to enjoy all the little traditions that go along with it.''

Luke swallowed the urge to argue. If this sort of feminine fussing was what a woman considered necessary for her wedding day, he supposed he had no choice but to go along with it. He could hardly start his marriage off by denying his bride her heart's desire. But the thought of spending the summer traipsing back and forth to town, attending the sort of gatherings Dorinda Williams thought appropriate... He barely restrained a shudder.

''Two weeks sounds just fine to me.'' It was the first time Eleanor had spoken since the discussion began, and three pairs of eyes immediately swiveled in her direction, reflecting varying degrees of surprise, as if her presence had been all but forgotten.

''Don't be absurd, Eleanor.'' Dorinda was the first to speak, her voice sharp. ''You have no idea the amount of work that goes into a proper wedding.''

"I can't think of anything that can't be done in two weeks," Eleanor said mildly.

Dorinda recognized the set of her niece's chin and knew there'd be no budging her. How such a quiet girl could have such a stubborn streak, she'd never understand. Heaven knew, she'd done her best to break her of it and there'd been times when she thought she'd succeeded. Then something would come up and the girl would set her chin in that particular way and Dorinda would know that nothing less than a team of wild horses would be able to change her mind.

Eleanor ignored the knot in her stomach and met her aunt's angry gaze. If Luke wanted to get married in two weeks, then two weeks it would be. It wasn't as if she were leaving behind a happy home, she thought. Besides, two weeks gave Luke less time to change his mind and decide that hiring a housekeeper would be better than taking a wife.

Luke smiled at his fiancée, thinking that he'd made a wise choice. They weren't even married yet and she was already anxious to please him.

"It's not possible," Dorinda said, but there was defeat in her tone.

"We'll manage." Eleanor's tone was quiet but implacable. She wondered if her aunt's desire to delay the wedding wasn't based on the hope that

Luke would come to his senses and choose Anabel, after all.

"A rushed wedding is bound to cause talk. People will wonder if there isn't a reason for hurrying things along." Dorinda's tone was concerned, but the look she shot between the two of them was suspicious, as if she were wondering if they knew each other better than she'd thought. "There'll be talk."

"Not in my hearing," Luke said. "Not more than once." The cool threat in the flat statement was enough to silence even Dorinda Williams.

So the date was set for two weeks from the coming Saturday. Not long after, Luke took his leave. As a newly engaged woman, Eleanor was allowed to walk him out to the front porch without a chaperon. Though, engaged or not, she couldn't see why she'd need a chaperon, not when the porch was in full view of anyone riding by.

Luke's horse stood in front of the house, reins looped through the iron handle that an enterprising blacksmith had attached to an old cannonball. The gray stood on three legs, drowsing in the late-afternoon sun, switching his tail occasionally to discourage flies.

Eleanor linked her hands together in front of her and tried to think of something to say. She'd just become engaged to this man. There must be a great many things that needed to be said, but not a one came to mind.

"I don't know if I'll be able to make it back to town between now and the wedding," Luke said.

"That's all right. I know you've a great deal of work to do and I'll be busy with the wedding preparations and suchlike." She risked lifting her eyes to his face and found him watching her with an unreadable expression.

"You're sure about this?" he asked abruptly. "About marrying me?"

"I'm sure. Unless... unless you've changed your mind." She had to force the words out through a throat that suddenly felt much too dry. If he'd changed his mind...

"I haven't." The flat reassurance slowed the pounding of her heart.

"I'll do my best to be a good wife to you, Mr. McLain."

"Don't try too hard. I don't want too high a standard to live up to." His crooked grin made her breathless all over again. "And I'd guess you'd better start calling me Luke."

"Is it short for Lucas?"

"Yes. But the only person ever called me Lucas was my mother, and that was only when she was scolding me."

"I'll try to keep that in mind. It might come in handy to have a way to let you know when I'm upset with you."

The quick, teasing smile surprised him and so did his reaction to it. He had the urge to pull her into his arms and press his mouth to hers, to see if that smile tasted as sweet as it looked. And probably scare her to death in the process.

He looked away from temptation, squinting out into the sunlight instead. When he looked at her again, her smile had faded but a trace of it still lingered around her mouth. She was looking at him with those big brown eyes, innocent as a newborn fawn. But the thoughts she inspired in him were far from innocent. The slight fullness of her lower lip drew his attention. He probably wouldn't see her until the wedding, which was over two weeks away, and it suddenly seemed impossible that he should leave without even a taste of her.

Eleanor's eyes widened as Luke's hand came up, his fingers cupping her cheek. The only other time he'd touched her had been when she'd spilled cherry pie all over his shirt. Then, the quick acceleration of her pulse might have been caused by the disastrous circumstances. But her pulse was beating just as rapidly now and there wasn't a disaster in sight.

She could feel the roughness of calluses on his hand and she suddenly thought of Andrew Webb's hand, pressing hers in greeting, soft and vaguely damp, lacking the work-roughened strength of Luke's.

"Do you suppose there'd be any objection to a man kissing his future wife?" His voice was husky, his face close enough that she could feel the brush of his breath against her skin.

Eleanor tried to find her voice, swallowed and tried again, but nervous anticipation had closed her throat, stealing her voice. She settled for an almost imperceptible shake of her head, not certain herself whether it was permission or protest.

And then it was too late for either. His mouth was touching hers, and all her innocent imaginings about what a kiss would be disappeared in a rush of heat.

She closed her eyes, lost in sensation. His mouth was warm and dry, softer than she'd imagined it would be. Even as she thought that, Luke's lips firmed against hers, his hand cupping the back of her neck as he tilted her face up to his, deepening the kiss. Drawn off-balance, Eleanor set her palm against his chest to steady herself and was immediately aware of the strong beat of his heart beneath her hand.

Luke felt the light touch burn through the fabric of his shirt, heating his skin as if she held a branding iron. He momentarily forgot that he was standing on the banker's front porch in broad daylight and that the girl in his arms was as innocent as a child. His tongue came out, tracing the tempting fullness of her lower lip, coaxing her to let him inside.

Immediately she stiffened, drawing in a quick, shocked breath, her fingers suddenly tense against his chest. It wouldn't take much to change her shock to surrender, he thought, his fingers tightening against the back of her neck. But this was no dance hall girl or even the widow he'd once kept company with in a neighboring town until she'd realized that letting him into her bed was not going to put another wedding ring on her finger.

His mouth lifted from hers, his fingers loosening their hold on her nape. She sank back onto her heels and it was only then that he realized that she'd been standing on tiptoe to kiss him. He was reminded of his brother's words that there didn't seem to be much to her. But there was plenty, he decided, dropping his hand to his side and stepping back from her. Plenty to fill a man's arms and his bed.

Two weeks, he reminded himself. He settled his hat on his head. "I'll see you in church."

"Yes." Eleanor's agreement was hardly more than a breath. She couldn't have said another word if her life had depended on it. Luke looked at her, his eyes shadowed by the brim of his hat. He nodded, as if satisfied with what he saw, and then turned and walked down the steps.

She watched him bend and unloop the reins from the cannonball, and then he was swinging up into the saddle with an easy grace that made her breath catch. He reined the gray around, glancing back at her and touching his fingertips to the brim of his hat before nudging the horse into a canter.

Eleanor watched until he was out of sight. Only then did her heartbeat slow to something approaching normal.

She was getting married. And she was marrying Luke McLain. Wait till Letty heard about this!

Chapter Six

Two weeks later Eleanor stared at her reflection in the mirror over her dressing table and debated the possibility of climbing out the window and running to the railway station to catch the next train to anywhere but here. It was her wedding day, but the ashen girl in the mirror looked as if she faced a trip to the guillotine instead of a church.

She started to pick up the brush that lay on the dressing table but her hand was shaking so badly that she doubted her ability to hold the brush, let alone use it. She let her hand drop to her lap and stared at her reflection with frightened eyes.

Oh, Lord, what on earth had made her agree to this? True, she wanted to leave this house, and the past two weeks had certainly done nothing to change her mind. Aunt Dorinda had done most of the preparations for the wedding, but her cooperation had not been given out of concern for her niece but rather out of a desire that everything appear just as it should.

With everything being done in such a harum-scarum rush, it's important that we observe the proprieties. We don't want to give people anything more to talk about than we already have, she had added with a long-suffering sigh and an annoyed glance in Eleanor's direction.

No, it wasn't the desire to stay in her uncle's home that was making her have second thoughts. It was the sudden realization that she was marrying a total stranger. The few occasions on which she'd seen Luke McLain were hardly enough to qualify him as an acquaintance, let alone a husband. Of course, there was The Kiss, which she'd begun to think of in capital letters. When she thought about The Kiss, it wasn't quite so hard to think about marrying him. But there was more to being married than kissing.

A sharp knock on the door startled Eleanor half out of her skin. Without waiting for an invitation, Anabel pushed the door open and stepped inside. Looking at her younger cousin, Eleanor felt her heart sink. Anabel was wearing a white dress made of the finest lawn, trimmed in pale blue ribbons. A panel of matching blue, gathered on either hip, draped artfully from her tiny waist almost to her knees before being caught in the back and then falling gracefully to meet the two layers of pleats that marked the hem. With her golden curls framing the perfection of her face, Anabel was the very picture of beauty.

Luke will take one look at her and realize what a terrible mistake he made. The fact that he'd had plenty of opportunities to observe Anabel's beauty and had still proposed to her didn't mean anything to Eleanor. She didn't need to look in the mirror to know that her cousin would outshine her at her own wedding.

"You look pale as a ghost," Anabel offered by way of greeting. Leaving the door open behind her, she sauntered into the room and settled herself gracefully on the narrow bed. She studied her cousin, her pretty blue eyes bright with malice. "I know why he asked you to marry him."

"Do you?" Eleanor turned back to the mirror and willed her hand to steadiness as she picked up the brush and began dragging it through her thick dark hair.

"It's because you're plain," Anabel announced cheerfully.

"Is it?" Eleanor refused to allow so much as a flicker of emotion to color her voice. Her reward was the annoyance that flashed across Anabel's reflected face.

"Sometimes a man will marry a plain wife because he can leave her at home and forget about her. He won't have to worry about her attracting any unwanted attentions. Luke knows you won't make any demands on him because you'll be so grateful to him for marrying you in the first place. I'm only mentioning this so that you won't spend too much time worrying over the fact that you aren't a beautiful bride. Luke—"

"Luke is a very lucky man, and I'm sure he knows it." Letty's words preceded her. She sailed into the room, her dark eyes snapping with anger. "And you are a nasty little cat who would have benefited a great deal from a few good spankings when you were a child. I'm afraid it's too late for them to do any good now."

"How dare you speak to me like that!" Anabel's porcelain complexion took on an apoplectic tint.

"Don't bother throwing a tantrum." Letty began tugging off her gloves, eyeing Anabel's flushed features with indifference. "If you start screaming I'd feel obliged to dash the contents of the wash pitcher in your face."

Eleanor swallowed an hysterical giggle at the shocked disbelief on Anabel's face. In all her sixteen years, no one had ever spoken to her in such a fashion.

"You can't—"

"I just have." Letty arched her dark brows to convey her surprise that Anabel hadn't noticed. "I'd suggest that you try to restrain your natural tendency toward malice, at least for today. If you do anything to cause Eleanor even a moment's discomfort on her wedding day, I should feel obliged to speak to your mother about a certain scene I happened to witness between you and Johnny Rutherford."

Anabel gasped, her face flushing. Eleanor watched, fascinated, as she opened her mouth and then closed it again without speaking. There was a moment's silence when it seemed as if Anabel was groping for something to say. Failing that, she rose from the bed and flounced out of the room, throwing Letty a look of hatred as she passed. Letty shut the door behind the girl.

"That girl is a positive menace," she said, turning back to Eleanor.

"Did you really see her with Johnny Rutherford?"

Johnny Rutherford's father owned one of the three saloons that dotted Black Dog's main street. Aunt Dorinda had been campaigning to have all three closed, and if she found out that her own daughter was associating with Harvey Rutherford's son...

"No." Letty tucked her gloves into her reticule and set it aside before giving Eleanor a grin that was pure mischief. "But I've seen the two of them exchanging looks and it seemed a reasonable threat. I guess it worked. She looked as if I'd knocked the wind out of her. I don't think you'll have any more trouble with her today," she added, with pardonable satisfaction. "And you're not to listen to a word she said, either. You look absolutely lovely."

"Oh, Letty, I couldn't look lovely no matter what I did." Eleanor's smile wobbled on the edge of tears. "Maybe Anabel is right. Maybe he is marrying me because I'm plain and—"

"Don't be a nitwit," Letty snapped. Stepping over to the dressing table, she took the brush from Eleanor's nerveless fingers and applied it to her hair. "You're not plain. You're not as flashy as your cousin, I'll grant you that, but you're far from plain. And I'll tell you something else—you have a kind of beauty that will last. By the time Anabel is thirty, she's going to look like a box of chocolates left out in the sun."

Despite her shaky nerves, Eleanor snorted with laughter at the image of Anabel's prettiness melting away. Letty was deftly twisting her hair into place.

"You'll still look as fresh as spring long after Anabel looks like day-old mutton."

"I can't imagine that, but you're a dear friend to say as much. Oh, Letty, what on earth am I doing? Was I temporarily mad to agree to marry a man I don't know?"

"Women have been marrying men they don't know since time began," Letty said briskly. She pushed hairpins into place, and the heavy mass of unruly hair suddenly looked almost elegant. "I'd rather see you marry Luke McLain any day than throw yourself away on that stick Andrew Webb, which is what you were going to do. Would you rather be marrying him?"

"No." Eleanor didn't have to consider her answer. From the moment she'd accepted Luke's proposal, she'd hardly given a thought to Andrew, except to be glad she no longer had to consider marrying him. "It's just that...he scares me," she said, as much to herself as to Letty.

"Joseph scared me half to death. I nearly fainted before I could say 'I do.' "

"But you said you loved him." Startled, Eleanor looked at her friend.

"I did, but that didn't mean I wasn't scared. It's a natural thing for a woman to be frightened of marriage. We're giving ourselves into a man's care, hoping that he'll be kind and that he'll provide for us, knowing there's little to be done if he turns out to be something much less than we'd hoped."

"If you're trying to reassure me, you're going the wrong way about it," Eleanor said.

"All I'm trying to do is make you understand that your fears are natural. I think Mr. McLain will make you a fine husband and I'm spiteful enough to like the idea that you're not only marrying before Anabel, but marrying so well. That will put the little cat's nose out of joint for some time to come."

"I can't marry just to spite Anabel," Eleanor protested with a laugh.

"No, but you might as well enjoy it." Letty's grin faded, her expression becoming more serious. "Has your aunt talked to you about your marital duties?"

Eleanor flushed and dropped her eyes to her lap. Not even with Letty could she be comfortable discussing such a personal topic.

"She said that there would be 'things' my husband would want to do, and that I would have to learn to endure them and to close my eyes and pray that they'd soon be over," she admitted in a whisper. Remembering Aunt Dorinda's solemn expression, she felt a shiver of dread go up her spine.

"What a lackwit," Letty snapped. "More likely, in this household, it's your uncle who's had to learn to endure," she muttered, half to herself. But Eleanor heard and was surprised to find herself giggling at the thought of her uncle being led, all unwilling, to his marriage bed.

"That's better." Letty took Eleanor's hands and drew her up off the hard little stool. "Come sit with me on the bed and I'll tell you what it's really like between a man and a woman."

Eleanor followed her, torn between curiosity and dread. She wasn't at all sure she wanted to know what happened between a man and wife, not when she was halfway to believing that she couldn't possibly go through with the marriage.

Eleanor stared at the gold band on her finger. It looked new and shiny and felt strangely heavy. She twisted it around her finger as if seeking a more comfortable position for it.

"Is it too big?" Luke's husky question made her jump, her head jerking toward him.

"Too big?"

"The ring." He nodded to the band she was still twisting. "Is it too big?"

"Oh, no." She forced herself to stop toying with the ring. "No, it's fine."

"I could have it made smaller," he offered. He took his eyes off the road and looked at her.

"No, really. It's fine. I guess I'm just a little nervous," she admitted.

"So am I." Luke grinned at her look of surprise. "First time I've been married."

"Me, too." Eleanor returned his smile, feeling a little of her tension ease. She didn't believe for a minute that he was nervous, but it was kind of him to pretend. Since he'd returned his gaze to the road, she allowed herself to glance sideways at him.

My husband. Thinking the words didn't make them seem real, any more than the wedding ring on her finger or the fact that he was taking her to the home they'd now be sharing. She'd stood in church and repeated her vows, heard him do the same, accepted the congratulations of the guests, changed from her wedding gown with Letty's help and left her uncle's house forever and she still couldn't make herself believe in the reality of what she'd done this day.

She'd been almost surprised to see Luke waiting for her at the church, so sure had she been that he'd have realized what a terrible mistake he'd made in asking her to marry him. Once she saw that he was there, she'd wished he hadn't come. Better to be jilted with an impersonal note than to receive the news that he didn't want her after all with the whole town looking on. But he'd only stood there on the church steps, the sun gleaming on his dark hair, and waited while she climbed those few steps. Then he'd taken her hand from her uncle's arm and led her into the church where everyone was already waiting.

And he'd actually married her.

Several hours later, the thought still amazed her.

"Won't be long now," Luke said, breaking the silence that had fallen between them. "House is just over that rise."

He glanced at Eleanor, and since she was looking in the direction he'd indicated, he let his eyes linger. The sun was almost gone but there was still enough light for him to see the soft curve of her cheek and the tempting fullness of her lower lip. Her mouth had lingered in his thoughts more than he'd liked. He'd had two weeks to think about it, two weeks to remember the softness of her lips under his.

Considering it had been nothing more than a kiss, it had certainly lingered in his mind. Of course, that really wasn't surprising, since she was going to be his wife. It was natural that he'd think about kissing her. He just hadn't expected to feel quite so much anticipation at the thought of doing it again. Not to mention everything that came after.

The house was nestled in a fold where the deceptively flat prairie suddenly dipped downward. There was a spring that ran clear and cool and had never gone dry during the years the McLains had been there. There were corrals and outbuildings, all the necessary clutter that went with running a ranch.

Luke left the buggy in the care of one of the hands, introducing him as Joe. In the near dark, all Eleanor could make out was that Joe appeared to be tall and thin. She could only hope that he wouldn't be offended if she didn't recognize him the next time they met. Luke unloaded her portmanteau from the buggy and set his free hand under her elbow, guiding her footsteps across the dark ground and up the steps onto the porch.

Daniel had stayed in town for the night and would be bringing her trunks out the next day. When Luke had first told her of this arrangement, she'd been grateful that she wouldn't have to deal with a brother-in-law as well as a new husband on her first night as a married woman. But when Luke pushed open the door and stepped inside to light the lamp, Eleanor would have given a great deal to have had half a dozen guests to troop inside with her.

Before she could give in to the urge to turn and flee as quickly as her new kid slippers would allow, Luke had the lamp lit, illuminating the front hall. He set the lamp on a table against the wall and turned to look at her, raising his brows when he saw her still hovering on the porch. He started to say something, stopped as if a thought had just struck him and grinned at her.

"I guess you can tell I haven't had much practice at this marrying business." He was coming toward her as he spoke, and before Eleanor could guess his intention, he'd bent and swept her up against his chest. She gasped and threw her arms around his neck, her reticule bumping against his back.

By the time he'd carried her inside, she'd realized that he was just following tradition by carrying her across the threshold. But the feel of his muscular chest pressed against her breast and the easy strength with which he held her were enough to scatter her wits to the four winds.

He set her down in the entryway and she reached up to straighten her hat, missing Luke's wince as the gesture drew his attention to the overdecorated atrocity. He wondered if she was fond of the hat and would be upset if some accident befell it, like perhaps a stray wind sweeping it into a horse trough. He filed the idea away for future consideration.

He saw her looking around the front hall, her eyes curious, and realized that she was probably anxious to see her new home. He wished suddenly that he'd put a bit more effort into getting the place cleaned up, maybe hired a woman from town to come out and put it in decent shape. He and Daniel had stirred themselves to clear out the worst of the mess, but he was suddenly conscious of the thick layers of dust on every surface, of floors that had seen neither broom nor scrub brush since the departure of the last housekeeper months before.

"Daniel and I aren't much for housework," he muttered, using the edge of his boot to brush cigar ash under the sofa while Eleanor was looking around the parlor.

"That's all right. I know a great deal about cleaning house, including how to get ash out of a carpet."

She glanced at the place where the ash had been before lifting her eyes to his face. Luke thought he'd never seen anything half so appealing as the teasing smile in those big brown eyes. He grinned back, and some of the nervous tension seemed to leave her face.

Luke showed her through the rest of the house but her impressions were sketchy at best. The place needed a thorough cleaning. It was obvious that it had been some time since it had known a woman's care. She knew she should be paying more attention to the things he was showing her. After all, this was to be her home from now on. But her thoughts kept jumping to the night that lay ahead. Her wedding night.

"Daniel has moved his gear out to the bunkhouse," Luke said as he opened the door to one of the three bedrooms upstairs. "He figured we ought to have the house to ourselves for a while."

"He didn't have to do that," she protested, thinking that the last thing she wanted was to have the house—or her new husband—to herself. "This is his home."

"I think he's figuring to move back in a few weeks. Since we didn't take time for a trip or anything, maybe he figured this was the next best thing."

"Well, it's very nice of him but not necessary," Eleanor said briskly. For one wild moment she considered suggesting that they should drive back to town and tell Daniel as much, maybe bring him home with them.

"This will be our room," Luke said, pushing open the door at the end of the hall.

Our room. Eleanor swallowed a lump in her throat the size of a melon and forced herself to the threshold of the room. Luke had carried her portmanteau upstairs with them, and he set it on the bed. One bed. One not terribly large bed. She swallowed again and dragged her eyes from that terrifying piece of furniture.

This room, like all the others, showed signs of neglect. Dust covered every surface, the floor was in desperate need of a good coat of wax and the curtains needed washing. Certainly, there was more than enough work here to keep her busy.

Her eyes drifted back to the bed and she couldn't repress a nervous shiver. For a moment she wished quite desperately that Luke had hired her as a housekeeper rather than married her. Never mind that her uncle would have seen her tarred and feathered rather than let her become housekeeper to two bachelors. Never mind that Luke's gray eyes had haunted her dreams from the moment they'd met. And most especially never mind that she'd thought of little else but his kiss for the past two weeks. A kiss on her uncle's front porch was one thing, sharing a bed was something else entirely.

If Luke noticed that she didn't allow more than the toe of her slipper to enter the room they were to share, he didn't comment on it. Leaving the portmanteau on the bed, he came toward her, and Eleanor quickly backed out of the doorway, anxious to avoid accidentally touching him. Her knees were still a little wobbly from the feel of him carrying her across the threshold.

Letty had thought to provide a light supper for the bridal couple, packing it in a wicker basket that had sat next to Eleanor's feet on the way to Luke's house—her house, she reminded herself as she picked at a plate of cold chicken and cold boiled potatoes dressed with Letty's special dressing. She'd been too nervous to eat at breakfast, too stunned at finding herself actually married to eat at the wedding supper her aunt and uncle had provided. The last decent meal she could recall was noon the day before and she knew she should be hungry, but she couldn't force down more than a few bites.

If Luke shared her nervousness, it didn't seem to have affected his appetite. He ate three pieces of chicken and a second helping of potatoes. Having run out of small talk, Eleanor let her eyes drift around the kitchen, which appeared to have suffered more abuse than the rest of the house. No wonder Luke had decided to get married. The place was falling apart around his ears.

Though she had no interest in food, she was sorry to see the meal end. Because once the food had been put away and the dishes had been scraped and set ready for washing the next morning, there was nothing to stand between her and the reality of that bed upstairs.

"Why don't you go on ahead," Luke said when there was no longer any excuse for lingering downstairs. "I'll smoke awhile and then come up."

Eleanor nodded wordlessly and left the kitchen, carrying a lamp with her to light the way. He was being considerate, she thought as she climbed the stairs. He was giving her time to unpack a few of her things and to change in privacy. If he was really considerate, perhaps he'd give her time to climb out a window and flee.

The image of herself dashing across the empty prairie in the middle of the night was so absurd that she smiled. But the smile wavered and crumpled as she pushed open the bedroom door and confronted the reality of the bed she was expected to share with her husband in a short while. It hadn't grown any larger since she'd last seen it. Two people sleeping in that bed would certainly be... intimate.

Trying to keep her mind a blank, Eleanor opened the portmanteau and took out what was necessary. She could finish unpacking tomorrow when she had a better idea of where her things might go, when Daniel arrived with her trunks. When her hands weren't trembling quite so badly.

She hurried through her ablutions, terrified that Luke might come in while she was in a state of undress. Tugging her nightdress on over her head, Eleanor froze as a sudden thought assailed her. Smothered in layers of fine muslin, she caught her breath, her eyes wide. He wouldn't expect to see her without her clothes, would he? Letty hadn't said anything about that. Surely he wouldn't expect to take all of her clothes off. No one had seen her naked since she was a baby.

Her heart thumping, she quickly finished pulling the nightdress down over her head and reached for her wrapper. Her pulse didn't slow until she had the wrapper on and buttoned all the way up to her throat. She pulled the pins from her hair and dragged a brush through it, trying to subdue the unruly curls into some semblance of decorum.

When she'd done the best she could, she tied the heavy mass back with a blue ribbon.

And then she waited.

Her hands clasped together in front of her to control their trembling, she tried to remember what Letty had told her, tried to forget Aunt Dorinda's grim expression and tried most of all not to think of how big and strong Luke was, of how easily he could overpower her. Despite Letty's reassurance, she couldn't prevent a shiver of fright from working its way up her spine when she heard a door close downstairs. Luke would be coming up soon. This was their wedding night and it wasn't likely that he planned to spend it alone.

Chapter Seven

Eleanor heard Luke moving around downstairs, perhaps checking to make sure the lamps were out and that windows and doors were closed against the cool night air. The sound of his boots on the stairs made her feel almost dizzy with fright. She threw a wild look at the bed, wondering if she should dive beneath the quilts and pretend to be sound asleep. But the last thing she wanted was to be anywhere near the bed when Luke came in.

So she stayed where she was, her hands gripping one another, the knuckles white with tension, her eyes huge in her pale face. When he entered the room, Luke thought she looked like nothing so much as a virgin sacrifice, waiting to be thrown into the maw of a volcano or fed to the lions.

He was already half aroused just from thinking about having her in his bed, but it was immediately obvious that it was going to take considerable effort to get her *into* that bed in the first place. Schooling himself to patience, he pushed the door shut, closing them in the room together. If possible, Eleanor's eyes grew even bigger.

He'd left his hat downstairs, and now he reached up to run his fingers through his dark hair, still slightly damp from washing up in the pump outside. The ice-cold water hadn't done much to quell his hunger. But even the simple motion of combing his fingers through his hair made her jump, and Luke suppressed a sigh of regret. It had been foolish to think she wouldn't be nervous.

"I'm not going to pounce on you," he said, keeping his tone light and easy.

She didn't smile but only looked away as he shrugged out of the black coat he'd worn for their wedding. He draped the coat over the back of a chair and turned to look at her again, debating the best way to go about seducing his wife.

"You knew we were going to share a bed, Eleanor." The words were neither statement nor question but hovered somewhere between the two. He saw her throat work as she swallowed. When she spoke, her voice was so low he had to strain to hear her.

"I just wondered . . . I wasn't sure . . ." Eleanor couldn't seem to lift her gaze from the floor.

"You wondered what?" The calm inquiry in Luke's voice gave her courage and she managed to raise her eyes as high as his chin. "What did you wonder, Eleanor?"

"I wondered if maybe you didn't have in mind a real marriage at all." She spoke the words in such a rush that they nearly slurred together. "That perhaps you really needed a housekeeper but couldn't find one and knew that my uncle would never allow me to work for you because it would mean living here alone with you and your brother and so you decided you'd marry me instead."

She stopped abruptly, holding her breath as she waited for his response. Luke's chest rose and fell as he drew a deep breath and slowly expelled it. The silence stretched out so long that she dared a nervous peek at his face. He was watching her, and she flushed and looked away, as if caught in some guilty crime.

"I had in mind a marriage real in every way," he said finally. "I'd hoped you'd want children."

"Oh, I do," she said, her mind filled with an image of a dark-haired baby with gray eyes.

"Well, then, having children requires a real marriage," Luke said reasonably.

"I know." Eleanor's voice dropped to a whisper and she returned her gaze to the floor again.

Luke couldn't help but notice the soft thrust of her breasts against the thin muslin of her nightdress and wrapper. The voluminous cut of the garments failed to conceal the womanly curves of her and he thought again that, while she might not be statuesque, there was certainly plenty there to fill a man's arms.

"Are you afraid of me?"

"No." He liked the way her chin immediately came up as if her pride had been stung. But her eyes skittered away the moment they met his. Her chin came down. "I'd just like a little more time before we . . . before we become . . . intimate."

Luke's first impulse was to give her what she asked for. Despite the pulsing beat of arousal that thrummed in his blood, he had no intention of starting off his marriage by forcing his bride to share his bed. But he hesitated, his eyes on her downbent head. That time he'd kissed her on her uncle's front porch she'd responded with a warmth that had made it damned uncomfortable to sit a saddle.

There was passion there and he wanted to taste it again. Whether she admitted it or not, she was scared to death, if not of him, then of what he might do to her. He could give her the time she asked and spend it trying to show her that she had nothing to fear from him. That might work. Then again, her fear might simply grow the stronger.

"When I was a little boy, I fell out of a tree and broke my arm," he said slowly, speaking apparently at random. "It wasn't a bad break but my mother didn't want to set it herself and risk leaving me crippled, so she sent for the doctor. It took him several hours to get there and I had plenty of time to think about what he was going to do when he got there and how bad it was going to hurt. By the time he got there, I'd scared myself so much that I started to cry the minute he set foot in the door."

He was pleased to see that Eleanor was looking at him, her eyes full of sympathy for the child he'd been. "Was it very bad?"

"No." Luke's mouth twisted in a rueful smile. "The waiting and worrying was a lot worse than anything he did. I'd scared myself half to death for nothing."

She blinked at him as his meaning sank in. "Are you saying that...marital duties are no worse than a broken arm?" she asked finally, looking both confused and even more apprehensive.

Luke nearly groaned aloud at the results of his clumsy attempt at reassurance. "What I'm saying is that the waiting and worrying are a great deal worse than reality."

"So you're suggesting that we just . . . get it over with?"

"That wasn't exactly what I meant." Luke choked back a laugh at her choice of wording. "But it's close enough, I suppose."

Eleanor chewed on her lower lip while she considered that possibility. She was still uncertain, but the longer Luke stood here talking to her, not jumping on her, the more the fear receded. It was difficult to hold on to her fear when he hadn't done anything frightening. And Letty had said that, with the right man, there was nothing to fear. If only she was sure that Luke was the right man. She was suddenly struck by the absurdity of that thought. He was her husband, which made him the right man in the eyes of God and the law. Perhaps he was right, and waiting would only make it worse.

"All right." The words exploded out of her as if she had to get them out in a hurry or not get them out at all. "If you think it's best."

It wasn't exactly an enthusiastic agreement, but it was as much as he'd hoped for to start with. Luke released the breath he hadn't realized he'd been holding and considered the best way to proceed from here. The blood thrumming in his veins demanded that he strip them both naked, throw her on the bed and slake the thirst she'd created in him.

Odd how much he wanted her. He'd known more beautiful women. Women who trembled with anticipation rather than fear at the thought of taking him into their beds. But there was something about this slip of a girl with her big brown eyes and sensuously full lower lip that had edged its way under his skin.

Just as well. It would make the job of producing a son a pleasure rather than a duty. And he'd make it a pleasure for her, too, he thought arrogantly, once he'd convinced her that he wasn't going to pounce on her and ravish her like some animal in the jungle.

"Did your aunt talk to you about what happens between a man and a woman?" As he spoke, he moved closer. Eleanor trembled but stood her ground, not pulling away even when he reached around behind her head and tugged loose the ribbon that held her hair at the nape of her neck.

"Yes." She managed to answer his question despite the shiver that ran down her spine as she felt his fingers brush her skin.

"What did she tell you?" Luke's tone was almost conversational as he gathered a handful of her thick hair and let it sift through his fingers to fall almost to her hips against the front of her gown.

"She said that a woman had to fulfill her marital duties and that I would learn to endure—that I should close my eyes and pray." She couldn't prevent a shudder as she remembered the stern expression in her aunt's eyes.

"Do you think I'm going to do something so horrible to you that you'll have to close your eyes and pray?" Luke didn't sound upset, only curious, and she dared a quick glance at his face.

"I . . . I don't know. My friend Letty said that it was more likely Uncle Zeb who'd had to learn to endure." Luke's quick bark of laughter reassured her. Whatever was going to happen couldn't be so terrible if he was laughing. Could it?

"What else did Letty say?" He kept his tone conversational, almost as if they were discussing the weather over a dish of brown Betty. So casual was his pose that it took Eleanor a moment to realize that he was deftly undoing the row of small pearl buttons that ran down the front of her wrapper. By that time they were nearly undone and it seemed foolish to protest.

"Letty said that...it might hurt a bit the...first time. But that after that, it could be quite pleasant." Her cheeks felt as if they were on fire when she finished speaking. Husband or no, she was not accustomed to discussing such things with a man.

"Did you believe her?" He made no move to push the wrapper off her shoulders, though it was completely open now.

"Yes . . . no . . . I'm not sure," she whispered finally.

"Would you believe me if I told you the same thing?" Luke's fingers slid along the line of her jaw to her chin, tilting her face up to his. It took every ounce of courage she possessed but Eleanor met his eyes.

"I'd try to."

Her careful honesty made him smile. But the smile faded when her tongue came out to lick her lips. The nervous gesture left a faint sheen of moisture behind and Luke thought he'd never seen anything so inviting in his entire life.

"Try real hard," he whispered as he lowered his head to hers.

Her mouth was just as he remembered it, soft and sweet, tasting faintly of the tooth powder with which she'd brushed her teeth. Her lips were stiff against his for a moment but gradually softened, allowing him to deepen the kiss. Luke's fingers drifted down her throat, his thumb resting on the pulse that beat steadily at its base. His tongue stroked across that tantalizing lower lip of hers.

Just as before, she sucked in a quick, shocked breath, stiffening under his touch.

"Open your mouth for me, Eleanor," he whispered without lifting his head. After a moment's hesitation she did as he asked, and then shivered in surprise as his tongue slid inside, claiming her mouth for his own.

At first she merely accepted his possession, standing rigid as a fence post beneath his touch. But Luke was patient. If it took the whole night to draw a response from her, then the whole night he'd use, even if the torture of it killed him.

But it wasn't going to take that long. He felt the change in her pulse first, felt it skip and then speed beneath his thumb. And then he felt it in the way her mouth opened wider beneath his, offering him greater access to the sweet warmth of her. Luke curled his tongue around hers, coaxing a response from her.

Eleanor was so absorbed in the wondrous feelings stirred by his kiss that she didn't notice his hands settling on her shoulders and then moving down her arms, taking her wrapper with them so that it pooled like a white shadow at her feet. His hand settled on her hip, warm and heavy, the heat penetrating her nightdress, making her aware that one layer of protection was gone.

She shifted uneasily but before she could murmur a protest, if that's what she'd intended, his hand left her hip. She hadn't had a chance to decide whether she was relieved or disappointed when she felt him touch her again. The breath was driven from her in a shocked little whoosh as his fingers brushed the side of her breast, once, twice, then cupped the firm globe as if laying claim to it. Eleanor dragged her mouth from his, her hand coming up to catch his wrist.

He left his hand exactly where it was. "Have I hurt you?"

Her eyes, wide and uncertain, stared up into his. She swallowed hard but shook her head. His eyes held hers as he brushed his thumb across the peak of her nipple. At the light touch, sensation rocketed through her, making her tremble.

"If you want me to stop, all you have to do is say so," he said.

Eleanor opened her mouth to tell him to stop, and he caught her nipple between his thumb and forefinger, squeezing gently. Her breath left her on a sigh that was nearly a moan. She wanted him to stop. Of course she did. But it was so difficult to think when he was doing that. Her fingers still held his wrist. She was completely unaware of using the hold to press him closer.

But Luke felt the subtle pressure, felt her lean into his touch. He lowered his mouth to hers. Her tongue came up to meet his with a hesitant eagerness that made his pulse beat with a thick, heavy rhythm. He no longer questioned the depth of his hunger for her. It was enough that he wanted her and that she was there, in his arms, yielding to his touch.

Afterward, Eleanor remembered his promise to stop if she asked him. And that she'd started to tell him to stop but somehow never quite got the words out. And then it had been too late. Much, much too late. Her fear and uncertainty had somehow disappeared beneath a wave of unfamiliar sensation. Instead of pushing him away, she'd found herself pulling him closer, wanting more of his touch.

She hardly noticed when his hand settled on her hip, his fingers gathering the fabric of her nightdress, drawing the folds of it upward, slowly baring her legs. Lost in the pleasure of his mouth on hers, his hand on her breast, she obeyed the subtle urging of his knee and shifted her legs apart. It wasn't until she felt the roughness of fabric against the softness of her inner thigh that she realized that she was nearly bare to the waist. She dragged her mouth from his, feeling something akin to panic flutter in her chest.

"Luke..." His name was a breathless whisper that ended on a sharp, indrawn breath as he slid his hand beneath the fragile protection of her nightdress, flattening his palm against her buttocks, urging her closer to his hard strength. At the same time his mouth slid down her throat, his tongue tasting the frantic pulse at its base.

"Luke, please."

She couldn't have said just what she was asking for. She wanted him to stop. Of course she did. The stroke of his hand on her buttocks, the pressure of his fingers on her breast were sinful. Anything that felt so wonderful had to be sinful. But she didn't think she could bear it if he stopped. No doubt she'd pay for the sin of enjoying the deliciously wicked things he was doing to her. But the threat of punishment in the hereafter wasn't as real as the pleasure he was giving her here and now.

Luke felt the uncertainty in her and knew she was hovering between pleasure and protest. But pleasure would win. There was too much passion in her for it to be otherwise. He eased his leg farther between hers, pressing his hard thigh upward against her soft warmth, feeling her start of surprise, feeling the dampness that revealed her need. He pressed harder, forcing her thighs wider so that she all but rode his leg.

Her shaken whisper was smothered beneath layers of muslin as he swept her nightdress up and over her head. His mouth swallowed any protest she might have offered, his tongue thrusting boldly inside, stealing her breath, stealing her ability to think. No one had seen her completely naked since she was a baby. The very thought had seemed horrifying just a little while ago. Yet here she stood, without a stitch of clothing on, uttering not a word of protest.

She should protest, she thought vaguely. Even though he was her husband, she was quite certain that what he was doing was not at all proper. But there was a liquid heat throbbing low in her belly and instead of pulling away, she found herself with the shocking urge to press closer to him. He pushed his leg harder against her most private places and she opened to him, helpless to do otherwise.

Luke's mouth left hers and Eleanor sucked air into her lungs, only to have it leave her on a startled shriek as she felt the wet heat of his tongue on her nipple. Her hands had been gripping his shoulders. Now they flew to his head, her fingers clutching his dark hair to pull him away. His mouth opened over her, drawing her into his mouth, and the strength left her hands.

His cheeks flexed as he drew on her nipple, already pebbled to hardness by the touch of his fingers. Eleanor felt that drawing at her breast, felt it echo deep inside her. Her protest became a whimper. Her head fell back, the thick fall of her hair covering Luke's arm where it lay across her lower back, supporting her, holding her. She'd never felt anything like this in her life, never even imagined such feelings were possible. How could pleasure be so intense that it was almost pain?

Luke felt her complete surrender in the yielding softness of her body against his, heard it in the barely audible whimper that escaped the back of her throat. He'd known there was passion in her. He'd counted on patience and skill to draw it out of her. What he hadn't counted on was the strain that patience would put on his control.

He wanted her. His gut ached with need, with a hunger that would have surprised him if he'd been in any condition to consider it. But at the moment all he could think of was laying his bride on the bed, stripping his clothes off and sheathing his aching hardness in the damp welcome of her body.

Eleanor felt the world spin as Luke lifted her in his arms and carried her to the bed. The linens were cool against her skin, which felt as hot as if she were burning up with fever. She opened her eyes and saw

Luke standing next to the bed, his fingers on the buttons of his shirt. He stripped the garment off his shoulders and his hands dropped to the waistband of his pants.

She told herself she should look away, that it had to be sinful to stare at a man's body, even when that man was her husband. But she couldn't drag her eyes from him. A mat of dark hair covered the muscled width of his chest, narrowing to a fine line that tapered down his belly, disappearing into the waist of his pants. And then he was shoving his pants over his hips and Eleanor's eyes widened, her mouth forming a round O of surprise.

Letty had said that her husband would be putting his manly part inside her. Though the thought had been shocking, Eleanor had seen animals mate and she'd thought she had some understanding of the process. But she'd had no idea . . .

"Luke, I don't think—"

"Shh." He was beside her on the bed and she could feel him pressed against her hip. The heat that radiated from him surprised her into silence for a moment, long enough for Luke's fingers to burrow into her hair, tilting her face up so that his mouth could claim hers.

Her thoughts grew fuzzy. She needed to talk to him, to explain that what he had in mind just wasn't possible. But it was so hard to think when he was kissing her like this, when his fingers were touching her breasts, her quivering belly, her—

She bolted against him, the breath whooshing out of her. He couldn't, he mustn't— But his fingers had already found her, discovered the embarrassing dampness of her most private feminine secrets. His thigh lay between hers, preventing her instinctive move to close her legs. And then he was stroking her, teasing her sensitive flesh, and instead of drawing away, she was arching into his touch, wanting more, wanting...something. Something that lay just out of reach, something she couldn't define, couldn't even imagine.

Her hands clung to Luke's shoulders as he rose above her, his legs sliding between hers. She felt the hair on his chest brush her nipples, already sensitized by his mouth. She felt him lower still, probing against the heart of her. Fear and uncertainty worked their way past the hunger he'd created and she caught her lower lip between her teeth, staring up at him with huge, dark eyes.

"Trust me," Luke whispered, seeing her uncertainty. Every fiber of his body screamed for him to find the satisfaction that lay so close, but he waited until he felt a subtle easing of her tension.

He lowered his head and covered her mouth with his as he consummated their marriage with a slow, steady thrust. He tasted her sharp gasp of pain as her maidenhead yielded to him, felt the shock of his possession ripple through her body. He forced himself not to move, to give her time to adjust to the reality of sharing her body with a man.

He waited, beads of sweat breaking out on his forehead as he struggled for control. And then she shifted beneath him, an almost infinitesimal movement that made him bite back a groan. He moved, retreating from the heated warmth of her. Her hips lifted slightly, as if in protest. He gave her what she asked and heard the startled gasp that broke from her at the sensation that resulted.

He'd known there was passion in her, and he'd been right. But he was surprised by the depth of her passion. He'd always prided himself on his control, on his ability to bring a woman to pleasure, but Eleanor's untutored response strained that control to the limits.

Eleanor was oblivious to Luke's struggle. She was awash in sensation, spinning out of control. Tension coiled in her, starting in the place where they were joined and spiraling out to encompass her entire body. The coil wound tighter and tighter until the tension was unbearable. She stiffened, suddenly frightened by the power of it.

Luke murmured something indistinguishable in her ear, some reassurance. And then his hand slipped between their bodies, finding her, touching her. And she shattered into a thousand pieces. She spun outward, the broad strength of Luke's muscled shoulders the only solid thing in the world. She heard Luke groan, a low guttural moan of something akin to pain, and then felt him shudder in her arms, his release spinning her higher still until it seemed as if they touched the stars.

It seemed a long time before Luke could gather the strength to lift himself away from Eleanor's lax body. She shivered slightly as cool air brushed over skin warmed by his loving. Luke tugged the quilt up over them, pulling her against his side as he sank back against the pillows. She snuggled into his warmth, her head pillowed on his shoulder, her small body curled into his.

Luke allowed his eyes to drift shut, his mouth curling into a satisfied smile. It wasn't often a man had reason to be glad he'd drawn the short straw.

Chapter Eight

Eleanor woke to the sound of someone moving around nearby. Startled and still half asleep, she jerked upright in bed, thinking that she'd overslept and Aunt Dorinda had come to get her up. But instead of her aunt's stern face, she found herself staring at the muscular width of a man's naked back. What had started out a scream emerged as a squeak when the intruder turned and she found herself staring into Luke's face.

Luke. Her husband. Memory rushed back. The wedding, the drive out to the ranch house, him showing her around her new home, her terrified anticipation of him joining her in the bedroom. And then it hadn't been terrifying at all, at least not in the way she'd anticipated.

"Good morning." His voice was even deeper than usual, husky with sleep.

"Good morning."

"How are you this morning?" His eyes searched her face and Eleanor felt her cheeks warm at the intimacy of that look.

"I'm fine." Her voice seemed to be caught somewhere in the back of her throat, emerging as little more than a whisper.

"You look fine." There was pure, masculine appreciation in his look as his eyes drifted downward. "You look more than fine."

With a horrified gasp, Eleanor snatched the blankets up to her chin, covering her bare breasts. Her cheeks felt as if they were on fire and Luke's husky laugh did nothing to cool the heat. It was probably foolish to feel embarrassed, considering the liberties she'd allowed him to take with her person the night before. Just the memories of those liberties was enough to make her tingle all over. But it was morning now, or close to it, she amended, noting the gray light that filtered through the thin curtains. And what was acceptable in lamplight seemed like brazen sin in daylight.

Luke took pity on her flushed cheeks and bent to scoop her wrapper up off the floor. She mumbled her thanks as she took it from him, but didn't immediately move to put it on. Seeing her uneasy glance in his direction, he sighed and turned away from her to pick up his shirt. Obviously it was going to take a while for her to lose her shyness. But he could be patient. Patience had its rewards, he thought, remembering her response the night before.

As he finished buttoning his shirt and began shoving the bottom of it into his pants, Eleanor walked past him to the dresser and picked up her hairbrush. Luke's movements slowed as he watched her drag the brush through the wild tangle of dark curls in a slow rhythm. Arousal thrummed low in his gut, but he restrained the urge to reach for her. He had a ranch to run and he couldn't do it from his bed, no matter how tempting it was to try. Besides, from the way she was avoiding looking at him, he suspected it would take considerable effort to persuade her to come back to bed.

Eleanor could feel Luke's eyes on her as she brushed her hair, but she couldn't bring herself to look at him. The memory of her abandoned behavior the night before was enough to make her cheeks flush with embarrassment. Not that he'd seemed to object at the time. Her eyes met his in the mirror and immediately darted away.

"I'll have breakfast ready shortly," she said, grasping at the prosaic as a way to distract her thoughts from what had happened the night before.

"Don't worry about it this morning. I'll grab some bread and meat on my way out. That'll hold me till supper."

"I'll have supper ready at noon for you and the hands, then." She picked up one of the ribbons she'd worn in her hair the day before and used it to tie the heavy mass at her nape.

It was exactly what he'd expected her to say, but Luke hesitated, feeling a twinge of something that could have been guilt. She looked so young this morning. Young and ... almost fragile. It occurred to him that in offering her this marriage that gave him everything he wanted, he might not have given as much thought as he should have to what *she* might have wanted.

He doubted many women dreamed of getting up the day after their wedding and cooking for half a dozen cowboys. Not to mention cleaning up three years of neglect. He wondered if he should have offered to take her on a wedding trip, maybe to Denver for a few days. And he could have hired someone to come in and clean up the house.

Luke shook his head. It was too late now, at least for the cleaning. And they could take a trip to Denver later in the year, when things slowed down a bit on the ranch. Besides, theirs was a marriage based on practicalities. Eleanor was hardly likely to expect romantic gestures from him.

"Just ring the bell outside the kitchen door when supper's ready," he said.

"All right." She'd turned to look at him, those big brown eyes solemn and just a little watchful, as if she wasn't quite certain what to expect from him. Well, that made two of them, Luke thought. He'd thought he knew exactly what he was getting when he decided he needed a wife. But now that he had one, he wasn't so sure.

"Do whatever you want with the house." He gestured vaguely. "Make whatever room you need for your things in here. And move whatever you like." He frowned at her, thinking that she really wasn't very big. "Don't try to move anything heavy. If I'm not around, one of the men can help."

"All right."

Luke hesitated, thinking there should be something else to say. But nothing came to mind and he shifted uneasily under the questioning look in her eyes.

"Well, I'll see you later, then." He turned and left without waiting for a reply, but he couldn't quite shake the feeling that there was something he'd forgotten. He was frowning as he went downstairs. This business of being married was going to take a little getting used to.

Eleanor watched Luke leave and told herself it was foolish to feel hurt just because he hadn't kissed her. He'd married her for practical reasons, not romantic ones, and she had no reason to expect kisses for no reason. It was just that, after last night ... She shook her head, telling herself not to be a goose. She had much too much to do to spend her time moping.

Eleanor's impressions of her new home the night before had been vague. Her mind had been on other things and she'd come away with only a rough idea that the whole house needed a good cleaning. In the daylight it was obvious that "a good cleaning" was putting it mildly. If there was a surface that wasn't coated in dust or grime, she didn't find it before the time came for her to start supper.

She wondered again why Luke hadn't simply found himself a housekeeper rather than a wife, but then a memory of the night before brought a flush to her cheeks. Perhaps he'd had more in mind than just a clean house. He'd said he wanted children, and certainly a housekeeper couldn't provide those.

The thought of a child made Eleanor smile. She pressed one hand to her flat stomach. She could be pregnant already. Her smile widened and her spirits rose. She'd always wanted children, just as she'd always wanted a real home. That was why she'd been willing to gamble on marrying Luke. Maybe there was more of her father in her than she'd thought. Certainly he'd never risked more on a turn of the cards than she'd risked by agreeing to this marriage. But unlike a game of poker, where once the cards were dealt, chance decided the outcome, she could make her own luck. Or so she hoped.

She looked around the kitchen, seeing beyond the grime to the future, a future that she and Luke could build together, here in this house, on this land. For the first time in her life she was settled in one place. She wasn't an unwelcome guest in her uncle's home anymore. She had a home of her own, a place to put down roots. She had her dream.

Her smile faded slightly as she considered that a husband who loved her had always been a part of her dream. But love could grow, and good marriages had been built on less than what she had with Luke. Or so she hoped. He desired her. Innocent as she was, she had no doubt of that. And if she provided him with a comfortable home and, God willing, children, who was to say love couldn't come of such things?

Her hopeful mood lasted until the noon meal. She'd spent the morning cleaning the kitchen, scraping three years' accumulated grime from every surface, then scrubbing everything with strong lye soap and a heavy scrub brush. It was going to take more than one morning's work to get the room really clean, but she'd made a dent in the job.

At least the larder was well stocked. Her husband and brother-in-law might have let the housekeeping slide but apparently they hadn't forgotten to eat. The state of the kitchen was testament to the fact that someone had been cooking in it, she thought, grimacing at the abundance of evidence left behind.

At midmorning she paused in her cleaning long enough to get a pot of stew started. That done, she got down on her hands and knees and began the monumental task of scrubbing the floor. By noon the kitchen was almost up to acceptable standards, the stew was done and a huge pan of biscuits was ready to go in the oven. She'd taken a guess at the amount of food necessary to feed half a dozen hungry cowboys and then she'd doubled her estimate.

She slid the biscuits in the oven, then went outside to ring the bell to call the men in to eat. By the time they'd washed up, the biscuits would be out of the oven, piping hot and flaky. She hoped they wouldn't take too long washing. Biscuits were at their best right out of the oven.

Her fingers were shaking a little with nerves as she quickly untied her apron and reached up to smooth her hair, patting hopefully at the eternally unruly curls around her forehead. This was her first test as a wife—well, maybe not her *first* test, she amended, blushing a little. But this was her first *public* test, and she wanted everything to be just right.

Eleanor was pouring coffee into thick cups when the squeal of the back door's hinges announced the arrival of the ranch hands. The room was instantly filled with large, masculine bodies. They crowded into the kitchen, smelling of sweat and manure.

She saw immediately that she needn't have worried about the biscuits cooling while the men washed up. The idea of using soap and water before eating was apparently hers alone. They appeared in her newly cleaned kitchen wearing whatever dirt had attached itself to their persons during the morning. Luke and Daniel entered last, and she was relieved to see that they'd at least washed the dirt from their hands, but they hadn't bothered to wipe their feet. In a matter of seconds the floor looked just as it had before she'd scrubbed it. "Sure smells good, ma'am." The words came from a tall, skinny young man, who looked barely old enough to shave. He gave her a gap-toothed smile.

"This is Gris Balkin," Luke said as he sat down at the head of the big oak table. "Slim White. Shorty Danvers. Joe Small."

Eleanor had already lost track of which face belonged with which name. She smiled and nodded as each man dipped his head in her direction and sat down at the table. She turned to pull the biscuits from the oven, sliding them into a big earthenware bowl, pleased to see that they were lightly browned and looked exactly right.

She turned back to the table and stopped dead, her eyes widening. She'd set the heavy pot of stew in the center of the table and put a big ladle beside it. The ladle was bypassed in favor of a more direct method. She watched as Shorty—or was it Gris?—served himself by dipping his bowl into the stew pot. Gravy dribbled across the table as he set the bowl in front of him and proceeded to lick his fingers clean where they'd apparently been dunked in the stew.

She waited in vain for someone to say something about this amazing display of bad manners. But since the other men were quickly following suit, in obvious appreciation of this expedient method of serving, it was hard to know just who should utter the necessary reproach. Trying to conceal her distaste, Eleanor edged up to the table and set the bowl of biscuits next to the stew.

"Biscuits!" One of the men—Slim?—greeted the addition with a pleased exclamation. The fact that his mouth was full did nothing to dim his enthusiasm.

The level in the bowl dropped instantly as hands flew across the table, snatching at the golden brown biscuits.

"Hot damn." The man who spoke began tossing the steaming biscuit back and forth between his hands, trying to cool it. "They's hotter than a witch's—"

"Gris!" Luke's snapped reprimand held a stern warning. He jerked his head in Eleanor's direction.

Reminded that there was a lady present, Gris flushed a deep shade of red. "Beggin' your pardon, Mrs. McLain."

Eleanor managed a weak smile to indicate her forgiveness for his language. If she'd thought that being reminded of her presence might have a beneficial effect on the men's manners, she was disappointed. While she watched, one of them picked up his bowl to slurp the gravy that remained in its bottom and then promptly dipped it into the stew pot for a second helping.

From the way the men were eating, she wondered if it wouldn't have served just as well to throw a raw haunch of meat into the center of the table and let them devour it like a pack of wolves. Certainly, wild animals couldn't have shown fewer table manners.

It didn't seem to have occurred to anyone to say grace, but then she couldn't really see the point of asking the Lord to bless the scene she was witnessing. Hands flew across the table, silverware clanked against bowls—thank heavens it was good, solid china; the sheer force with which they stabbed at chunks of meat would have shattered anything less sturdy.

They slurped their coffee and talked with their mouths full, at least when they weren't shoveling food into those same mouths. And shovel was the operative word. They ate with a speed that might have been flattering if she hadn't suspected that they'd have done the same with boiled shoe leather.

Her husband and brother-in-law were marginally better. At least they didn't stuff food into their mouths with their fingers, she thought. But then Daniel wiped his mouth on his sleeve and the smidgen of relief disappeared. She could only watch in awe as the mound of biscuits and the huge pot of stew were devoured in no time at all.

She'd never seen anything like it, and if there was a good side to the spectacle, it was that they were gone almost as soon as they arrived, nodding to her as they left the table, one or two mumbling a thank-you as they tromped out the door. Luke lingered behind the others.

"That was a fine meal, Eleanor."

"Thank you." She summoned up a smile.

"Are you settling in all right?"

"Yes." At least, she had been until now.

She wanted to say something about the scene she'd just witnessed but she couldn't find the words. Just a short while ago she'd been feeling so hopeful about the future but, looking at him now, she was reminded that he was still a stranger to her, no matter what intimacies they'd shared the night before.

"I'll take your trunks upstairs tonight. Unless you need them sooner."

"No. Tonight will be fine."

Luke hesitated, looking for something else to say. When he'd thought about marrying, he'd assumed he'd bring his new wife home, get her settled and not give much more thought to her. But he'd damn near lost a finger this morning because his mind was on his bride instead of the balky cow he'd just roped.

Looking at her now, he couldn't say just what it was about her that had made it so hard to keep his mind on his work this morning. It wasn't that she was a raving beauty, because she wasn't. But there was certainly something to be said for hair that was never quite tamed and eyes as big and soft as a fawn's.

Remembering the way her eyes had turned almost black with passion, Luke felt arousal stir in his gut. His jeans suddenly felt constricting and he had the urge to forget all about the work waiting to be done and take his wife upstairs to bed.

He could kiss away the dusting of flour on her short, straight little nose. And from there, he was only a whisper away from her mouth. That full lower lip of hers had haunted him since the first time he'd seen her. And now he had reason to know that it tasted every bit as good as it looked.

"If there's nothing you need, I'll be getting back to work," he said abruptly. If he didn't get out of here, he wasn't going to be able to resist the urge to kiss her, and once he kissed her, he wouldn't have bet a plugged nickel that he'd get out of the house anytime soon.

"There's nothing I need. Thank you."

"I'll see you later, then." It was just that he was new to marriage, Luke told himself as he strode out. He paused at the top of the back steps, settling his hat on his head to cut the glare from the noontime sun. It was like driving a herd new to the trail; it took a few days to settle in.

No doubt, it was going to take time to settle into being married, Eleanor thought. She dragged her eyes from the door through which her new husband had departed and surveyed the disaster that had, a short while ago, been a clean kitchen. The floor, which had been mopped less than an hour before, was coated with dirt and mud and substances she didn't want to identify. The table was a wreck of greasy dishes and spilled food.

She'd planned to eat after the men, but her appetite was gone. Forcing herself to move, she began clearing the table. Time, she told herself as she pumped water into a kettle and set it to heat, she just had to give it time. Hadn't she read that women provided a civilizing influence on the frontier? Obviously, the Bar-M-Bar hands had been too long away from such influence.

Eleanor spent the afternoon the same way she'd spent the morning—cleaning and cooking, though her enthusiasm for both was considerably diminished. At least she wouldn't have to worry about running out of things to do, she thought with a touch of sharp humor.

By the time the evening meal was on the table, she was too tired to care if the men ate with their feet, which was just as well because the scene was a repeat of the one at noon. She'd baked two pies, using dried apples she'd found in the big pantry. Both disappeared in a heartbeat, devoured literally out of hand since it didn't seem to occur to anyone to use a plate or fork.

Once the meal was finished, the hands returned to the bunkhouse, Luke and Daniel disappeared into the den to go over some paperwork and Eleanor was left with the wreck of her kitchen. Her jaw set with annoyance, she cleaned up the new mess as quickly as possible, then heated water to take upstairs so that she could wash up.

Luke had just struck a match to light his cigarette when he heard Eleanor's footsteps on the stairs. He promptly lost track of his conversation with Daniel. Was she going up to bed? He didn't have to close his eyes to picture the way she'd looked the night before, with her hair tumbling almost to her hips and her dark eyes soft with innocence and passion, a potent combination. Would she put on the same nightdress? He'd enjoy taking it off again, sliding his hands under the layers of fine muslin to find the even softer skin beneath. He'd—

"Dammit!" The curse exploded from him as the forgotten match burned down to his fingers. He dropped the match, shaking his singed hand and glaring at his brother, who was grinning unsympathetically.

"Thought you might have forgot about it," Daniel said.

"You could have said something." Luke blew on his fingertips to cool the burn.

"Could have," Daniel agreed, still grinning. He struck a match on the heel of his boot and lit his own cigarette before leaning forward to do the same for his brother. "But I figured you'd remember the match before it did any permanent damage."

"Thanks," Luke said dryly. He heard Eleanor moving around in their bedroom, which was directly over the den, and it took a considerable effort to keep his mind from drifting to what she might be doing.

"She's done a lot of work." It was obvious that Daniel knew what had distracted his older brother. "Place looks better already."

"Yeah." Luke agreed absently. The truth was, he hadn't paid much attention to what the house looked like. Somehow, after last night, he found himself less concerned with his bride's housekeeping skills. But now that Daniel had mentioned it, he noticed that the layers of dust that had coated every surface were gone.

"And she bakes a damn fine pie," Daniel added. He drew on his cigarette, squinting at his older brother through the smoke.

"Best biscuits I've ever eaten," Luke said, feeling a stir of pride.

"Can't argue that."

But Luke lost the conversational train again as a floorboard creaked overhead. Was she getting undressed? Or maybe she was already undressed and was now taking her hair down, running a brush through the thick, dark curls.

He jerked, startled, as Daniel leaned forward and plucked the cigarette from between his fingers.

"You burn yourself again and you're not going to be fit to handle a rope," Daniel said as he crushed the butt out in the ashtray on the desk.

Luke flushed, annoyed with himself for becoming distracted again. Dammit, what was it about her that made it so hard to put her out of his mind? Mercifully, Daniel refrained from commenting on his distraction, though the laughter in his eyes suggested that there was plenty he could have said, if he'd chosen.

"The boys were planning a poker game tonight. You going to join in?"

Luke opened his mouth to say he would and the floorboards shifted again overhead. "Not to-night."

He ignored his brother's knowing grin as he said good-night and went out to the bunkhouse. But once alone, Luke didn't immediately go upstairs. He deliberately took time to roll another cigarette and smoke it, proving to himself that, when it came to his new wife, he was in complete control. Only when the cigarette had been smoked to a stub did Luke allow himself to blow out the lamp. He climbed the stairs at a slow, deliberate pace, ignoring the steady beat of arousal that urged him to hurry.

She was leaning over the bed to turn back the quilt when he entered the room, but she straightened and turned to look at him, her eyes dark and unreadable. She was wearing the same nightdress she'd worn the night before but her wrapper lay across the foot of the bed. As she moved, Luke saw the gentle sway of her breasts beneath the thin muslin and hunger grabbed him by the throat.

Eleanor had planned to be in bed asleep—or feigning sleep—before Luke came upstairs. She was tired from the work she'd done, but more than that, she was no more certain that marrying Luke had been the right thing to do than she had been before she married him. And that uncertainty was all the more unsettling for the intimacy they'd shared the night before.

But Luke had come up to bed sooner than she'd anticipated. She watched him now, wondering what he'd say, wondering what she should say in return. They'd spent so little time talking, so little time getting to know each other.

But Luke didn't seem to be in a conversational mood. Without saying a word, he came toward her, unbuttoning his shirt as he walked. Eleanor felt her breath catch as he shrugged out of his shirt, letting it drop to the floor. Her gaze was filled by the thick muscles of his chest. She remembered the feel of those muscles against her breasts, the sweet abrasion of his chest hair against her nipples.

She swallowed and tried to find her voice, though she wasn't sure what she planned to say. Luke's hand came up, his fingers deft as he untied the ribbon that held the end of her braid. In seconds her hair was spilling over his hand. Eleanor opened her mouth—to protest?—but Luke's lips covered hers and whatever sound she might have made vanished in a sigh. Somehow, her fingers were sliding into the thick darkness of his hair, her mouth opening to invite his possession.

Held like this, pressed so close to him, her uncertainty faded. Luke's arms were so strong, his touch so sure. Something so sweet couldn't possibly be a mistake, could it? And then he was easing her back onto the bed, following her down, and Eleanor stopped thinking altogether.

Chapter Nine

"They eat like a bunch of savages, Letty."

"Men *are* savages." Letty's calm response drew a quick laugh from Eleanor but it ended in a discouraged sigh.

"I don't know what to do," Eleanor admitted. "I've read about the civilizing influence a woman's supposed to have on men but I haven't seen much evidence of it so far."

"It's only been two weeks, Ellie. They've had three years to revert to behavior more natural to them. It's going to take time and persistence to change their bad habits."

The two women were seated in the newly cleaned parlor of the McLain house. Letty had driven out to visit. After two weeks spent in exclusively male company, Eleanor would have been grateful to see any woman, but she was especially grateful to see Letty. She refilled their cups from the teapot that had been Letty's wedding present to her and settled back into her chair.

"I thought maybe just knowing I was there would make them remember their manners," she said. "But yesterday one of the men grabbed a handful of meat off the platter and dropped it on his plate. I'm surprised he didn't growl while he was eating it."

Letty smiled sympathetically. "You have to be firm with them, Ellie. Subtlety doesn't work with men. Unless they're hit over the head with something, chances are they won't pay any attention to it."

"I can't scold them as if they were children."

"Why not? In my experience, men frequently *act* like children. It might do them some good to be treated as such."

"It might, but I'm not going to be the one to do it." Eleanor's imagination quailed at the thought.

"Then ask Luke to say something to them," Letty suggested.

"Luke?" Eleanor's tone was so blank that Letty's brows rose again.

"Luke. Your husband," she said.

"I know who he is." Eleanor flushed and looked away.

"I thought you might have forgotten."

"Of course not." Eleanor took a sip from her teacup, using the action as an excuse to avoid her friend's eyes for a moment. Forget Luke? It would be easier to forget her own name. "I couldn't ask him to speak to the men," she said as she set her cup back in its saucer.

"Why not?"

"I just couldn't." She caught Letty's look and sighed. Letty could be annoyingly stubborn at times. "I don't really...know him well enough," she said slowly, trying to put her feelings into words. "We've only been married two weeks and I just don't feel comfortable making demands."

Letty considered that for a moment and then shook her head. "I think you're wrong, Ellie. The longer you go not making any demands, the harder it's going to be to make them." She lifted one hand to still the argument she could see in Eleanor's eyes. "I'm not suggesting that you turn into a shrew overnight, but you don't have to be a doormat, either."

"I'm not a doormat," Eleanor protested.

"Have you had a fight with Luke?"

"No, but—"

"Then you're a doormat." Letty's tone brooked no argument.

"But we've only been married two weeks," Eleanor protested.

"Past time for a fight. Or at least a small quarrel. You spent too many years living with your aunt, learning to hold your tongue because it did you no good to do otherwise."

"I can't just pick a fight with Luke over nothing."

"There's always something to quarrel with a man about." Letty spoke with the voice of experience and Eleanor smiled despite herself.

A comfortable silence fell between the two women. Eleanor sipped her tea and felt herself relax for the first time in two weeks. There was mending to be done and in a little while she needed to start preparations for supper—feeding the animals, as she'd come to think of it. But for now she wouldn't think of anything beyond enjoying the moment.

"What about his brother?" Letty asked abruptly.

"Daniel? What about him?"

"What's he like? I mean, have you found him to be pleasant?"

"Yes." Eleanor's answer was slow. She wondered at the reason for Letty's question. "Why do you ask?"

"I just wondered." Letty seemed interested in a minute spot on the skirt of her rose-colored silk dress.

"You're attracted to him." Eleanor's tone was gleeful.

"Don't be ridiculous," Letty snapped. Her cheeks were pinker than they had been. "I was just making polite conversation, that's all."

"He *is* attractive," Eleanor said, ignoring her friend's feeble protest. Of course Daniel was attractive. He was practically the spitting image of his brother. How could he be anything else? "Oh, Letty, it would be such fun if you married Daniel! Then we'd be sisters by marriage."

"Marry him? I don't even know him!" But Letty's protest wasn't as vehement as it might have been.

"We can take care of that. Once he meets you, he'll fall in love with you."

"We've been introduced and he showed no signs of being smitten. He barely nodded to me at the wedding," Letty observed with a hint of annoyance.

"There was so much hustle and bustle, I doubt he could have pointed out the bride," Eleanor said soothingly.

It was all she could do to refrain from rubbing her hands together with glee. In the years she'd known Letty, this was the first interest her friend had ever shown in someone of the opposite sex, despite the fact that several eligible bachelors had put considerable effort into courting the young widow. That it should be Daniel who'd attracted Letty's eye was simply too perfect.

"You could invite us to dinner," she suggested. "That would give Daniel a chance to get to know you."

"Absolutely not!" Letty's teacup clattered against the saucer as she set them both down. "I won't stoop to chasing the man. Besides, you're jumping to conclusions. I never said I found him in the least attractive."

"But you didn't say you didn't, either." Eleanor's tone was sly. She was not in the least discouraged by Letty's attitude. All she had to do was make sure their paths crossed and trust Daniel to have the good sense to see what a wonderful wife Letty would make.

"I don't know what you're plotting, but I want no part of it," Letty said when she saw the look in her friend's eyes. Her movements were agitated as she stood and reached for her reticule and gloves. "I should be getting home."

She appeared relieved when Eleanor didn't pursue the topic of Daniel's suitability as husband material. Letty asked if Eleanor and Luke would be attending the upcoming Fourth of July celebration in Black Dog, easily the town's most festive holiday of the year. Eleanor didn't know but said she'd ask Luke.

"Don't forget to do so. It wouldn't be much fun without you." Letty brushed a kiss on Eleanor's cheek. "And don't forget that a good quarrel now and then can do wonders for a marriage. Besides, it can be such fun to make up," she added with a wicked smile that made Eleanor blush.

Eleanor stayed on the porch, watching as Letty drove her smart little buggy out of the yard. She waited until it was out of sight before turning back to the house. She mulled over Letty's suggestion that she needed to be more demanding but discarded it almost immediately. Letty just didn't understand. True, she had been married, which made her the voice of experience. But Letty had been in love with her husband and he with her. Their situation had been altogether different from hers and Luke's.

Ask Luke to speak to the men? How could she? Aside from the time they spent in bed together, she felt as if she barely knew him. And the fact that she'd come to know him very well indeed in the Biblical sense only clouded the issue. Outside the bedroom they rarely exchanged more than a few sentences in a day. And they didn't talk much inside the bedroom, either, she admitted, flushing as she considered what they did do.

Still, wonderful as his lovemaking was, it wasn't enough to satisfy the part of her that insisted that there was more to a marriage than that. Other than in bed, she might almost have been invisible for all the attention Luke paid her. Not that he was ever rude, but she wanted more than politeness from him. She wanted . . .

She wanted him to love her.

No matter how often she told herself that it was a foolish, romantic notion, that marriage didn't require love, she couldn't give up the dream of having a husband who loved her the way her father had loved her mother.

Eleanor grinned as she considered Letty's suggestion that she pick a fight with Luke. Somehow, she couldn't quite believe that that was the best way to make a man fall in love with her. Obviously, she'd have to think of something else.

In the meantime, there was dinner to prepare and she still had to think of some way to persuade the men that eating like a pack of wolves was not the best form of behavior. If only she knew how this feminine "civilizing influence" was supposed to work. Lord knew, she needed a double dose of it here.

If Luke had suspected that Eleanor was less than content with their marriage, he would have been surprised. As far as he was concerned, marriage was a great deal better than he'd ever anticipated. When he'd listed the attributes he required in a wife, he'd had little hope of fulfilling them all, but he'd managed to do just that.

Dust no longer coated every surface. Meals were neither burned nor raw. In fact, if he had a complaint about his wife's cooking, it was that it was too good. It took a considerable effort of will to drag himself from the table and climb back into the saddle. His clothes were clean and mended, he was well fed, the house was becoming a home again and, on top of all that, he'd married a woman who had all the sweet passion a man could possibly want.

He'd made a good choice, he thought now, his gaze pardonably smug as he looked around the parlor, admiring the gleaming surfaces and the renewed color of his mother's treasured rug, which had been thoroughly beaten a few days ago and then relaid over a bed of fresh straw.

"Place looks like it used to," Daniel commented, his thoughts moving along the same lines as his brother's.

"Yup." Luke noticed that the ashes on his cigar had grown dangerously long, and reached for the ashtray. The ash dropped off before he got there and he used the toe of his boot to rub it into the rug before tapping the remainder off in the ashtray.

Eleanor had already gone upstairs, so there was no possibility of her seeing him drop ashes on her freshly cleaned rug. Not that she would make a fuss, even if she did, he thought. Didn't have a bad-tempered bone in her body, near as he could tell. He thought he heard a sound from upstairs, but Daniel spoke before he could decide whether or not he'd really heard something.

"Best pie I've ever laid a tooth to." The ashtray was beyond Daniel's reach, so he tapped his ashes into a cut-glass bowl that held decorative waxed fruit.

"She can cook." Luke allowed a trace of smugness to color his words.

Hearing it, Daniel grinned. "Got just about everything you wanted."

"Yup."

"No regrets?"

"Nope." He wondered if Eleanor was in bed yet. The thought of going up to join her held more interest than smoking another cigar with his brother, he decided, examining the tip of the one he held. He tilted his head toward the door, thinking he'd heard something but, again, Daniel spoke before he could decide for sure.

"I never thought I'd envy you for drawing the short straw when we decided one of us had to get married," Daniel said ruefully.

He would have said more, but this time they both heard the same sound. A startled gasp, followed by a soft flurry of movement from the direction of the hall. Luke was on his feet and in the doorway in the space of a heartbeat. He caught only a glimpse of Eleanor's ankles as she disappeared up the stairs in a swirl of muslin.

He winced as the sound of their bedroom door being slammed echoed through the house.

His face expressionless, Luke turned back into the parlor. Carrying his cigar over to the ashtray, he rubbed it out, taking great pains to extinguish every trace of embers. Daniel cleared his throat.

"You hadn't told her about us drawing straws?" he asked.

"Didn't seem much point in it." Luke shrugged.

"Women can be a little peculiar about things like that." Daniel stood and stubbed out his own cigar in the ashtray.

"She may be a little annoyed but she's a sensible girl. I'll have a little talk with her," Luke said in his best husbandly tone.

"There's room in the bunkhouse," Daniel offered.

"She's not the sort to throw a fit."

Daniel gave him a doubtful look as he bent to pick up his hat from where it had rested on the sofa. He put it on, looking at his older brother from beneath its shadow. "I said it before but I'll say it again. Ain't the woman been born that can't throw a fit, given the right circumstance."

"My wife doesn't throw fits," Luke said firmly, confident that he was right.

"There's room in the bunkhouse," Daniel repeated. He clapped his hand on Luke's shoulder before leaving.

Luke waited until he heard the front door shut behind Daniel before heading upstairs. If Eleanor *was* going to throw a fit, he had no desire for Daniel to hear it. Not that he thought for a minute that she was going to do any such thing. But it did occur to him as he reached the second floor that he really hadn't spent all that much time with his bride, other than in bed, of course. Maybe he didn't know her as well as he might.

He reached for the doorknob and felt a surge of relief when it turned easily beneath his hand. He'd half expected the door to be locked against him. She might be a little upset. Maybe she'd even shed a few tears, but she was a sensible girl and she'd be reasonable. Luke pushed open the door and stepped into the room, prepared to comfort his weeping bride.

"What the—" He ducked as a book sailed past his ear and slammed into the wall beside the door. His eyes followed its trajectory back to the source and his reasonable explanation for what Eleanor had overheard vanished from his thoughts.

His gentle, sensible bride stood on the other side of the bed, the fury in her eyes at odds with the flowing femininity of her nightdress and wrapper. Maybe she wasn't going to be reasonable after all, Luke decided as he pushed the door quietly shut behind him.

Chapter Ten

"You low-down, stinking polecat!" Another book sailed across the room to land with a thud against the wall.

There wasn't a tear in sight, Luke noticed as he dodged the missile. But if looks could kill, he'd have died right where he stood. Since looks alone wouldn't accomplish the task, Eleanor was apparently more than willing to try direct methods.

A silver-backed hairbrush and matching comb were fired in his direction with the speed and accuracy of a gunfighter throwing lead. Luke winced as the brush bounced off his shoulder.

"You are the most disgusting, filthy excuse for a human being I've ever had the misfortune to meet in my entire life," she told him as her fingers closed around the handle of the wash pitcher.

"Eleanor—"

The pitcher sailed past his head, smashing against the wall and splattering Luke with water and shards of china.

"Stop this right now," he said. But his stern tone was made less effective by the fact that he was forced to hop to one side to avoid the bowl the pitcher had been sitting in. The sound of shattering china seemed only to fuel her rage.

"I'd have been better off marrying a one-armed leper," she snarled as she groped for the mirror that matched the brush and comb.

"Don't you throw that," he ordered. The mirror just missed his head. "Dammit, woman, stop throwing things and let me explain!"

"There's nothing to explain." She'd found another book and sent it hurtling across the room.

"You don't know what you heard," Luke protested, dodging the book and starting toward her.

"I may have been dumb enough to marry you, but that doesn't mean I'm deaf, too," she snarled. Out of ammunition, she jerked off one of her slippers and threw it at him as she backed away from his advance. "I heard exactly what Daniel said. You married me because you drew a short straw and had to find yourself a wife. *You married me because you lost.*" Her normally soft voice rose to something close to a shriek.

"It wasn't like that," Luke said, knowing it had been exactly like that.

"You stay away from me," she demanded, taking another step back. She brandished her remaining shoe, her dark eyes snapping with rage.

Luke kept an eye on the shoe. She'd proven to have uncomfortably accurate aim.

"You calm down and stop acting like a...a woman," Luke told her, unable to think of a more suitable comparison.

"Acting like a woman is better than acting like a jackass."

"Put that shoe down right now."

Luke edged a little closer. The shoe stayed where it was, her arm poised to throw.

"Stay away from me."

"If you don't put that shoe down this minute, I'm going to put you over my knee, I swear I will!" He'd never laid a violent hand on a woman in his life, but he was starting to think he might make an exception for his wife.

"You wouldn't dare." She looked more infuriated than intimidated, and the shoe didn't move.

"If you're going to act like a child, I'll treat you the same way."

"Better a child than a skunk," she snapped.

"I've had just about enough of this," he warned, and took an authoritative step toward her.

The shoe clipped the side of his forehead, the shock of it staggering him more than the blow itself. The little witch had actually thrown it, despite his warnings. Luke lifted his hand to touch the injured area, drawing away fingers streaked with blood from where the hard heel had cut the skin.

Anger grabbed him by the throat. He lifted his eyes to his wife. Her face was white, as if she were as shocked by her action as he was. Her eyes met his, reading the steely intent in his look. With a squeak of dismay she turned to flee the beast she'd roused.

Luke caught her before she'd gone two steps, tumbling her back onto the bed in a tangle of muslin skirts. She fought like a wildcat, her legs churning as she tried to kick him. She managed to land a few blows but accomplished little more than bruising her bare toes against his shins, which were protected by the tops of his boots. She tried to bring her hands up to strike him but she was no match for Luke's superior strength, and it wasn't long before she found herself pinned facedown across her husband's lap, her legs caught between his, the solid weight of his forearm across her shoulders.

"Don't you—" Eleanor's muffled warning ended on a shriek as the flat of Luke's hand came down across her derriere. The muslin of her nightdress provided little cushioning, either for that blow or the two that followed in quick succession.

Luke's hand came up, ready to deliver another swat, but with a pitiful little cry Eleanor went limp, her face buried in the covers, her shoulders shaking in an apparent paroxysm of tears. Guilt slammed into him. Good God, what was he doing? He hadn't lost his temper like that in more years than he could remember. And here he was, losing it with his wife, *beating* her, for God's sake! He'd reduced her to tears, probably scared the life out of her. Staring down at her trembling back, Luke felt lower than a snake's belly.

"Eleanor." He eased his hold, reaching out to draw her up, intending to apologize, to offer comfort.

The moment his grip loosened, Eleanor twisted with the speed of a striking snake and fastened her teeth in the first portion of his anatomy that presented itself, which happened to be his thigh.

If it hadn't been for the protective denim of his jeans, Luke thought she might have drawn blood, which was what she seemed to be after. Denied that, she still managed to inflict considerable discomfort.

With a howl of mingled outrage and pain, Luke shot to his feet. Since Eleanor was still sprawled across his lap, his sudden move dumped her onto the floor, breaking her grip on his leg at the same time.

For the space of several heartbeats they stared at each other, Luke's eyes almost coal black, Eleanor's brown eyes snapping with a mixture of anger and a touch of fear. Luke was savagely pleased to see the latter. The guilt he'd felt a moment before at striking her had shifted to regret that he hadn't continued the spanking. The little witch had bitten him!

He bent, reaching for her. Eleanor scrambled backward and stumbled to her feet, hampered by the enveloping layers of muslin. She darted toward the door but his hand closed around her upper arm, spinning her around and tumbling her back onto the bed.

This time Luke felt less hesitant about using his strength against her. The struggle was brief, the outcome clear from the start. In a matter of seconds he'd pinned her to the bed, holding her there with the hard length of his body.

Panting and breathless, she lay beneath him, taut as a fence wire and nearly as full of barbs, Luke thought, feeling the bruises she'd managed to inflict. Her hair had come loose during the wild struggle and now it covered her face, blinding her. She huffed, trying to blow it out of the way.

Seeing her dilemma, Luke caught her wrists in one hand and pinned them against the tangled covers over her head. He used his free hand to brush the hair away from her face. She gave him a glare by way of a thank-you, her eyes no longer the soft brown of a fawn's but almost black with rage instead.

"Now you're going to listen to me," he said sternly.

"You hit me!"

"You deserved it," he retorted, ignoring the niggling twinge of guilt. "You damn near took my leg off with your teeth."

"Too bad it wasn't your head," she snapped, showing no repentance.

"You're acting like a child. I don't know what you're so fired up about in the first place."

"Did you draw straws to see which of you had to get married?" she demanded.

"Yes." There was no sense in denying that much.

"And did you draw the short straw and have to marry me because of it?"

"I didn't have to marry *you*. I just had to marry someone." If he'd thought that bit of information would cool her ire, he was mistaken.

"You married me because you *lost*." She all but spit the last word at him.

"It wasn't like that. It didn't have anything to do with you personally. We just figured one of us ought to get married and—"

"Why?" she interrupted without apology.

"Why what?" With her stretched out beneath him, it wasn't easy to keep his mind on the conversation. His body, tuned to fever pitch by the fight, was starting to occupy itself in other directions.

"Why did one of you have to get married?" Obviously, Eleanor was not having the same problem with her concentration.

"Well, there was the house. It needed a woman's touch."

"It needed blasting powder. It looked like a bunch of hogs had been living here."

Luke didn't think that was quite fair, but she was angry and he'd allow her the exaggeration. With her eyes shooting sparks at him the way they were and the length of her body pressed to his, he was willing to allow her just about anything she wanted.

"We knew the place needed a woman," he said, bringing his mind back to the conversation at hand with an effort.

"Why not hire a housekeeper?"

"We thought of that. But we'd had trouble with the last couple of women we hired. A wife seemed a better idea," he admitted—a mistake, apparently.

"Ooooo!" The sound was somewhere between a wildcat's scream and a steam whistle, and it was the only warning she gave. She arched abruptly, trying to dislodge his weight. The movement was sudden enough and he'd been distracted enough that she nearly succeeded.

There was a frantic scramble for control with Luke hampered by the need to avoid hurting her. Eleanor felt no such need. A pained grunt escaped him as her knee caught him on the thigh. Considering where she'd been aiming, Luke considered himself fortunate to escape with a bruise. By the time he'd managed to regain control, they were both breathless.

"What the hell is wrong with you?" he demanded furiously.

"Get off me!"

"Are you going to stop trying to kill me?" Her eyes gave him the answer and he judiciously tightened his hold on her wrists.

How could he have thought she didn't have a temper? he wondered, staring down at her flushed face. He'd seen rabid coyotes look friendlier—less dangerous, too, he thought, feeling the assorted bruises she'd managed to deliver. He'd been in barroom brawls and come out with fewer injuries. But then, in a barroom brawl, he'd never had to concern himself with protecting his opponent.

"I don't know what you're so riled about," he said, his exasperation plain. "It isn't as if we married for love."

Eleanor had been straining her arms against his hold but, at his words, she stilled. She stared up at him for a moment, her eyes unreadable. And then her lashes lowered, shielding her expression from him.

"No, we didn't marry for love," she murmured, the first sign of reasonableness that Luke had seen since he entered the room.

"Then why are you so angry?"

Instead of answering his question, she asked one of her own. "Why didn't you hire a housekeeper?"

Luke considered the question, wondering if the truth was going to set her off again. But since he didn't have a plausible lie, the truth was going to have to do. Besides, it wasn't as if there was anything wrong with the truth, dammit!

"A housekeeper couldn't give me a son," he said. "I told you I wanted children, and that takes a wife."

He waited, wishing he could read something in her expression. But she kept her eyes lowered and her face utterly still, leaving him to guess what might be going on in that female head of hers.

Angry or not, she felt remarkably good beneath him. His body, oblivious to the taut atmosphere, was reacting to the feel of her stretched out against him. Hardly conscious of moving, Luke shifted, his hips nudging more firmly between her thighs so that she cradled his growing arousal against her feminine softness.

He wanted her in a way he couldn't ever remember wanting a woman before. Dammit all, he didn't even know what they were fighting about! What difference did it make *how* she'd come to be his wife? She was, and that was what mattered.

Feeling his hardness, sensing the change in his mood, Eleanor went utterly still, like a rabbit sensing the nearness of a hunter. Her eyes met his and she saw the hunger in the tightness of the skin stretched over his cheekbones, in the way his eyes had darkened to the color of smoke.

"No." She gasped the word out, turning her head to the side as he bent to kiss her. Deprived of her mouth, Luke settled for nuzzling the taut line of her neck instead.

"You're my wife." His breath whispered over her skin. The light touch sent a shiver of awareness through her. He'd taught her too well these past two weeks, she thought bitterly. Her body responded to his touch like a finely tuned instrument to the hands of a master. But she'd rather die than give in to him now.

"You'll have to force me." Her voice was hard as tempered steel, not an inch of give in it.

Luke lifted his head to stare down at her, reading the determination in her face. He could make her give in to him, even wring a response from her, whether she was willing to admit it or not. Hell, she was his wife; there'd be no one to blame him if he took what he wanted, willing or not.

But he'd never forced a woman in his life and had nothing but contempt for a man who would do so, whether she was his wife or not. With a curse he released his hold on her, rolling off the bed and out of reach as he did so. If she took another swing at him, he couldn't vouch for his temper. The next time she hit him, he'd either turn her over his knee again or flip her skirts over her head and bury himself in the sweet warmth of her.

But Eleanor didn't try to renew her attack. She was more concerned with pulling her nightdress down over her bare legs as she scrambled off the bed on the side opposite him. She watched him without speaking, her dark eyes wary. With her hair lying in tangled curls on her shoulders and her breasts still heaving with exertion, she might have been a painting labeled Temptation. The thought put an extra edge to his voice.

"Let me know when you're through with your temper tantrum," he said coldly. Without another word he turned and stalked from the room, his boot heels ringing on the wooden floor.

He snatched his hat up on the way out the front door, slapping it on his head as he strode across the yard to the barn. There were lights on in the bunkhouse and he briefly considered Daniel's suggestion that there was room for him to sleep there. But he discarded the thought as soon as it came. He'd be damned before he'd have every cowboy on the place knowing that his wife had thrown him out of their bed.

The barn was warm and smelled of fresh hay and animals. The gray gelding recognized the sound of Luke's footsteps and put his head over the stall door to snort a greeting. *At least my horse is happy to see me,* Luke thought sourly. He stopped to rub the gelding's forehead.

He still couldn't believe Eleanor's display of temper—a temper he'd have just about bet the ranch she didn't possess. It seemed Daniel was right—there wasn't a woman born who didn't throw fits.

He wasn't an unreasonable man, Luke thought, feeling somewhat aggrieved. He could understand how a woman might not much like to hear that she'd been married because her husband had drawn a short straw. Not that it seemed to him that it should matter all that much. They were married, and that was all there was to it. But a woman might not see it that way and he could understand Eleanor being upset. If she'd cried, he would have been more than willing to dry her tears.

But instead of tears, she'd tried to kill him. Might have succeeded, too, if he'd been a little slower. Luke fingered the shallow cut on his forehead. It was little more than a scrape but the severity of the injury was not the point. The point was that

Eleanor had inflicted it, along with more bruises than he could count.

Eleanor—his quiet, biddable bride.

He still couldn't believe the display of temper he'd witnessed. Damned if she hadn't looked as if she'd have been happy to see him dead.

"She could have killed me," he said aloud.

The gelding nodded his head in sympathy. Or maybe he was just trying to make sure Luke's scratching fingers reached a particular itch.

"How was I supposed to know that she had a temper like a catamount with its tail caught in a trap?"

The gelding snorted.

"Females," Luke muttered in a tone laced with disgust. "I should have stayed single."

She should never have married Luke McLain. That was the one thought that penetrated Eleanor's storm of weeping. She'd have been better off staying with her aunt and uncle. At least *they* hadn't drawn straws for her as if she was a . . . an unwanted package that someone had to take.

She caught her breath on a sob. No, that wasn't true. They'd never made much secret of not wanting her. If they could have drawn straws to get rid of her, they might have done so, despite Uncle Zeb's aversion to gambling. So she'd gone from a home where she wasn't wanted to a husband gained because he'd lost a silly, childish gamble.

Gulping to stem the flow of tears, Eleanor rolled onto her back and stared up at the ceiling. Her chest ached with a mixture of hurt and anger. Was there something wrong with her? Had she committed some sin, that she should be punished by being forced to live where she wasn't wanted?

But Luke hadn't said he didn't want her. He hadn't said that at all. She sat up, her breath hitching in her chest with residual sobs. What was it he'd said?

I didn't have to marry you. *I just had to marry someone.*

So once he'd drawn the short straw, he'd still had to choose a bride. And he'd chosen her.

Eleanor slid off the bed and padded across the room to get a clean handkerchief. She wiped her eyes and blew her nose. Her breath still catching a little, she sat down on the wooden rocking chair in the corner next to the window and drew her bare feet up under the edge of her nightgown.

Luke had married her by choice.

She rolled that thought around and felt some of the tightness in her chest ease. However he'd gone about deciding to get married, he hadn't married *her* as a result of drawing a short straw. And as he'd pointed out, it wasn't as if they'd married for love.

The reminder had been painful but she couldn't deny the truth of it. Luke had never said he loved her. And if she had been foolish enough to fall in love with him—and she wasn't entirely ready to admit that she had—then she couldn't blame him for her change of heart.

The problem was, she'd gone into this marriage with too many stars in her eyes. She'd told herself that she was being practical but she'd really been a romantic child, dreaming about happily ever after. The past two weeks should have beaten that out of her. Hadn't Luke made it abundantly clear that he'd wanted a wife for cooking and cleaning and not much else?

Well, for a few other things, she admitted as her glance fell on the bed. Now the covers were rumpled from their struggle, but most mornings their tousled condition was caused by something else entirely. Certainly, she had no complaints about that part of her marriage. And she didn't think Luke did, either.

A short straw! Eleanor winced at the thought. It was a far cry from her romantic fantasies. But it was done and they were married and she was simply going to have to make the best of it. Now that her temper had cooled a bit and she was able to think a little more clearly, she had to admit that things could have been worse.

Whatever his reasons for marrying her, Luke had proved to be a kind husband so far. He'd treated her gently. Most of the time, she amended, aware of a tenderness in her nether regions. She shifted uncomfortably in the hard rocker, her eyes darkening with renewed anger at the remembered abuse he'd delivered.

Of course, he *had* been provoked, she admitted, thinking of the bloody scrape on his forehead. Perhaps she shouldn't have thrown that shoe. Eleanor considered that possibility for a moment and then shook her head. He'd deserved that—and worse. Her only real regret was that she hadn't managed to inflict more damage. Luke should never have drawn straws over something as important as marriage.

No doubt he'd been congratulating himself on having gotten a docile bride, one who'd cause him little trouble while providing the sons he wanted. She'd given him little enough reason to think she was anything other than that these past two weeks.

"If you act like a doormat, you've no cause for complaint if people treat you as such," she muttered to herself. She stood, putting one hand to her bruised derriere, her small chin firming in a way that might have made Luke nervous if he'd been witness to it.

She couldn't change the past. She was married and that was all there was to it. And marriage to Luke McLain, no matter how it had come about, was certainly better than being an unpaid and unwelcome drudge in her aunt's home. It was even, though she'd admit it only to herself, better than finding herself married to Andrew Webb and his four children.

No, she couldn't say, even with anger still churning inside her, that she was sorry she'd married Luke. But it was time and past that she made a few changes around here. More than simply dusting and cleaning. Luke might have got himself a bride and, God willing, he'd have the sons he wanted, too, she thought, setting a hand against her stomach. But he was going to find out that she wasn't quite the biddable girl he might have thought her.

Of course, considering the encounter just past, he might already have a hint of that. Eleanor smiled at the thought and crawled into bed, feeling better than she'd have thought possible an hour ago.

Chapter Eleven

Luke wasn't sure what to expect from Eleanor when he saw her at breakfast. But since a pile of hay had proved a scratchy and uncomfortable bed, he'd had plenty of time during the night to contemplate the possibilities.

His favorite image was of Eleanor repentant over her display of temper the night before. He'd walk into the kitchen and find his breakfast laid out for him—mounds of fluffy biscuits, bacon sizzling on the stove, fried potatoes in the warming oven and Eleanor poised to cook his eggs. Those big dark eyes of hers would be soft and warm—and just a little red from crying tears of regret. Her smile would be a little trembly around the edges—her look asking for forgiveness.

He might not give it right away, he decided, touching the wound on his forehead gingerly. But eventually, he'd forgive her and they'd make up. A faint smile curved Luke's mouth as he considered just what form that making up might take. When he was a boy, he'd once heard his pa say that making up was the best part of having a quarrel. He hadn't understood it then, but he could certainly understand it now.

Maybe Eleanor would offer to kiss every bruise she'd inflicted, he thought, letting his imagination run wild. She could start with the scrape on his forehead and work her way down to the bite on his thigh. The image brought a new ache to join the ones he already had.

The hay rustled under Luke as he shifted uncomfortably on his scratchy bed. Dammit all, he didn't see why making up had to wait until morning. What was he giving her time to think about, anyway? He was her husband. He had certain rights, and the least of them was the right to sleep in his own bed. If Eleanor didn't want to share it with him, let *her* spend the night in the barn.

Righteous indignation had him sitting up, ready to go back to the house and inform his recalcitrant bride of his decision. He was halfway to his feet when he suddenly saw Eleanor's soft brown eyes, flashing with rage but with an underlying hurt in them. He sank back on the blanket, the righteous indignation fading into something uncomfortably close to guilt. Maybe he'd allow her some time to think things over, after all.

He just hoped that her temper would wear off by morning. If it hadn't, he might be wise to insist on her tasting any food she served him. Mad as she'd been, he was likely to find himself with arsenic in his biscuits.

As it turned out, Luke didn't have to worry about the possibility of finding hazards in his food. Nor did he have to concern himself with his bride's mood. Eleanor solved both problems for him by not making an appearance at the breakfast table. Which suited him just fine, Luke told himself as he sliced bacon into a skillet. The last thing he wanted was to deal with a temperamental female first thing in the morning.

He'd just poured his first cup of coffee when his brother came in. The past few days Daniel had been having breakfast at the main house.

"There's coffee," Luke said, by way of greeting.

While Daniel poured himself a cup of the syrupy black brew, Luke sliced more bacon into the skillet.

"Where's Eleanor?" Daniel asked, after taking his first swallow of coffee and finding it nearly thick enough to chew and strong enough to strip paint off a house—just the way coffee should be.

"She's sleeping in," Luke said shortly.

As if on cue, they both heard the sound of footsteps in the bedroom overhead. Luke clenched his teeth and cut another slice of bacon, nearly taking a piece of his thumb with it.

"She feeling all right?"

"She's fine."

There were a few minutes of silence while they both watched the bacon sizzle in the pan. Luke knew his brother well enough to know he wasn't likely to let it rest there. He used a fork to pull the bacon out of the pan and then began cracking eggs into the sizzling fat that remained. Daniel found a loaf of the bread Eleanor had made the day before and began cutting thick slices off it. It wasn't as good as the fresh biscuits Eleanor would have made, but fried in the bacon fat, it would be filling.

"Was she upset about what she heard last night? About us drawing straws, I mean?"

Luke had known the question was coming and he had an answer ready. "She was a bit upset, but I talked to her." That was true enough. They *had* talked.

"She didn't throw a fit?" Daniel brought the bread over and tossed it in the skillet as Luke removed the eggs.

"She saw reason," Luke said firmly, hoping it was true. He got out two plates and set them on the table, dividing the scorched bacon and overdone eggs between them. A moment later Daniel plopped slices of fried bread on each plate and they sat down to eat.

"I thought she might throw you out," Daniel said as he picked up his fork. "Figured we'd be seeing you in the bunkhouse."

"I'm master in this house," Luke said with repressive dignity. Eleanor hadn't thrown him out; he'd decided to leave.

"Seems odd, though," Daniel shook his head as he started to eat.

"What seems odd?" As soon as he said it, Luke had the feeling he was going to regret the question. He was right.

"Well, if Eleanor had thrown you out, it would have seemed natural. But if she didn't—you bein' master in this house and all—it's a puzzle how you got that hay in your hair."

Daniel looked up from his plate, his grin pure devilry. He was not measurably disturbed by the glare Luke sent in return.

* * *

Eleanor set bowls of potatoes, green beans simmered with a chunk of bacon and a mound of hot biscuits on the table. A big platter of fried steaks sat on the back of the stove, keeping warm. Gravy simmered in the big iron skillet, almost thick enough to be poured into the bowl she had ready and waiting. Wiping her hands on her apron, she walked to the door and stepped outside to ring the dinner bell.

There was a faint tremor in her fingers as she went back to the stove to stir the gravy. She hadn't spoken to Luke since their quarrel the night before and she wasn't sure of the best way to handle this first meeting. She'd thought about little else all day and she was no closer to an answer now than she had been this morning.

The men piled into the kitchen just as they always did, unwashed and unkempt. After two weeks she could now connect names with faces and was starting to know them as individuals apart from the large mass of male bodies invading her kitchen once or twice a day.

She poured the gravy into its bowl and carried it to the table. Neither Luke nor Daniel had appeared yet and, apart from a few sidelong glances and a polite nod or two, the men didn't seem aware of her existence. Eleanor set the gravy down on the nearly full table and stood watching the usual display of flying fingers as they grabbed at the food before them. They ignored the serving utensils in favor of the more expedient method of picking up the entire bowl and dumping a portion of its contents onto their plates. Biscuits flew across the table like fat golden brown leaves caught in a tornado.

When Gris and Joe grabbed for the same steak, there was a brief tug-of-war across the tabletop before Joe's fingers slipped loose, leaving Gris the triumphant owner of the piece of meat. He grinned, displaying a mouthful of biscuit and potatoes.

"Ya'll just ain't fast—ow!"

His sentence ended on a pained yelp and the steak landed on the tabletop with a plop as Eleanor's big wooden spoon caught him across the knuckles. The bowl of potatoes pinged against the wood as Slim's wrist received a sharp rap from the same source. Never slow on the uptake, Shorty Danvers hastily dropped the biscuit he'd just grabbed and moved his hands prudently out of reach.

There was a stunned silence as they all turned their eyes toward the small but fierce-looking woman who stood at the end of the table. Eleanor held the wooden spoon like an avenging angel's sword. Her dark eyes sparkled with anger as she looked at the men before her.

"I've seen hogs with better manners," she said sharply. "You come to this table and fall on my food like wolves on a freshly killed deer. You walk in here without so much as wiping your feet and track dirt and manure over my clean floors." She used the spoon to point to the trail of mud that led from the door. All heads turned and looked guiltily at the evidence.

"I'm right sorry, ma'am," Slim said. "Never thought about it none."

The humble apology was not enough to mollify her. Eleanor pointed the spoon at him and Slim pressed his back against his chair, actually seeming to pale beneath the force of the gesture.

"Did you think about washing the filth off your hands and face?" she demanded.

"No, ma'am." There was a chorus of mumbled agreement as her eyes swept the table. Guilty looks were cast at grimy hands.

"Were you all raised in barns?"

"No, ma'am." That was Shorty. "Leastways, I wasn't, and my mama would've been madder than a wet hen if I'da come to her table without washing."

"Then why do you come to *this* table in that condition?" Eleanor demanded, pointing her spoon at his dirty hands.

Though it was Shorty she was looking at, the question was directed at all of them. But no one said anything, leaving it to Shorty to come up with an answer that might satisfy their diminutive interrogator. He glanced uneasily at his companions, hoping for assistance. When none was forthcoming, he swallowed and lifted his eyes to Eleanor's face.

"I don't reckon there's a good reason, ma'am. 'Ceptin' maybe, us bein' just men for so long, we done forgot the manners our mamas taught us."

The others nodded their agreement with this theory, fixing their eyes hopefully on Eleanor's flushed face. There'd been some doubts about the wisdom of Luke's decision to get married but, in the two weeks she'd lived on the Bar-M-Bar, the men had decided that the boss had made himself a pretty good deal. His bride not only made biscuits light as a feather but she had a way of smiling at a man that made him think twice about the benefits of being a bachelor. None of them liked the idea of the little missus being permanently riled at them.

"Do you think you could remember some of those manners if you tried?" Eleanor asked, her voice softening a little. Ridiculous as it was, considering the tough cowboys sitting before her, she suddenly felt as if she was scolding a bunch of youngsters.

"Yes, ma'am. I reckon we could."

Shorty stood and the other men followed his lead, then they trooped back out the door to wash their hands at the pump. Eleanor's eyes followed them, skidding to a halt on the two men standing just inside the doorway.

Luke.

And Daniel, she added belatedly. Peripherally, she was aware of the amused sparkle in her brother-in-law's eyes. Obviously, they'd been there long enough to overhear at least a portion of the scene just past. Equally obvious was the fact that Daniel had found it highly amusing. Luke's reaction was not so easily read, at least not in the darting glance that was all Eleanor could manage in his direction.

"I don't think I've ever seen anyone or anything back down Shorty Danvers," Daniel said, brushing past Luke as he walked farther into the kitchen. "Most of those men would tackle a herd of buffalo bare-handed if the notion struck them, but they looked meek as lambs after that dressing-down, Eleanor."

"I don't see any cause to eat like a pack of wolves," she muttered.

She picked up the steak Joe and Gris had used in their brief tug-of-war and set it back on the platter. Using a towel to wipe the table where it had been gave her a good excuse to avoid looking at Luke as he pulled out his chair at the table.

"You want to check behind our ears to see if we washed well enough?" he asked in a slow drawl that sparked Eleanor's anger all over again, making her momentarily forget the cool, calm image she'd determined to present to him.

"It might not be such a bad idea at that," she snapped.

She jabbed a fork into the platter of steaks, wishing it was some portion of her husband's anatomy instead. Just seeing him brought memories of last night's quarrel rushing over her, most vividly the humiliation of finding herself facedown across Luke's lap.

"It seems to me that the hands aren't the only ones who've forgotten how to behave like civilized men instead of unreasoning brutes."

The glance that slashed his way left Luke in no doubt as to the direction of her thoughts. It didn't sound as if having had a day to think things over had inspired a mood of repentance in his bride. He stared at the fork that stood upright in the middle of a thick steak and knew she'd just as soon it was stuck in him.

Across the table he caught Daniel's questioning look, caught also the amusement in his eyes, and knew Daniel was remembering his determination to get himself a docile bride. Daniel didn't know the half of it, Luke thought, rubbing his fingers absently over the bruised place on his thigh where Eleanor had sunk her surprisingly sharp little teeth into him.

If she hadn't had other things on her mind, Eleanor would have been amused by the careful display of manners at the dinner table that night. Not that any of them were ready to dine in high society, she thought, watching Gris pick up the gravy bowl and carefully pass it across the table to Joe. But at least there seemed no danger of blood being spilled in the melee to fill plates.

She ate almost nothing herself. Every time she glanced in Luke's direction she was reminded that they hadn't exactly settled anything the night before. She was annoyed to see that Luke ate with his customary hearty appetite. Obviously, he wasn't going to let a little thing like beating his wife get in the way of his dinner, she thought angrily. A small voice of reason suggested that perhaps "beat" was a trifle strong and pointed out the damage she'd inflicted in turn. Eleanor did her best to ignore it.

The men departed as soon as they'd eaten and, despite her preoccupation, Eleanor was amused by the careful way each of them thanked her for the meal and wished her good-night.

She was grateful when Luke and Daniel went with them. The longer she could put off talking to her husband, the better, as far as she was concerned. And as for Daniel, she was in no better charity with him than with his brother. It had been the pair of them drawing straws to see which would have to get married, and it was humiliating to think that someone else knew the circumstances of her marriage.

Luke's footsteps were slow as he climbed the stairs. If he hadn't known better, he would have thought that Eleanor had gone to bed. But he'd seen the bedroom light burning and he knew she was awake. In the weeks before the wedding, there had been times when he'd imagined what it would be like to have a wife waiting up for him. He'd fancied the idea that she'd be keeping the bed warm, pictured the welcoming smile on her face, the eagerness in her eyes.

After last night, it seemed the only eagerness he was likely to see in his bride's eyes was for his blood.

Considering the way she'd torn a strip off the men at supper, he wasn't holding his breath in expectation of seeing her fall over herself to repent for last night's display of temper. He had to admit to a certain reluctant pride at the way she'd dealt with the hands. If he hadn't seen it for himself, he wouldn't have believed that five foot nothing of female could buffalo his cowboys. Gris Balkin, as tough a man as Luke had known, had damn near shuffled his feet like a schoolboy in trouble for putting a frog in the teacher's pocket.

It had certainly been something to see, but if Eleanor thought she'd be able to run roughshod over him the way she had over the men, she was wrong. He had no intention of letting his wife rule the roost.

The bedroom door was partially open and Luke approached it somewhat cautiously. Her aim the night before had been uncomfortably accurate and she'd had all day to restock her arsenal. He pushed the door open and stepped inside, prepared to duck, if necessary.

Eleanor was sitting in the rocking chair, her slender fingers busy picking apart the seams on a dress. Luke vaguely recognized the garment as having been his mother's. There were trunks of her things in the attic and he'd told Eleanor to make use of them if she wanted.

Though she must have heard him enter, she didn't look up immediately but continued clipping threads to open the seam. She presented a picture of domestic tranquillity, as calm and cool as a spring shower. If it hadn't been for the fact that her fingers were shaking so hard it was a wonder she didn't drop the tiny scissors she held, Luke might have thought her completely indifferent to his presence.

Eleanor could feel Luke watching her, and it took every ounce of concentration she could muster to keep her eyes on the material in her lap. The small black circles that patterned the rich green silk blurred together as she waited for him to speak.

He shut the door behind him and she jumped as if the quiet click had been a gunshot.

Aware that she could no longer control the unsteadiness of her fingers, she set the scissors aside and folded her hands in her lap. With an effort she lifted her head and, for the first time since their quarrel the night before, she forced herself to really look at her husband.

He looked back at her, his eyes wary. She could hardly blame him for that, Eleanor admitted, letting her eyes flicker up to the scrape on his forehead. Seeing where her attention was directed, Luke lifted his fingers to the small injury.

She knew she should apologize, should say she regretted throwing her shoe at him, not to mention the books, water pitcher and her hairbrush. But the truth was, she wasn't in the least sorry. Though she'd gotten over the worst of her anger, it still seemed as if whatever small injury she'd inflicted was the least he deserved. Besides, he'd gotten his revenge quite thoroughly, she thought, shifting a little on the pillow she'd put down to cushion her slightly tender posterior from the hard seat.

Seeing her shift uncomfortably and knowing the cause, Luke felt a twinge of guilt. But it was only a twinge. The way she'd come at him last night, it was a wonder she hadn't done permanent damage. And if her butt was tender, it couldn't be more so than his forehead or the bruise where she'd sunk her teeth into his thigh.

"Don't try and bring any of those trunks down out of the attic by yourself," he said abruptly, nodding to the pile of fabric in her lap. "They're too heavy. If I'm not around, ask Daniel or one of the men to help you. After the talking-to you gave them, I'd guess if you said jump, they might ask how high."

Eleanor didn't smile at his slight attempt at humor. "I got tired of watching them eat like animals."

"I think you made that pretty clear." *Maybe we could just forget last night,* he thought with considerable relief. He walked farther into the room and reached for the buttons on his shirt.

"I'd prefer it if you slept elsewhere." The words were rushed as if they'd had to be hurried out or not said at all.

Luke's fingers stilled, his eyes taking on a chill as they settled on her face. Eleanor swallowed but met his gaze steadily, hoping she looked more calm than she felt.

"We're married," he said flatly, as if that answered everything.

As if she should just ignore the fact that her marriage had come about because he'd gambled and *lost.* Anger stirred in the pit of her stomach. She forced it down. She didn't want to quarrel with him.

"I know," she said, proud of how calm she sounded. "I know you've every right to sleep in that bed."

It wasn't exactly sleeping I had in mind, Luke thought.

"And to demand your marital rights," she continued, as if reading his thoughts.

"You haven't exactly objected to those demands," he snapped, stung by her cool tone.

She flushed, but continued as if he hadn't spoken. "I'm just asking you to give me a little time. I knew our marriage was hardly a...love match, but it's been a shock to find out that you married me because you lost a bet."

"It had nothing to do with you, dammit!" Luke didn't apologize for the profanity.

"I know." She nodded, seeming to grow more calm in the face of his annoyance. "I understand that, but it's not exactly pleasant to find that you drew straws to see who'd *have* to get married."

"It wasn't you we were drawing straws over." Luke was aware that his voice had risen.

"I know that, but I can't help but wonder what would have happened if Daniel had drawn the short straw."

Luke stared at her. "What does that have to do with it?"

"If he'd drawn the short straw, wouldn't he have been the one who had to find a wife?"

Luke nodded reluctantly. He didn't like the direction the conversation had taken.

"Well, then, it's possible he'd have thought I'd suit his purpose, the same way you did. Whether it was you or Daniel, you still needed someone to cook and clean and have sons." Eleanor's mouth twisted in a rueful smile. "If he'd drawn the short straw, I could have ended up marrying your brother."

"No!" The sharpness of his denial brought Luke up short. He drew a slow breath and continued more calmly. "That wouldn't have happened."

Eleanor lifted one shoulder in a half shrug. "Maybe not. Daniel might have thought some other girl would do a better job of cooking and cleaning and having babies. But the end result would have been the same: You and I wouldn't be married."

"But we *are* married," he snapped.

"I'm not trying to deny that."

"There are those who think that sharing a bed is part of being married," he said, heavily sarcastic.

She was unmoved. "I know, and I'm not asking you to move out permanently. I'm just asking you to give me a little time to adjust my thinking."

"How much time?" He was aware that, in asking that question, he was admitting defeat. The relief in Eleanor's eyes said that she knew it, too.

"A few days, perhaps. That's not too much to ask, is it?"

It is much too much. An hour is too much. He'd been aching to have her since last night. She sat there, wrapped in layers of fabric, modest as a nun, and all he could think about was peeling those layers from her, of laying her back on the bed and easing his way into her welcoming body. Only, something in the set of her jaw told him it wouldn't be welcoming.

Damn, who would have thought that such a little female could be so pigheaded? He could have dealt with another tantrum. He'd even half looked forward to that. If she'd been throwing things and shouting at him, he could have tossed her onto the bed and kissed the anger out of her.

But how the hell was a man supposed to deal with this kind of calm reason?

"I'll give you time," he snapped finally.

"Thank you." Now that she had what she wanted, she gave him a sweet smile.

"Let me know when you've had enough time to think." The sneer in his voice made his opinion of her request obvious. He jerked open the door and cast her a warning look over his shoulder. "Just don't think I'll wait forever."

He stalked out without bothering to wait for an answer. The door closed behind him with a final-sounding click.

Halfway down the hall he hesitated outside his old bedroom. When he'd married Eleanor they'd moved into the room his parents had shared. There was no reason for him to sleep in the barn when there was a perfectly good bed going to waste. A quiet sound from inside the master bedroom had him moving down the hall to the stairs.

He'd sleep better in the barn than he would in the house knowing Eleanor was just across the hall, alone in bed—the bed he had every right to be sharing with her.

The gray gelding stuck his head over the stall door, giving Luke a surprised look as he stalked past.

"Don't get used to it," Luke snarled. "I don't plan on making a habit of this."

It had to be his imagination that made the gelding's snort sound full of disbelief. Wrapping himself in a blanket, Luke settled into a mound of hay and tilted his hat down over his eyes. He wished he'd never heard of the institution of marriage. As far as he could see, the main thing it seemed to ac-

complish was to cut up a man's peace and drive him
out of his own home.

Give her time, she'd asked. Well, he'd give her
time. But she'd better not expect him to wait forever. He was getting too damned old to be sleeping
in the barn.

Chapter Twelve

"They drew straws?" Letty's dark eyes were wide with shocked disbelief. "They actually drew straws to decide which of them would marry?"

"And the one who drew the shortest straw—the one who *lost*—had to find a bride." Anger simmered in Eleanor's voice. She'd had a week to adjust to the idea, but the time had done nothing to cool her ire. "Since Luke drew the short straw, he had to get married."

Letty stared at her friend, and Eleanor found a certain grim satisfaction in the fact that the other woman was struck speechless. She'd felt much the same way when she'd found out the truth. Not exactly *speechless*, she corrected herself, remembering her fight with Luke.

"I just can't believe that they'd make such an important decision in such a...childish fashion,"

Letty said finally. "Drawing straws. It just doesn't seem possible."

"It's possible," Eleanor assured her grimly. "Luke admitted as much."

"Amazing." Letty shook her head as she set her teacup on the small table beside her.

They were sitting in the parlor of the McLain house. With the drapes drawn back, sunlight spilled across freshly polished wood surfaces. A soft, early-summer breeze drifted through the open windows. The room was spotlessly clean and shone with the care that had been lavished on it in recent weeks.

She'd always wanted a home, Eleanor thought as she watched dust motes drift through a beam of sunlight. She had gained that when she married Luke, but in the past couple of weeks she'd realized that having a place to call her own had been the least important part of her dream. Without someone to love, someone who loved her, a house was just a house. It needed more than four walls and a fireplace to fill the emptiness in her heart.

"He didn't have to marry *you,* did he?" Letty said slowly, searching for a bright spot in her friend's situation. "He still had to choose a bride, and he chose you. That has to prove something."

"Probably that I'm the most gullible-looking female he could find," Eleanor said glumly.

"Now, that's not true. You know as well as I do that there's not an unmarried woman in Black Dog—and more than a few of the married ones—who wouldn't have jumped at the chance to marry Luke McLain. And unless he's blind, deaf and dumb, Luke knew it, too, what with every one of them making cow eyes at him. Don't forget, your cousin Anabel practically threw herself at him. So obviously he had a reason for courting *you.*"

"That's true." Eleanor felt her mood brighten a little. Letty wasn't telling her anything she hadn't already told herself but, hearing the words from someone else, they sounded more reassuring. But it still stung to think about Luke and Daniel drawing straws over who would *have* to get married.

"Does Luke know that you found out about this?"

"He knows."

"I hope you let him know exactly what you thought of what they did."

"I think he has a pretty good idea," Eleanor murmured. Hitting him in the head with her shoe seemed to have gotten the point across.

"Good. Drawing straws, indeed!" The more Letty thought about it, the more indignant the idea seemed to make her. "I'd thought better of Daniel. And of Luke, of course," she added quickly, catching Eleanor's interested look.

"Of course," Eleanor agreed, but she took note of the reference to Daniel. It wasn't the first time Letty had mentioned him. Despite her current annoyance with her brother-in-law, Eleanor had grown fond of him. If he and Letty were to fall in love... Eleanor barely restrained a grin. Wouldn't it be wonderful to have Letty as a sister by marriage? She filed the thought away for future reference. Perhaps if she could throw them together a little bit....

The opportunity came sooner than she'd imagined possible.

Half an hour later the two women were standing on the porch, lingering over their farewells, when Daniel rode into the ranch yard. He didn't recognize the buggy sitting in front of the house but, seeing that Eleanor had a female guest, it wasn't hard to guess her identity. He'd taken note of Letty Sinclair at his brother's wedding. What man wouldn't notice a trim figure with curves in all the right places and masses of dark hair that fairly begged for him to pull out the pins so that it could spill into his hands? She was a widow, if he remembered right. He'd always been partial to widows. A nudge of his heel turned his horse in their direction.

He stopped his horse at the foot of the steps. Taking off his hat, he gave them his best smile, the one he'd once been told would melt any woman's heart. Come to think of it, it had been a widow woman who'd told him that.

"Afternoon, Eleanor. Mrs. Sinclair."

"Afternoon, Daniel." He was surprised by the warmth of Eleanor's greeting. She hadn't been exactly friendly toward him since finding out about him and Luke drawing straws to see who'd have to marry.

"Mr. McLain." Letty's greeting seemed a bit on the cool side, and it occurred to Daniel that Eleanor might have told her the whole story. It was not a comfortable thought.

"Oh, heavens! I just remembered that I need to check my bread dough," Eleanor said suddenly. "Excuse me."

"I'll say goodbye, then," Letty said.

"No, I want to say a proper goodbye. I'll only be a moment." Eleanor's skirt swished against the porch floor as she turned and hurried into the house. She left complete silence behind her.

"Nice day," Daniel said.

"Yes."

He waited, but she didn't seem to have anything to add. She'd been putting on her gloves when he rode up and now she concentrated her attention on smoothing every tiny wrinkle from the soft kid. Must be shy, he decided. A shy widow—not exactly what he'd been hoping for, but he didn't mind a bit of a challenge.

"It's a long drive from town," he said, trying another angle.

"Not really."

"Long way for a woman to travel on her own."

"I'm accustomed to looking out for myself." Her tone was cool but Daniel persevered.

"It's not safe for a woman alone."

"A woman alone is quite safe, Mr. McLain. It's when she's in the company of men that she finds herself at risk."

Daniel grinned. She had spirit. He liked that. "Perhaps I should escort you home, Mrs. Sinclair. Make sure you get back to town safe and sound."

"That won't be necessary. Thank you." The last was added so grudgingly that Daniel's grin widened.

"If you're not careful, ma'am, you'll give me the idea that you don't care to have my company." If he'd thought to embarrass her, he failed.

"And here I was beginning to think that you weren't nearly as intelligent as I'd thought, Mr. McLain." Her smile was so brilliant that it took Daniel a moment to realize that he'd just been insulted. It had been so neatly done that he couldn't decide whether to be angry or amused. He raised one dark brow.

"I'm starting to get the impression that you don't like me, Mrs. Sinclair."

"I don't know you." His calm response had sparked Letty's temper and she found herself saying more than she'd intended. "And I've no wish to know a man who'd draw straws to decide a woman's future."

"We were deciding our own futures," he corrected her. His voice was sharper than he'd intended. He'd grown fond of Eleanor, and the hurt he'd seen in her eyes lately hadn't made him feel particularly good about what he and Luke had done. He didn't need someone else to point out the error of his ways.

"You're splitting hairs, Mr. McLain. It was a schoolboy's game, certainly not what one would expect from a pair of mature adults making such a critical decision."

Daniel's amusement lost out to annoyance. He didn't like being scolded, particularly not by a woman several years his junior—a very pretty woman. And the fact that she was probably right didn't make him like it any more.

"I can see my presence is distressing to you, ma'am," he said with cold formality. "I'll take my leave now. Good day."

"Good day to you, sir." Letty's nod was regal enough for royalty.

Daniel's mouth tightened as he set his hat back on his head. With a nod as icy as her own, he reined his horse around and rode out of the ranch yard.

Females. Who needed 'em.

Eleanor returned to the porch in time to see her brother-in-law ride away. "Where is Daniel going?" she asked.

"I have no idea."

"Did you two quarrel?" Eleanor asked, studying her friend's flushed cheeks and too-bright eyes.

"Certainly not! I don't know Mr. McLain well enough to quarrel with him. And you needn't think that I don't know exactly what you're up to, Eleanor." Letty fixed her friend with a stern look. "I don't need you to play matchmaker for me."

"I don't know what you're talking about." Eleanor widened her eyes innocently. "I had to check on my bread, else it might have risen too high."

Letty's snort of disbelief made clear her opinion of the thin excuse. "If I want to catch Daniel McLain—and, mind you, I'm saying *if*—I'll go about it in my own time and in my own way. I don't know that I'll bother." But her eyes drifted after Daniel, watching as he rode out of the ranch yard.

"He's very handsome, don't you think?" Eleanor followed her friend's gaze. Next to Luke she thought Daniel was the most attractive man she'd ever seen.

"Handsome is as handsome does," Letty said repressively.

Eleanor was kind enough not to ask her what she meant. She followed the other woman down the porch steps to where Letty's buggy waited. Unlooping the reins from the hitching rail, Letty climbed up and settled herself on the padded seat. She looked at Eleanor.

"You've concerns enough of your own without trying to matchmake for me."

That was certainly true enough, Eleanor thought as she watched Letty drive away. She had more than enough concerns of her own. She sighed as she turned and went back into the house. It had been almost two weeks since her quarrel with Luke, since she'd asked him to give her time to adjust to the real reason he'd married her. He'd given her what she'd asked for. But she was starting to wonder if she might have made a mistake in the asking.

Eleanor went into the parlor and began gathering the tea things onto a tray. What bothered her wasn't that their bed seemed shockingly empty without Luke in it. It was that he hadn't, by word or glance, given her any reason to think that he was all that anxious to return to that bed. Since the night he'd slammed out of their bedroom he'd treated her with a cool politeness that sent a chill right through her. She could have been the housekeeper he and Daniel might have hired if he hadn't married her.

Had it been a mistake to ask him to sleep somewhere else? What had she really hoped to accomplish? They were married. Nothing was going to change that. Just as nothing was going to change the circumstances under which their marriage had begun.

Eleanor sighed as she carried the tea things into the kitchen. Maybe she'd let her temper get the best of her. What if all she'd accomplished was to remind Luke of how easily he could get along without her? It wasn't as if she were a beauty, like her cousin Anabel, the kind of woman a man couldn't help but want. Maybe she'd just given him a chance to realize that he'd *prefer* to sleep alone.

Setting the tray down on the kitchen table, Eleanor began putting things away. Her teeth worried at the inside of her lower lip as she worked. She'd remade two of his mother's dresses, and the deep, rich colors suited her better than anything she'd ever owned. She knew, without vanity, that she looked almost pretty in them. She might never be as beautiful as Anabel but she wasn't unpleasant to look at.

She smoothed one hand over the deep rose skirt and wondered wistfully if Luke had noticed how she looked.

Luke had noticed.

He'd noticed the warm glow of her skin, the lustrous darkness of her hair, the way her brown eyes sparkled when she smiled—not that she'd thrown a whole lot of smiles in his direction lately. He'd noticed the soft curves of her body, the feminine sway of her hips. There wasn't much about Eleanor that he *hadn't* noticed.

Luke tipped his hat back on his head, allowing the late-afternoon breeze to cool the sweat on his forehead. Reaching for the makings, he rolled himself a smoke, letting the roan choose his own path home. He'd spent most of the day clearing away a rock fall that had blocked a spring, one of the few in the area that could be depended on to give water all summer long. Depended on as much as one could depend on anything in nature, anyway. Lighting the cigarette, Luke squinted against the bright sunlight. If the past few weeks were anything to judge by, it was going to be a hot summer.

Of course, if you looked at it another way, it could be mighty cold. His thinking circled back around to Eleanor, something it did all too frequently these days. His wife's attitude was as chilly as the weather was hot. He'd thought getting married was going to make his life simpler. He should have known better. When had a woman ever made anything simpler?

Look how she'd complicated things by falling into a fit of the sulks over him and Daniel drawing straws, something that hadn't had anything to do with her. He hadn't even known she existed when he drew that damned short straw, he thought, annoyed all over again. What difference did it make *how* they'd come to be married? They were married and that was all there was to it. She was just being stubborn and...female about the whole thing.

Luke took a deep drag on his cigarette, his dark brows hooking together in a frown as the house came into sight. He should never have let Daniel convince him that one of them had to get married.

They'd been doing fine without a wife. Good food and a clean house hardly balanced out the trouble of having to deal with a woman. And at the moment those were the only benefits he was getting out of this marriage.

Thinking of the benefits he was missing, his frown deepened into a scowl. He was getting damned tired of sleeping in the barn. But he'd be double damned before he'd move to the bunkhouse and let the hands know that he'd been thrown out of his own bed. The way they were treating Eleanor these days, they'd probably assume he'd done something to deserve it, Luke thought sourly. She had his cowboys acting like schoolboys anxious to impress a new teacher.

Luke's jaw set with determination. She might have managed to buffalo his men but he was made of sterner stuff, and he wasn't going to let a snip of a female dictate to him. If she thought he was going to come crawling, asking her to let him back into *his* bed, she had another think coming. A man didn't *ask* to share his wife's bed—it was his right in the eyes of God and the law. The only reason he hadn't insisted on claiming that right was that he was being gracious, giving his bride time to get over her snit. Pretty soon he'd put his foot down and make it clear to Eleanor that he was through playing this little game of hers. Maybe he'd even do it tonight after supper.

The thought of spending the night between cool linen sheets rather than on a bed of scratchy hay was enough to lighten Luke's mood. But it wasn't the sheets alone that made his mouth curl into something approaching a smile. He'd missed a comfortable bed, but if that was all he'd wanted, he could have slept in another bedroom. What he really wanted was Eleanor in that bed with him. There was more to marriage than good food and a clean house, dammit! He'd been more patient than most men would have been, more patient than he had any reason to be.

He'd lay down the law tonight.

As Luke rode into the ranch yard his eye was caught by movement at the back of the house. The sheets he'd just been thinking about were hanging on the line, their pristine whiteness catching the last of the afternoon sun. He tried to remember the last time he'd seen a row of sparkling white sheets hanging on a line. Maybe somewhere in town, he decided. It sure hadn't been here, not since his mother died, anyway.

His fingers tightened on the reins, drawing the gelding to a halt. Between housekeepers he and Daniel had done wash as seldom as possible and had dried their wet clothes by draping them over a bush. When he'd married Eleanor, one of the first things she'd done was to replace his mother's rotted clothesline and chase the spiders out of the bag of wooden clothespins. It hadn't taken long to get used to the pleasures of having clean clothes again, holes patched and tears mended.

When it came to the cooking and cleaning Eleanor had certainly done everything a man could want. She'd turned the house into a home again and managed to restore the kind of civilized atmosphere his mother had always insisted be maintained. His mother would have liked Eleanor, Luke thought, watching the sheets undulate in the breeze. Lucinda would have admired Eleanor's spirit, and probably would have thought that banishment to the barn was the least he deserved, he admitted reluctantly.

The back door opened and Eleanor came out. She walked toward the clothesline. Luke settled back into the saddle, admiring the sway of her hips beneath her skirts, the way the sun picked out red highlights in her dark hair. He felt desire stir in him, a hunger that went deeper than the purely physical.

He missed her, dammit! It wasn't just her presence in bed that he missed, though he damn sure missed that. He missed seeing her smile, missed the sound of her laughter. If he'd known marriage was going to be such a complicated thing, he'd have brained Daniel and dragged *him* to the altar.

Eleanor began taking the clothes off the line. Luke stayed where he was. He'd never given much thought to the act of hanging clothes on a line, but he thought about it now. She lifted her arms to unpin a sheet. Her breasts lifted with the movement. The stiff breeze that blew across the prairie might be perfect for drying clothes but it had other, less prosaic benefits, like the way it molded her rose-colored skirt to her legs, outlining the lush curves of her body. Luke's mouth went dry. His jeans were suddenly uncomfortably snug.

He started to nudge the roan into a walk, but a figure hurrying out of the bunkhouse stopped him. Gris Balkin moved across the ranch yard at a pace that made Luke's eyes widen. Three days ago Gris had stepped in a prairie dog hole and twisted his ankle so badly 'they'd had to cut his boot off. Eleanor had helped bind the ankle and Luke had told him to stay off his foot and out of a saddle until the swelling went down. Gris hadn't been happy about being confined to the ranch yard, but he'd been spending his time working on the tack, doing some much-needed repairs.

And cozying up to *his* wife, Luke thought, his eyes narrowing as the younger man hobbled over to the clothesline. Eleanor turned and smiled at Gris, and Luke's mouth tightened with annoyance. If she wasn't going to smile at *him* she had no business smiling like that at another man. Ignoring the small voice that pointed out that it wasn't Gris she was angry with, Luke nudged his heel into the roan's side and moved toward the couple standing by the clothesline. Eleanor was his wife. Maybe some people needed to be reminded of that.

"Let me help you with that, Miz McLain."

Eleanor turned to look over her shoulder, frowning when she saw Gris· limping toward her. "You're supposed to be resting that ankle," she told him, her tone gently scolding.

"If I stay settin' in one place much more, I'm likely to take roots."

"I doubt that," Eleanor said, laughing softly. "From what I've heard, cowboys are about as rootless as they come."

She bent to pick up the clothes basket, but Gris was there before her, lifting it and carrying it farther down the clothesline. With a nod of thanks, Eleanor continued taking the clothes off the line, dropping the pins into the big pocket on her apron.

"I'd guess that's so for a goodly number of us, ma'am," Gris said, his voice thoughtful. "I'd never given much thought to settling down myself. My folks was always movin', always wantin' to see what was over the next hill, so I ain't never stayed in one place too long. I figured that's the way it'd always be but lately I'm startin' to think it might be kinda nice to have a little place of my own, maybe a woman, too. If'n I could find one that'd have me," he added with a self-conscious grin.

"Is there someone in particular you're thinking of?" Eleanor asked over her shoulder as she plucked a pair of clothespins from the line. It took Gris so long to reply that she turned and looked at him, her brows raised in question. "Do you have a girl in mind?"

"There's a girl," Gris admitted in a strangled voice. "I met her last time I was in Denver." Having got that much out, he suddenly waxed eloquent. "She's got yellow hair and big brown eyes. Made me think of a palomino filly I seen once."

Eleanor swallowed a chuckle and kept her expression solemn. "She sounds lovely."

"She's the prettiest thing I ever seen," he told her fervently. "Her daddy owns a dry goods store, though, and I doubt she'd even look at me."

"You won't know until you try. I think a woman would be lucky to have you," Eleanor said. She folded one of Luke's shirts and set it in the basket, her expression taking on a wistful edge. Gris's dream wasn't that different from her own—a home and someone to love.

"I ain't much to look at," he observed with painful honesty. "Women set store by such things."

Eleanor turned to look at him, her expression considering. Gris ducked his head self-consciously. "A woman wants a great deal more than good looks in a man. She wants someone who'll love her and cherish her, someone who'll make her feel as if she's the most important thing in the world to him. Besides, I think you're a very handsome man," she added, stretching the truth just a bit. Gris wasn't likely to make a girl's heart melt at first glance, but there was a certain appeal in his gap-toothed smile and the natural friendliness of his gaze.

Gris looked at her as if she'd suddenly sprouted wings and a halo, his brown eyes hopeful. "You mean that, Miz McLain?"

"Mean what?" The unexpected addition to their conversation made Gris and Eleanor both jump.

Luke ducked between a pair of sheets to confront them. He'd deliberately angled his approach so that the clothes hanging on the line blocked their view of him. He wasn't sure why he'd felt it necessary to employ tactics more suited to fighting Indians than to approaching his wife and one of his ranch hands. He hadn't expected to catch them exchanging guilty secrets. But, seeing Eleanor smile at Gris, he'd felt something he couldn't quite define, something that had made him want to punch Gris in the nose and then throw Eleanor over his shoulder and carry her off.

"Mean what?" he asked again when neither of them spoke.

Eleanor drew a deep breath, trying to still the rapid beat of her heart. She very much wanted to believe that it was sheer surprise that had increased her pulse but, the truth was, her heart was inclined to behave erratically whenever Luke was near. And the fact that she was angry with him—which she still was—didn't seem to make any difference at all.

"I was just offering Gris some advice," she said repressively.

"Oh?" Luke's gaze swung from his wife to Gris. There was nothing overtly unpleasant in either his tone or his look, but Gris was suddenly put in mind of a fish he'd seen a picture of one time—a huge creature with rows of fierce-looking teeth bared in a smile a lot like the one his boss was giving him now.

Gris swallowed hard, his prominent Adam's apple bobbing. He shifted, trying to take weight off his bad ankle. He wished suddenly that he'd stayed in the bunkhouse, working on the tack. "I was goin' to carry the basket for Miz McLain," he said, feeling the need to offer an explanation.

"I can manage just fine, Gris." Eleanor came to his rescue when Luke said nothing, but simply stood there looking at him. "But thank you for offering." Her smile made Gris flush and duck his head. He mumbled something incoherent, shot Luke another uneasy look and then turned and limped away.

"He's a nice boy," Eleanor said, her nerves jumping with the knowledge that she and Luke were alone.

"Boy?" Luke's dark brows rose. "He's at least six years older than you are. Hardly a boy."

"He seems young to me." She shrugged and turned back to the clothesline. It took a conscious effort to keep her fingers from trembling as she tugged a clothespin free.

"What were you offering him advice on?"

"This and that." She moved a little farther down the line, anxious to put some distance between them, but he simply moved with her, seeming to loom over her.

"What kind of this and that?" Luke's tone was pleasant, but there was an underlying note of steel in it.

Eleanor's back stiffened. Wasn't it just like him to ignore her for two weeks and then subject her to this catechism over her conversation with Gris? She dropped the last of the clothes into the basket and turned to face him, bracing her hands on her hips and giving him a look that made no secret of her annoyance.

"If you must know, Gris was concerned that he might not be handsome enough to attract a woman."

Luke's brows shot up and he was foolish enough to snort with laughter. "That skinny kid?"

"As you pointed out, he's considerably older than I am. Old enough to be thinking about having a family."

"I guess that's so." Luke no longer cared what Gris had been talking to Eleanor about. She'd unbuttoned the top button on her bodice, revealing the hollow at the base of her throat and the pulse that beat there. His fingertips itched to feel that soft flutter of movement, to hear her sigh with pleasure when he kissed her there. Her hair was drawn back into a prim bun at the back of her head, but a few unruly curls had drifted loose to caress her forehead and neck. It would take only a moment for him to loosen her hair so that it tumbled over his hands in a thick, dark curtain. He could slide his fingers into that curtain and tilt her mouth up to his. A few kisses and she'd melt into his arms.

"I think it's sweet that Gris is thinking about going courting." Eleanor's words broke into Luke's increasingly lustful imaginings. "Maybe he'll bring his girl flowers or read her a poem."

The idea of Gris reading poetry made Luke grin. "I don't think the poetry is such a good idea. The one time I heard Gris recite anything that rhymed, it was after he'd drunk half a bottle of rotgut whiskey. And the poem wasn't exactly fit for a lady's ears. He'd better hope the flowers do the trick."

"Maybe he could learn a poem that was fit for a lady's ears," Eleanor said.

Luke was distracted by the way the sun was picking out red highlights in her hair and missed hearing the tightness in her voice. "Maybe. But I just can't picture Gris spouting poetry."

Eleanor's eyes narrowed. "Maybe he could see if his girl would like to draw straws," she said. The silky tone of her voice was reminiscent of a diamondback's warning rattle just before it struck. "How would it work, do you think? If she draws the short straw, she has to marry him?"

"That had nothing to do with you," Luke snapped, seeing his fond hopes of seducing his wife disappearing.

"So you've said." There was more weariness than anger in her tone. She bent to pick up the willow clothes basket. "I have bread in the oven," she said as she brushed by him.

Luke stared after her. She kept throwing that damned short straw into his face as if there was something he could do to change it. He wanted to be angry with her. But he suddenly remembered what she'd been saying to Gris when he'd approached them, before she'd known he was there. *A woman wants a great deal more than good looks in a man. She wants someone who'll love her and cherish her, someone who'll make her feel as if she's the most important thing in the world to him.* And when she'd talked about Gris going courting, bringing flowers to his girl and reading poetry, there'd been a wistful note in her voice that made him feel lower than a snake's belly.

He hadn't done much by way of courting. He'd seen Eleanor, decided she'd fulfill his needs for a wife and made his offer. He'd been relieved that she hadn't insisted on all the nonsense that usually went along with getting married. He had, he realized uneasily, done exactly what Sean Mulligan had told him he couldn't do—he'd chosen a wife in much the same way he'd have chosen a horse. He'd looked for good lines and a pleasant disposition and had been arrogant enough to think that that was all there was to it.

The back door shut behind Eleanor, and Luke turned away from the house. He was frowning as he walked to where he'd left the roan ground hitched. Marriage wasn't turning out to be quite as simple as he'd expected, but he was willing to adapt his thinking some. There was more than one way to skin a cat—or to win a wife.

Chapter Thirteen

When Eleanor opened her eyes, the first thing she saw was the flowers. They were lying on the pillow next to her. She squeezed her eyes shut and then opened them again. The flowers were still there. When she slid one hand out from under the covers to touch them, she half expected to find they were figments of her imagination, but the coarse stems were solid beneath her fingertips.

Luke.

She sat up abruptly and looked around the room, but she was alone. He'd brought the small bouquet in and left it lying on the pillow for her to find when she woke. The idea that he'd been in the room, perhaps stood by the bed watching her sleep, made Eleanor's heart beat a little faster. Had he been tempted to wake her, maybe with a kiss? She felt a small twinge of something that could have been—

but certainly wasn't—disappointment that he hadn't done just that.

She picked up the bouquet and lifted it to her nose. It had a herbal, slightly medicinal smell. Eleanor thought it was wonderful. Her mouth curved and tears stung her eyes.

Luke had brought her flowers.

Luke saw the flowers as soon as he came in for breakfast. Eleanor had put them in his mother's cut glass vase and set them on the windowsill. He remembered his mother using that same vase, filling it with roses from her gardens and setting it on a mahogany sideboard in the dining room of the big old house back before the war. The ragtag bunch of wildflowers looked pathetic in comparison to that memory, and Luke winced. Maybe the flowers hadn't been such a good idea. He'd probably just reinforced Eleanor's annoyance with him.

But when Eleanor turned away from the stove and saw him, her face softened in a shy smile and there was no mistaking the warmth in her eyes. Luke felt something loosen in his chest, a tightness he hadn't even realized was there until it began to ease. He'd missed that smile, missed seeing it turned in his direction. She looked as if she was about to speak but, if so, she changed her mind when Daniel entered the kitchen behind him.

"Breakfast's ready," was all she said as she turned back to the stove and began dishing up the food.

Luke took his place at the table, his eyes lingering on the soft curves of his wife's body. She was wearing a plain dress in a warm shade of golden brown. It covered her from throat to toes and couldn't, by any stretch of the imagination, be called seductive. But in his mind's eye Luke saw her the way she'd looked this morning when he'd crept into their bedroom to leave the flowers on the pillow.

Her face softly flushed with sleep and the lush curves of her figure outlined beneath the covers, she'd looked like temptation personified. His fingers had itched to loosen the heavy braid that confined her dark hair, and it had taken every ounce of self-control at his command to resist the urge to lift the covers and slide into bed next to her, to wake her with a kiss. His instincts told him that she wouldn't have resisted but he'd learned something of his bride's stubborn pride these past couple of weeks and he knew that, while she might have given in to him, she'd have bitterly resented it—and him. He wanted an end to this war between them, not a new battleground, so he'd turned and walked away, leaving her in her solitary bed.

Breakfast was normally a quiet meal, and this morning was no exception. The cowboys cooked their own breakfast in the bunkhouse, so it was just family in the big kitchen. Since the night Eleanor had found out about him and Daniel drawing straws, the meal had generally been marked by hot food and a chilly atmosphere. Luke knew it wasn't his imagination that there was a definite warming in the air, a warming that had nothing to do with the cast-iron stove that radiated heat into the room.

Several times he was aware of Eleanor sliding quick glances in his direction, glances that did not come with the rapier edge most of her looks had held lately. If he'd known a few flowers would have such an effect, he'd have picked her a washtub full, Luke thought, feeling a little smug. He finished his bacon and eggs, enjoying the meal more than he had any in recent weeks. Things were definitely looking up.

"Could I speak to you a minute?" Eleanor's voice stopped him on his way out of the kitchen.

Daniel glanced from his brother to his sister-in-law, one eyebrow raised in silent question. It was the first time in two weeks that Eleanor had shown any desire to spend a moment more than she had to with Luke. Luke caught his eye and gave him a look that promised severe—and painful—retribution if he said anything. Daniel's mouth quirked and Luke could see him almost visibly swallowing whatever he'd been about to say.

"Breakfast was real fine, Eleanor." Daniel pushed open the door and went out, slapping his hat on his head as he walked down the steps.

His departure left a pool of silence in the kitchen. The room was filled with the smell of bacon and biscuits. Heat radiated from the big iron stove, comforting in the chill dawn hours. Crisp muslin curtains hung at the windows, pushed open now to show the pale gold of first light spreading across the prairies.

Luke was struck again by how much things had changed since he'd married Eleanor. A few weeks ago this room had been more nearly a pigsty than a kitchen. She'd worked hard, making the house into home. If a little bit of courtship made her happy, maybe it wasn't too much to ask.

"I wanted to thank you for the flowers. They're very pretty." Her smile was warm but held a touch of wariness that made Luke wonder if she thought that he might be expecting a reward in exchange for the bouquet—like maybe an invitation to return to their bed. The fact that the thought *had* crossed his mind made Luke feel a little guilty and put a gruff edge on his voice.

"They're not much."

"They're wonderful!" Eleanor's quick defense of the small gift added to his guilt. "No one's ever given me flowers before," she added with a shy smile. "Thank you, Luke."

"You're welcome." They stood there looking at each other for a moment, the air full of things unsaid. It was Luke who broke the silence. "I'll see you later." He smiled at her and then pushed open the door and stepped outside.

His smile lingered as he strode across the ranch yard. A little time spent courting his wife was a small enough price to pay for putting a smile back on her face. If he played his cards right, it wouldn't take him long to convince her to forget about the broom straws that had caused all this trouble. A few more days and he'd be back where he belonged—in his own bed with a warm and willing Eleanor beside him.

"I can't believe you paid that kid two bits for that mangy hunk of fur." Daniel shot a disgusted look at the small basket Luke had tied to the saddlehorn. The plaintive mews emanating from the basket made it clear that the occupant was no happier about the situation than Daniel was.

"It's for Eleanor," Luke told him, not for the first time. "Women like cats."

"They can have 'em." Daniel pulled the makings out of his pocket and began rolling a cigarette. "Nasty, sneaky critters with claws the size of daggers."

"The whole damn kitten isn't any bigger than a table knife," Luke noted. "I don't think you have to fear for your life just yet."

"Just you wait." Daniel ran his tongue along the edge of the paper and sealed the cigarette with a deft roll of his fingers. He gave the basket a dark look as he set a match to the tip of his smoke. "It'll grow."

"You sound like you're speaking from experience."

"I used to see a widow woman who had a whole houseful of the things. There was one—a huge white critter with claws a yard long and a yowl that'd raise the dead—that hated me. Used to lie in wait and then jump out at me and sink its claws into anything handy. I had nightmares about that cat."

Luke's unsympathetic bark of laughter echoed across the prairie and earned him a sour look from his brother.

"You can laugh, but I've got scars from that thing. Haven't been able to abide cats ever since."

"I noticed the widow Sinclair bought a kitten," Luke said, sliding Daniel a look of sly malice.

"Maybe widows have a particular fondness for cats."

Daniel grunted, narrowing his eyes against the smoke and looking out toward the horizon.

"Too bad they don't all share a fondness for you. Letty Sinclair doesn't seem bowled over by your charms."

"It's those damned straws we drew," Daniel snapped. "Your wife has her all het up about it. It didn't have a thing to do with her! Hell, it didn't even have anything to do with Eleanor."

"Women have a different take on things," Luke said, glancing down at the basket. The kitten was the latest step in his campaign to soothe his bride's temper. The flowers had been such a success that he'd been at a loss about what to follow up with. Though the atmosphere between them had been distinctly warmer for the past two days, Eleanor hadn't shown any inclination to invite him back into their bed. Obviously he needed something with which to follow up the posies. The kitten was the perfect choice. What woman could resist a kitten?

"I never thought I'd see the day when you'd be trying to bribe your wife to let you back into your own house," Daniel said, glaring at the basket as if its occupant was somehow to blame for the situation.

"I'm not bribing her." But Luke was aware that there was an uncomfortable element of truth in his brother's accusation. He liked to think of the flowers and the kitten more as peace offerings than bribes. And what difference did it make what they were as long as it made Eleanor happy and persuaded her to forget all about that miserable broom straw?

"Looks like a bribe to me," Daniel said.

"Seems to me that it might not hurt you to watch and learn a little from your older brother. Unless you like having Letty Sinclair glare holes in your back."

"I don't much care what she does," Daniel said with studied indifference. "There's plenty of other fish in the sea."

"I haven't noticed you looking at any of those other fish the way you look at her."

Daniel shrugged. "She's a pretty woman."

"I hear tell Andrew Webb thinks so, too," Luke said casually.

"That stick?" Daniel snorted his contempt of the storekeeper. "She wouldn't look twice at him."

"Maybe not, but I wouldn't bet on it. He's got a solid business, and a widower with four kids is the sort of thing that's inclined to fill a woman's heart with all kinds of maternal urges." Luke shook his head, narrowing his eyes as he looked out across the prairie. "No telling what a woman might do if she thinks there's kids that need taking care of."

"She wouldn't have him, kids or no." But Daniel's tone was less sure than his words.

"Probably not," Luke agreed after letting the silence stretch long enough to convey his doubts. "Still, those kids are a powerful draw."

He slanted his brother a quick sideways glance, barely restraining a whoop of laughter at the set of Daniel's jaw. Just as he'd thought, his little brother had it bad for the widow Sinclair. And, from the way she'd all but snubbed him in town today, Daniel had his work cut out if he was planning on making any progress in that direction.

"She'd never have Webb," Daniel said again, more forcefully.

"Of course not," Luke agreed. As far as he knew, Letty Sinclair didn't have anything more than a nodding acquaintance with Webb. But he provided a handy prod. It was the least Daniel deserved for causing him so much trouble. And if Daniel took a dislike to the skinny little storekeeper it was the least Webb deserved for the proprietary looks he'd given Eleanor before their marriage. Not to mention selling her that god-awful hat. He still hadn't figured out a way to get rid of the wretched thing.

But he could worry about the hat later. Right now he needed to concentrate on persuading Eleanor to forget that damned straw. The kitten was the next step in that particular campaign.

"A kitten! Oh, Luke, thank you!" Eleanor cradled the tiny ball of gray fur between her hands as she smiled up at her husband, her eyes sparkling with pleasure.

"I thought she might be good company," he said, stroking the kitten's head with one finger.

"She's adorable." Eleanor felt as if her heart was literally swelling with joy and she had to blink against the sting of happy tears. "It's the most wonderful present anyone's ever given me."

On an impulse she rose on tiptoe and pressed a kiss to Luke's mouth. She'd intended to simply brush her lips against his, but he moved automatically to steady her, setting his hands on her hips, and the feel of his mouth tantalized her into lingering. He tasted of smoke and coffee and tobacco. The scent of sunshine and horse clung to him— warm, masculine smells that reminded her of hungers she'd been doing her best to pretend she didn't feel. With her hands full of kitten she couldn't push him away, even if she'd wanted to, and the sudden weakness of her knees made stepping back an impossible option.

Luke tasted her surrender and deepened the kiss, his tongue coming out to stroke the fullness of her bottom lip, coaxing her to let him inside. He could have her right here and now, he thought as her mouth opened for him. No more nights in the barn. No more crawling around on the damned prairie looking for flowers or paying small robber barons to part with kittens. He could end it all right here. She wanted him. He could feel it in the yielding curve of her body, taste it in the soft surrender of her mouth. If he carried her upstairs right now, she wouldn't offer so much as a whisper of protest.

Only she'd hate him for it.

Luke shut out the warning voice that insisted that he was about to take one step forward and two back. He drew Eleanor closer, sliding his foot between hers and shifting his hands so that his fingers cupped the fullness of her bottom. She gasped, the sound muffled against his mouth, but she didn't pull away. Instead, her mouth softened even more, her tongue meeting his with a shy hunger that made Luke's body harden with need.

It was the kitten, still cradled in Eleanor's hands, who put an end to the moment. She'd been willing to tolerate close quarters, but when Luke slid his hand up Eleanor's back, pressing her closer to him, the quarters went from close to downright confining and the kitten's patience came to an abrupt end. With a shrill mew of annoyance she sank her claws into the nearest surface, which just happened to be Luke's shirtfront.

"Ouch!" Luke jerked back with a startled oath. His quick movement didn't allow the kitten time to loosen her grip, with the result that she was jerked from Eleanor's hold. She responded in the only way possible, digging her tiny claws deeper still into Luke's shirt and, by sheer coincidence, into the skin it covered. Feeling as if a dozen needles were stabbing him in the chest, Luke grabbed for the kitten, who, thoroughly upset by now, dug her claws in even tighter and yowled her displeasure.

"Don't hurt her," Eleanor said, taking a quick step forward as Luke managed to wrench the kitten loose.

"Don't hurt *her?*" he asked. "You're warning *me* not to hurt *her?* Seems it ought to be the other way around. I think she just tried to kill me."

"She was just scared," Eleanor said in defense of her pet.

"She's bloodthirsty." Luke glared at the kitten dangling from his fingers by the scruff of her neck. She glared right back at him, her green eyes promising future retribution. Remembering Daniel's words of warning, he wondered if maybe he wouldn't have been better off picking another bunch of wildflowers. At least they didn't have claws.

Daniel hitched his horse to the rail outside the general store. Luke had smirked when he'd announced that he was making the trip into town for the second time in less than a week, but he was definitely here to get something and that something had nothing to do with Letty Sinclair. It was just that when he'd seen her walking into Webb's, it had occurred to him that whatever he needed was most likely to be found in the general store.

He walked across the boardwalk and into the store, mentally mulling over the problem of just what it was about Letty Sinclair that had worked its way under his skin. She was pretty, but he'd known other pretty women. Maybe he'd even known some prettier, though he couldn't swear to that. But there was something about the way Letty looked at him. There seemed to be a challenge in her dark eyes, one he just couldn't ignore.

Daniel paused inside the door, letting his eyes adjust to the light. At first the store seemed empty. His eyes skimmed over stacks of canned goods and shelves laden with clothes, looking for Letty's slim figure. She'd been wearing a dress of some rosy pink color, he remembered. He was starting to wonder if he'd imagined seeing her enter the store when he heard a soft, feminine laugh, blending with a deeper, masculine chuckle. The sound made his hackles rise.

Daniel started toward the back of the store with long, predatory strides. So, Luke hadn't been lying when he'd said that Webb had his eye on Letty. The pasty-faced, underfed clerk actually thought he had a chance of drawing and keeping the attention of a woman like Letty. Well, he'd see to it that Webb was weaned from that notion.

Rounding a display of hats, Daniel nearly ran over Letty, who was walking toward the front of the store. He caught her by the shoulders, steadying her.

"Mr. McLain!" Letty's voice was breathless with surprise.

"Mrs. Sinclair." He let her go reluctantly and reached up to take his hat off. "My apologies, ma'am. I didn't see you. You're not hurt, I hope?"

"Not at all, Mr. McLain." Letty put her hand to her chest, as if to still the pounding of her heart. It was just that he'd startled her, she told herself. Her accelerated pulse had nothing to do with those gray eyes of his or the way his dark hair fell onto his forehead in that little wave that made her fingers twitch with the urge to brush it back.

Better that her fingers twitch with the urge to smack his face, she reminded herself sternly. If not for Eleanor's sake, then for her own. She hadn't been a widow for three years without learning to recognize the look of a man with improper notions. And the fact that she'd had an improper notion or two of her own about Daniel McLain only made her more determined to keep her distance.

"If you'll excuse me, Mr. McLain."

"Certainly, Mrs. Sinclair." He stepped back with a polite gesture for her to pass.

His response was the epitome of gentlemanly courtesy, but there was something in his eyes that made a mockery of her careful formality. Letty's back stiffened, her full mouth tightening with annoyance. Her skirts swished against the wooden floor as she swept past him, her chin thrust into the air. Andrew Webb followed behind her, his steps an anxious clatter. But neither the rustle of her skirts nor the sound of Andrew's footsteps was enough to drown out Daniel's soft, knowing chuckle.

He followed them to the front of the store. By tilting his head a little, he could look past Webb and admire the inviting sway of Letty's skirts. Her spine was rigid as a poker and he was willing to bet that her expression was just as stiff. He just couldn't seem to resist the urge to ruffle her feathers.

He waited while she paid for her purchases, making no pretense of having any business of his own to transact. When she turned from the counter, Daniel was amused to note that she managed to avoid noticing him, not an easy task, considering he was standing right behind her. She strode briskly toward the door, and it took some quick footwork on his part to get there ahead of her.

"Allow me," he said, bowing from the waist as he pulled open the door.

"Thank you." Frost dripped from her voice and her expression was hardly indicative of gratitude. As she swept through the door, even the swish of her skirts sounded annoyed.

Grinning, Daniel followed her out. He couldn't say just what it was about her that made him want to rile her, but the urge was irresistible. Two long strides took him to her side.

"Allow me, Mrs. Sinclair," he said, reaching for the parcel she'd carried from the general store.

"That's quite all right, Mr. McLain. I can carry it myself."

"I won't hear of it," he said with exaggerated gallantry. A brief tug-of-war ensued, with Daniel finally gaining control of the paper-wrapped package. He smiled at her, his eyes bright with mischief.

"Really, Mr. McLain, it's not at all necessary," she said between gritted teeth.

"Nonsense, Mrs. Sinclair. A lady should never carry her own parcels when there's a gentleman nearby."

"If there were a gentleman nearby, Mr. McLain, that might be relevant," she snapped, driven beyond endurance.

Daniel laughed aloud. Letty tried not to notice how attractive he was, but it wasn't easy. It simply wasn't fair that one man—one incredibly annoying man—should be so wickedly good-looking.

"If I didn't know better, I'd think you'd just insulted me," he said, grinning down at her.

"Please give me my parcel and let me go on my way," she said, her voice strangled. She was aware that they were receiving interested glances from passersby. "We're starting to draw attention."

"No one would look twice if you would simply allow me to walk you to your destination," he observed in a tone of such innocence that Letty's fingers curled into her palm against the urge to smack him.

Without a word she spun on her heel and stalked off down the boardwalk. Daniel was beside her every step of the way, looming over her, seeming to cut off the very air she was breathing. At least, she assumed that was why she felt so breathless. They walked in silence for a few yards. She was determined not to speak another word to the wretched man, not even if they walked from here to Denver.

"I guess I should apologize," Daniel said after a moment. "I just can't seem to resist the urge to ruffle your feathers. It's just that you—" He broke off as Letty stopped abruptly, rounding on him with a look in her eyes that spoke of violence to come.

"Mr. McLain, if you tell me that I look pretty when I'm mad, I'm afraid I just might forget that I'm a lady and attempt to enact a violence upon your person."

Daniel was so surprised that he actually took a step back, eyeing her warily. "I wasn't going to—"

"Yes, you were. Believe me, Mr. McLain, there isn't a clever line I haven't heard. In the three years since my husband's death I've had any number of gentlemen—and I use the word lightly—express their sympathies over my loss, tell me that they understand the loneliness I must be feeling and make a gracious offer to alleviate that loneliness. I neither need nor want that sort of assistance. I do not understand why men assume that when a woman loses her husband she also loses her morals. I assure you that I have not done so, so you can stop wasting your time and leave me in peace.

"Good day, Mr. McLain."

She wrenched her parcel from his suddenly slackened hold and nodded briskly before spinning on her heel and walking away, her heels clicking on the boardwalk, the sound as hollow as the empty feeling in her chest.

Daniel stared after her. She was prickly as a damned cactus but he was uncomfortably aware of the element of truth in her accusations. It *had* occurred to him that, being a widow, she might be open to a less than proper suggestion or two. His conscience nipped uncomfortably. Underneath the prickliness he'd seen something that looked suspiciously like hurt. He'd never meant to hurt her. Dammit all, he *liked* her.

Cursing under his breath, he strode after her. Catching up with her in front of the newspaper office, he reached out and jerked the parcel from her hand, the brown paper crackling in protest at his roughness.

"I said I'd carry your parcel," he snapped when she opened her mouth to protest.

"Your excessive graciousness makes it difficult to feel grateful, Mr. McLain," Letty snarled in return.

"Anyone ever tell you that you've got a temper like a catamount with its tail caught in a trap?"

"Why, no." She widened her eyes in mock pleasure and gave him a smile that carried a cutting edge. "Coming from you, I'll take it as a compliment."

"It wasn't meant as such."

They stood in the middle of the boardwalk, glaring at each other, oblivious to the curious glances being cast in their direction.

"What is it with you?" Daniel asked, his tone filled with frustration. "No matter what I say, you poker up like I've just insulted your mother. Are you still mad about those blasted straws Luke and I drew? That didn't have anything to do with you."

"A man who'd draw straws to decide a lady's future is not likely to inspire great trust in a woman."

"We weren't drawing straws to decide anybody's future but our own." He all but shook her abused parcel in front of her nose as he tried to make his point. "Luke didn't decide on Eleanor until after that."

"That's not the point."

"Seems to me that it's *exactly* the point," he said. He'd never in his entire life met such an exasperating woman. "Since we didn't know Eleanor, we weren't drawing straws for her."

"But if you hadn't drawn straws, Luke wouldn't have decided to marry Eleanor. And what made him pick on her, anyway?"

"He thought she'd be biddable."

The sentence seemed to hang in the air between them. They both considered how biddable Eleanor had turned out *not* to be. Despite her annoyance, Letty's mouth twitched.

"Biddable?"

"That's what he thought." Daniel had a sudden image of his sister-in-law standing over the table like an avenging angel, spoon in hand and fire in her eyes, and felt his mouth curve in a reluctant smile. "Guess he got a bit of a surprise."

"I'd say so. *Biddable* isn't exactly the first word that comes to mind when I think of Eleanor."

"I think Luke's figured that out." Remembering his brother's frustration with his bride, Daniel chuckled. Letty joined in, the anger evaporating from between them.

"Perhaps there's a greater justice at work here," Letty said, still smiling.

"Maybe." Daniel found himself wondering if her skin could possibly feel as soft as it looked. He didn't want to talk about his brother's marriage any more. "If I asked, very politely, would you allow me to carry your parcel for you, Mrs. Sinclair?"

Seeing the warmth in his eyes, Letty felt her cheeks flush. He really was impossibly good-looking. If she had the sense God gave a gnat, she'd rebuff him politely, reclaim her battered parcel and go on her way. Daniel McLain was trouble, even when he smiled. Most especially when he smiled.

"You may, Mr. McLain." Smiling up at him, she was aware that trouble had never looked quite so inviting.

Chapter Fourteen

The summer sun floated low on the horizon, its light softer than it had been earlier in the day, its brilliance drained by the approach of darkness. Eleanor pushed her toe against the porch floor, setting the rocker in motion. The ranch house tended to gather the day's heat and hold it inside, like a miser hoarding coals against the threat of winter. As the light faded and the prairie cooled, so would the house. But at this time of day there was no more pleasant place to be than the front porch.

A basket sat on the floor next to the rocker, filled to overflowing with a tumble of colorful fabric scraps. On Letty's last visit she'd brought the latest issue of a popular ladies' magazine. In it had been a picture of something the editors called a crazy quilt "an amusing trifle with which a lady might choose to fill her idle moments. Sure to add elegance to any home." Eleanor suspected it would take more than a silk-and-velvet throw to add elegance to the plain ranch house, but the picture in the magazine looked appealing.

She'd completed the first block, covering the muslin foundation with random shapes cut from the rich scraps she'd found in the attic, mute evidence of her mother-in-law's frugal nature. Her embroidery needle slid in and out of the fabric, leaving delicate trails of featherstitching along each seam. She smoothed the thread into place with the edge of her thumbnail and took a moment to admire her efforts.

At her feet, the kitten wrestled ferociously with a strip of lustrous emerald green velvet. The battle was fast and furious, the combatants tumbling back and forth across the floor in a titanic struggle for supremacy. Eleanor watched for a moment, interfering only when it began to look as if the fabric was getting the upper hand. She unwound the narrow length of fabric from the kitten's body and then twitched the end of it and Rascal promptly dived back into the fray.

"Makes a pretty picture," Daniel said, coming up behind Luke, who stood in the doorway of the barn.

"It does." Luke didn't shift his eyes from the porch. Eleanor had picked the kitten up and was holding it in front of her face, talking to it. He couldn't distinguish words, but the warmth of her tone carried easily on the evening air.

"She seems to like that mangy cat," Daniel said. "But I guess she didn't like it enough to let you back into the house. Maybe you should try a bigger bribe. A horse, maybe."

"Go to hell," Luke said, without heat.

"Course, it's going to be damned awkward having a horse in the house," Daniel said thoughtfully. "And there's going to be no end of trouble if she wants to let it sleep on the end of the bed. But the way it stands, I guess that won't make much difference to you, will it? Unless maybe you're hoping she'll let *you* sleep on the end of the bed."

"Don't you have somewhere to go?" Luke turned a cold gray glare in his brother's direction. It was Saturday and, generally, the cowboys all went into town.

Daniel grinned. "I was going into town with the rest of the boys but, if you'd like, I could stay here and keep you company."

"No, thanks."

"I hate to think of my older brother spending another long, cold night alone." Daniel managed an expression of solicitude that was at odds with the wicked sparkle in his eyes. "We could play a few hands of poker. We don't have to play for money, of course. Maybe we could play for broom straws.''

''I doubt the widow Sinclair would take kindly to you playing with broom straws. She wasn't much amused the first time around.''

''What I do is none of her concern.'' Daniel shrugged to show his indifference, but Luke was not fooled. He knew his brother too well.

''I thought you were escorting her to the Fourth of July celebration next week.''

''That doesn't mean she's got a ring through my nose,'' Daniel said.

''I don't think it's a ring through your nose you need to worry about. It's one on her finger.''

''You don't have to worry about that. I've got no plans to marry Letty Sinclair. Nor anyone else, for that matter.''

''I'm not worried,'' Luke said cheerfully. ''From what I've seen of Mrs. Sinclair, she's got more sense than to marry a worthless cowboy like you. When the time comes for her to remarry, I'd guess she'll be looking in other directions. That fellow Webb, for example.''

''She wouldn't look twice at Webb,'' Daniel snapped.

''Maybe not.'' Luke's smile grew wider still, his mood improving in direct proportion to his brother's annoyance. "But she strikes me as a practical sort of female and he's got himself a fine business, a nice house close in to town—and there's those children."

"You keep mentioning them, but I don't see why a woman would want to marry and find herself mother to a passel of kids she don't even know." But there was uncertainty in his tone—an uncertainty Luke seized on with affectionate malice.

"Women tend to take a different view of things," he said kindly. "And when it comes to children . . ." He let his voice trail off and shook his head, at a loss to explain the way a woman's mind worked. "Well, like I said before, they can be a powerful draw."

There was a moment of silence. From the corral behind the barn came the sound of the hands talking as they saddled their horses. Luke couldn't hear what they were saying but he knew what the gist of the conversation would be. Shorty would be boasting about his prowess with the ladies; Joe Small was undoubtedly claiming that he had a feeling in his bones that tonight was his lucky night and he was sure to make a killing at the poker tables. Luke didn't know about luck, but he did know that Joe was the worst poker player he'd ever sat across the table from, which meant that, unless luck parked itself on his shoulder and played the hand for him, he was bound to lose tonight, just as he did every night.

Gris and Slim wouldn't be saying much about their plans, but Luke knew how their evening would go. Slim would settle himself at a table in a corner of the saloon, order a bottle and drink himself into a stupor, trying to forget the family he'd lost to Comanches over a decade before, and Gris would drink a little, play a little poker and end the evening by pouring his friend back into his saddle and making sure Slim got back to the ranch in one piece.

A few weeks ago, before his marriage to Eleanor, he might have been going with them. Luke sought inside himself for a feeling of regret, but found none. He liked things the way they were. Well, not *exactly* the way they were, he amended, returning his attention to where Eleanor sat on the porch, still playing with the kitten. The situation needed a few adjustments, but he had plans for taking care of that.

"A stick like Andrew Webb would never interest a woman like Letty Sinclair," Daniel said, drawing Luke back to the conversation at hand.

"You're probably right," he said absently. He was losing interest in the game.

"Not that I care one way or the other," Daniel said, his voice a little too loud. "It isn't like I'm interested in getting leg shackled myself. If she wants to marry Webb, it's no skin off my nose."

"I never said it was," Luke observed. "Like you said, you don't want to get married, so why should you care what Letty Sinclair does?"

"Right." Daniel looked less sure than he sounded and at another time Luke might have taken advantage of his brother's uncertainty and continued his teasing. But he had other things on his mind tonight.

"Inviting a woman to go to a picnic with you isn't exactly a proposal," Luke assured him.

"No, it's not." Daniel seemed soothed by the thought. "The whole town will be there. We'd probably have bumped into each other anyway."

"Probably." Luke was relieved to hear Shorty call Daniel's name, his tone impatient. Ordinarily he would have welcomed the opportunity to prolong the discussion of his brother's intentions—or lack thereof—toward Letty Sinclair. After the way Daniel had been riding him about the situation with Eleanor, it would have been a pleasure to watch him squirm. But he had plans for this evening, and the sooner Daniel and the boys left, the sooner he could get started on them.

One thing he knew for sure—he'd spent his last night in this damned barn.

Luke entered the house with a carefully thought out plan of seduction laid out in his mind. His brother and the hands were on their way to town. He and Eleanor had the ranch to themselves and he was determined that this night would see an end to their current—unsatisfactory—sleeping arrangements. He'd worked out just the right approach, a masterful combination of reason and seduction. And the package in his hand might help to sweeten the pot a bit.

He'd expected to find Eleanor either sewing or reading but the sound of the piano, silent since his mother's death, had drawn him to the parlor doorway. Outside, the sun had nearly disappeared behind the faint blue line of the Rockies, just visible to the west. The glow of a kerosene lamp cast a soft light in the room. The kitten was asleep on an embroidered cushion near the empty hearth, its tiny body curled into a perfect gray ball. Eleanor sat on the oak stool in front of the instrument, her fingers drifting lightly across the keys. She sang softly as she played, her voice low and a little husky, the words of "Shenandoah" a wistful lament drifting across the dimly lit room.

There was something so peaceful about the scene—something that spoke strongly of home and hearth, of love and comfort, of roots and belonging. Luke felt something tighten in his chest, a sharp twinge of near pain. *This* was the real reason he'd taken a wife. A son to inherit the ranch was only a small part of it. He'd wanted something more in his life than cattle and dust and worry about snow in the winter and drought in the summer.

He'd wanted a home.

Eleanor had given him that. She'd taken an empty house and turned it into a home again. It wasn't the first time he'd had that particular thought, but this time it occurred to him that the house wasn't the only thing that had been changed by her presence. He'd changed, as well. Proof of that was the fact that he was standing here instead of being on his way to town with the hands.

The last notes of "Shenandoah" faded into the warm evening air, soft and sweet and wistful.

"That was beautiful."

The sound of Luke's voice made Eleanor's fingers jump on the keys, creating a discordant jangle of notes. She spun around on the piano stool, her skirts whispering against the floor. Luke stood just inside the parlor door. The lamplight didn't reach quite that far, making him visible only as a tall, broad-shouldered shadow.

"I didn't hear you come in," she said breathlessly.

"I didn't mean to startle you." Luke came farther into the room, stepping into the light. Eleanor felt her breath catch all over again. Surely there would come a time when just the sight of him would no longer make her feel as giddy as a girl meeting her first beau. "That was real nice," he said, tilting his head toward the piano. "I didn't know you played."

"I haven't played much in the last few years. I'm afraid I'm more than a little rusty."

"Not from what I heard." He was carrying a paper-wrapped parcel, which he set on the floor near the sofa before crossing to the piano. "Did you take lessons from that piano teacher from Boston, too?"

"Miss Brown?" Eleanor shook her head, surprised that he knew about the woman who'd spent several months in town, giving lessons to anyone who cared to pay her fee. "No. Anabel took lessons from her, though."

"Your aunt said as much. From what I heard, either Miss Brown wasn't much of a teacher or your cousin is tone deaf."

Eleanor turned back to the piano to conceal a delighted smile at his summation of Anabel's skills. "Miss Brown did her best," she said, avoiding direct criticism.

"So, why haven't you played much lately? Your aunt and uncle have a piano."

"Yes, but I kept quite busy helping Aunt Dorinda. There wasn't a great deal of time for playing the piano."

"Treated you like a drudge, did she?"

The question startled Eleanor into looking up at him. "No, of course not. It was just that, after they were kind enough to take me in, I felt as if I should do as much as possible to repay their generosity."

She'd offered herself the explanation so many times that she'd almost come to believe it. It had been easier to accept the endless stream of tasks if she convinced herself that she was doing it purely by choice.

"I'll bet that pinch-nosed aunt of yours made sure to remind you of just how obligated you were," Luke said shrewdly.

Familial obligation demanded a denial but Eleanor couldn't get one out. She lowered her head, one finger picking out an aimless tune on the ivory keys. "They didn't have to take me in," she said, reminding herself as much as Luke.

"I suppose not." Something in his tone suggested that he could have said a great deal more on the topic of her aunt and uncle's charity but, to Eleanor's relief, he didn't add anything to that simple agreement.

"So, if it wasn't Miss Brown from Boston, who taught you to play piano?"

"My father. After my mother died, we never lived in one place long enough to have a piano of our own. Not that Papa ever had the money for that kind of luxury," she added. "But there was usually someone in each town who was willing to let me use their piano."

"You moved around a lot?" Luke shifted position, leaning his elbow on top of the upright piano and looking down at her.

"We did a lot of traveling." Eleanor picked out the first few notes of "Aura Lee." "Papa couldn't seem to settle in one place after Mama died."

"Your uncle said he was a gambler."

"He was." Eleanor looked at him, her chin tilted up, as if daring him to say something critical.

"Can't be many gamblers who tote a child along with them. Must have been hard to always be on the move."

"I didn't mind," she said. It was a half-truth. She'd hated never having a home. It hadn't taken her long to learn that any friends she made would soon be left behind, so she'd stopped trying to make friends at all, preferring loneliness to the pain of saying goodbye. She'd longed for a real home and a chance to put down roots. But whatever roots Nathan Williams might have grown had been severed by his wife's death. She'd sometimes thought that he was running from his grief, always moving on for fear that, if he stayed in one place, he'd have to face the depth of his loss. And much as she'd hated always being on the move, she would have hated being left behind even more.

"Papa always made everything an adventure." She played a quick, light tune, her mouth curving in a reminiscent smile. "When I think of him, I always remember him laughing."

"Hard to imagine Zeb Williams having a brother like that," Luke said thoughtfully. "I'd be willing to bet the ranch that the only time Zeb laughs is when he gets a chance to foreclose on someone."

Eleanor gave a choked little laugh at his accurate summation of her uncle. "Uncle Zeb isn't exactly a jolly man," she admitted with careful restraint.

Luke had a sudden image of a fourteen-year-old Eleanor, all dark hair and big brown eyes, entering her uncle's house and finding scant welcome.

Though it was years past and he hadn't even known of Eleanor's existence, he felt angry on her behalf.

"Do you play?" Eleanor asked, breaking into his thoughts.

"Play?" Luke stared at her blankly, his thoughts elsewhere.

"The piano," she clarified, playing a rippling series of notes as if to remind him of the instrument's purpose.

"Not me." Luke shook his head, his mouth curving in a quick grin. "My mother tried to teach me a time or two but I can't carry a tune in a bucket. Can't play piano, and my singing is enough to set every coyote within forty miles howling in pain."

"You can't be that bad," Eleanor protested with a laugh.

"Worse." Luke shook his head regretfully. "My mother finally made me promise to stop practicing because she was afraid the noise I made might do permanent harm to her piano."

"So, she was the only one who played?"

"Daniel can hold his own. Or he could. He hasn't played much since she died. Running a ranch doesn't leave much time for piano playing."

"You must miss your mother a great deal," Eleanor said softly. She brushed her fingers across the keys, a quick, caressing movement that made Luke's thoughts turn in a slightly more carnal direction than music appreciation. "I was only six when my mother died. I hardly remember her at all." Eleanor's voice was wistful. "But I remember that she always smelled of lilacs. There was a beautiful lilac bush outside our house in St. Louis and when it bloomed in the spring, she'd cut big bunches of blossoms for the house. The smell seemed to linger on her clothes and hair all year round."

"Roses," Luke said, memory washing over him. "Before the war my mother grew roses. In the summer my father used to complain that the house smelled like a perfume shop because of all the roses she brought inside. When we came west, she brought cuttings of some of the bushes, but they didn't take here. Too hot and dry in the summer, too cold in the winter. I think leaving her gardens behind grieved her more than leaving the house."

"Where did you live?"

"Virginia. My father and his brother grew tobacco."

"I've never been to Virginia but I've heard that it's lovely."

"It's green." Luke stared at the window just past her shoulder but his eyes were unfocused as he looked through the closed curtains and into a past he rarely thought about. "In the summer I used to think even the air tasted green."

"It sounds beautiful."

"It was. Oakwood had been in the family since before the War for Independence. My great-grandfather built the house."

"Why did your family leave it?"

"After the war there wasn't much reason to stay in Virginia," he said simply.

"I was only a child when Lee surrendered, but my father used to talk about the damage the war did and wonder how long it would take for the country to heal."

"Some wounds never heal completely." Luke spoke softly, half forgetting that Eleanor was there. "My father didn't believe in slavery, but he did believe strongly in states' rights. He went south to fight for the Confederacy. My uncle believed in preserving the union at all costs. He went north. When they came home they vowed that there'd be no mention of the war, no talk of battles won or lost. The past was past. They'd fought, they'd survived, that was all that mattered."

"They sound like very wise men," Eleanor said quietly.

"But only men." Luke remembered half-heard arguments, ended but never resolved because no resolution was possible. The tension that had stretched between the adults had soon lapped out to encompass him and Daniel and their cousins. The quarrels their fathers were so determined to avoid were soon exploding among their children. Fights had become a weekly and then almost a daily event until his mother and his aunt had finally pointed out the truth no one wanted to face—there could be no going back to the way things had been before the war. The changes had been too fundamental for that.

"It didn't take long for it to become obvious that too much had changed," Luke said, speaking half to himself. "My uncle scraped up enough money to buy my father's half of the land and we moved west."

"It must have been a terrible time for your family." Eleanor's fingers stroked the keys.

"We were better off than many. My father came home sound of mind and body. That was as much as anyone could hope for and more than many got."

The haunting notes of "When Johnny Comes Marching Home Again" filled the silence after he spoke. The mournful tune brought back half-forgotten memories—the grim stranger who'd returned in his father's body, his mother's tears, the emptiness of the land, the taut silence of the house, broken by those carefully controlled nonarguments that were somehow worse than open fighting.

"It was a long time ago," Luke said as the last poignant note of the song faded. He straightened away from the piano, forcing the memories away. if there was one thing the war and its aftermath had taught him, it was that there was never any point in looking back. The past was past and there was nothing to be accomplished by thinking about it.

"Do you ever think about going home?" Eleanor tilted her head to look up at him, her dark eyes soft with sympathy for all the war had cost his family.

"This *is* home," Luke said without hesitation. "Virginia is just a place I once lived. A lot of sweat and blood has gone into building this place. Lord willing, our sons will build on what we leave behind."

Eleanor flushed a little at the mention of sons, her eyes dropping away from his, and it occurred to Luke that he'd all but forgotten his purpose in coming into the house tonight. The sound of the piano and Eleanor's gentle company had driven thoughts of seduction from his mind. Shaking off the last ghostly tendrils of the past, he focused on the present.

His present was tied to the woman sitting in front of him—a not unpleasant thought, despite the current situation. He noticed the way the lamplight picked out reddish highlights in her dark hair, which was swept up into a soft knot at the back of her head, baring the nape of her neck. His fingers itched to pull out the pins and see her hair tumble down her back, sable and silk in his hands, against his skin. He wanted to loosen the buttons that marched primly up the front of her dress all the way to her neck and set his fingers against the pulse that beat at the base of her throat.

"So many people come west looking for new beginnings," Eleanor said, speaking half to herself. She brushed her fingers over the keyboard, creating a quick ripple of sound. She slanted a quick look in Luke's direction. He was looking at her but the lamplight cast shadows across his face, making it impossible to read his expression.

Dropping her eyes back to the keys, she picked out an aimless little tune, her thoughts on the man leaning against the piano rather than on the music. When he'd first appeared, she'd thought it must be providence taking a hand in her life. She'd been wrestling with herself for nearly a week, ever since he'd given her the kitten. She wanted to tell him that she'd had enough time to consider their situation; that she'd realized it was time to move on with their lives.

It hadn't been an easy decision. She'd had to turn loose her girlish dreams of romantic love and accept reality. Luke didn't love her. It would be foolish to believe otherwise. But he must care for her, at least a little. How else to explain the flowers and the kitten and his patience with what many would consider her unreasonable attitude? Certainly, he would have been well within his rights to insist that they share a bed. The fact that he hadn't might have been the result of indifference rather than kindness but Eleanor didn't believe he was indifferent to her, any more than she was indifferent to him. No, he'd given her the time she'd asked for because he cared enough to try to please her. And if that wasn't the passionate love she'd dreamed of, it was more than she might have had.

But now, how did she go about telling him that it was time for him to come back to their bed?

"I have a present for you," Luke said, interrupting her thoughts.

"A present?" Eleanor's hands dropped into her lap as she lifted her head to look at him. "For me?"

"Didn't I just say so?"

"What for? It's not my birthday." Not that she'd received many birthday presents in recent years, she thought to herself.

"It's something I meant to give you a long time ago but I forgot."

Eleanor had been so absorbed in the simple fact of his presence that she'd barely noticed the package he'd been carrying when he entered the parlor. Now she looked at it with sudden interest as he picked it up from where he'd set it on the floor near the sofa and brought it over to her.

"For me?" she questioned again as she took it from him.

"Well, it's certainly not for the cat." Luke's teasing smile made Eleanor's heart thump against her breastbone.

She looked down at the package in her lap, half afraid of what her eyes might reveal. The way he was smiling at her and the warmth in his voice made her long for him to love her the way she'd always dreamed of being loved. She wanted to be the center of his world, the source of his greatest joy and deepest happiness. Eleanor plucked at the string that tied the plain brown paper package.

That hadn't been a part of their bargain, she reminded herself sternly. She might not have known about the short straw he'd drawn but she had known that Luke wasn't marrying her because he'd fallen in love with her. He'd made no secret of what he wanted—a wife to take care of his home and give him children. And she'd wanted desperately to escape her uncle's household. Theirs hadn't been a bargain based on love. If she'd come to wish otherwise—well, that was her problem.

"Are you going to open it or just stare at it until age turns the paper to dust?" Luke's dry question broke into her thoughts.

"I like to take my time when it comes to presents," Eleanor said. With an effort she pushed aside her thoughts and glanced up at him with a quick smile. "Patience is a virtue, remember."

"Maybe, but that ain't a side of beef that needs aging." He nodded to the package she held.

"I'm relieved to hear it." Focusing solely on the moment, Eleanor plucked at the knot that tied the string. When it didn't yield, she started to pick at it with her fingernails.

Luke clucked his tongue with exasperation. "A man could grow old and die waiting for you to undo that knot."

Without waiting for a response to his comment, he leaned over and took hold of the string with both hands. A quick jerk and it snapped in two.

"I was going to save the string for another use," Eleanor said, casting him a look of mild reproach. "One long piece is more likely to be useful than two short ones."

"I'll buy you a roll of the stuff," he promised, unimpressed by her frugality. He was anxious to see her reaction to the fabric. She'd seemed very taken with it a few weeks ago. He hoped she still felt the same. If he'd thought about it, he might have been surprised to realize that, at the moment, he was more concerned with the pleasure he hoped the gift would give Eleanor than in persuading her to let him back into their bed—at least for the time being. He had the feeling that there'd been too few presents in her life.

"Oh, my!" Eleanor exclaimed breathlessly as she folded back the paper to reveal the soft, rich length of blue grenadine. She stared at the fabric for a moment before brushing her fingertips across it as if to confirm its reality.

"That's the stuff you were looking at that day in Webb's," he said, a little uneasy in the face of her silence. "You seemed to like it."

"You remembered that and went back and found it for me?" Eleanor lifted her head to look at him, her expression full of wonder.

"Actually, I bought it then."

Her eyes widened. "You bought it that day? For me?"

"That's right."

She ran her palm across the fabric again, almost kneading it with pleasure. "Why would you have bought something like this for me when you didn't even know me?"

Luke shrugged. He'd wondered that a time or two himself. He offered her the only answer he'd come up with. "I thought it would suit you."

"It's a wonder you've a penny left to your name if you make a habit of buying fabric for strange women just because you think it would suit them. Besides it being highly improper."

"I don't think doing it once is likely to ruin me, and I was never much inclined to waste time worrying about what's proper and what's not. Do you like the fabric?"

"Like it?" Eleanor stroked it again, her fingertips caressing the rich weave in a way that made Luke's skin tighten with sudden awareness. "No one has ever given me anything half so beautiful."

Seeing the glitter of tears in her dark eyes, Luke felt a twinge of guilt at the ulterior motives behind the gift, but not enough of a twinge to change his mind. He'd had enough of sleeping in the barn. It was time to put this business of that damned broom straw behind them and get on with their lives. It was what Eleanor wanted, too. She was just too stubborn to admit it.

"Thank you, Luke." Eleanor set the fabric on the piano stool as she rose, the paper rustling against the oak. "It's a wonderful present."

She stepped toward him, rising on her toes to brush a quick kiss across his cheek. She'd baked an apple pie for dinner and Luke caught a faint whiff of cinnamon as if the scent still clung to her skin and hair. There was something remarkably sensuous about the wholesome smell, or maybe it was just the fact that he seemed to find that nearly everything about his wife aroused him.

When she started to step back, he caught her hand, holding her in front of him. "Is that all I get?" He saw Eleanor's eyes widen at the husky question and forced his mouth to curve in a teasing smile. "I seem to recall getting more than a peck on the cheek when I brought home that kitten. You're not going to tell me that you like that mangy cat more than you like the fabric, are you?" he asked lightly.

"I'm very fond of Rascal," Eleanor said, glancing at the kitten, who was still asleep on her cushion. When her eyes met Luke's he could read her uncertainty and knew she was remembering the last kiss they'd shared, a kiss that might have gone considerably further than it had if it hadn't been for the kitten sinking her claws into his chest. He did his best to look as if he wasn't remembering the same thing, as if he wasn't hoping for a repeat— minus the cat, of course. Perhaps he succeeded, because Eleanor's mouth curved in a smile that held more than a hint of coquetry. "But it really is very nice fabric," she admitted.

"Nice enough to deserve a proper kiss?" Luke asked even as he used his grip on her hand to draw her subtly closer.

"I suppose so." Their eyes met and held for a long, silent moment, and it seemed to Luke as if a message passed between them—an acknowledgment that this night would see an end to the distance between them, an end to this foolish game they'd been playing out.

Chapter Fifteen

Her mouth touched his, soft as a butterfly's wing. Luke's mouth softened in response, returning her kiss but letting her control the moment. She seemed to gain confidence from his passivity and she edged closer, her lips pressing more firmly to his. Moving slowly, Luke brought her hand up to his chest, pressing her fingers over his heart. His free hand came up to touch her shoulder, the delicate ridge of her collarbone, the nape of her neck, and then his fingers cupped her head, tilting her head back farther as his mouth opened over hers.

He traced his tongue over the fullness of her lower lip and felt her shiver in reaction. She started to ease back, started to speak—to offer a protest? But Luke's patience abruptly ran out. He told himself he had all night, that there was no need to hurry. But all it took was one taste of her mouth and his patience disappeared in a rush of hunger.

His mouth hardened over hers, swallowing whatever she might have said, drinking in her murmur of surprise as he pulled her against him. There had been too many nights spent alone, too many days spent wanting.

It was like being caught up in a tornado, Eleanor thought dazedly. One minute she'd been kissing Luke, a safe, gentle kiss that made her feel warm inside. The next, Luke was kissing her and there was nothing safe or gentle about it. She whimpered as his tongue plunged into her mouth, and the warmth became a conflagration that seared all the way to her soul. Her fingers curled into his shirtfront, clinging to him as the world spun around her.

Without giving her a chance to regain her balance, Luke slid one hand down the length of her back. Eleanor gasped in shock as he boldly spread his palm across her bottom, urging her forward until she stood between his thighs. Even through the layers of skirt and petticoats she could feel the rigid length of his arousal pressed against the most feminine heart of her. Her knees threatened to give out beneath her and she lifted her hands to his shoulders, holding on to him as the only solid thing in her universe.

The feel of her yielding softness in his arms shattered the last remnants of Luke's control. He opened his mouth again over hers, sliding his tongue between her teeth, tasting the sweet warmth of her surrender. He'd waited forever for this—for the feel of her mouth opening to his, her slender body curving against the harder planes and angles of his. It hadn't been the discomfort of making his bed in the barn that had kept him awake at night. It had been this need, this hunger he felt for his wife. She was everything warm and womanly, everything he'd ever wanted. And she was his.

Pins showered to the floor as his fingers burrowed into the twisted knot that held her hair. Eleanor murmured something—whether protest or approval, Luke was beyond hearing the difference. His pulse drumming in his ears, he felt an almost feverish urgency to confirm his possession in the most basic of ways, to feel her body welcome his. He fumbled with the buttons at the throat of her gown, urgency making his hands less than steady.

"Luke." She wrenched her mouth from his, turning her face aside. "Stop," she begged breathlessly.

"You don't want me to stop," he whispered against her throat.

"It's too fast." Her hands flattened against his chest, trying to wedge some distance between them. "Let me go."

Later—much later—Luke would be willing to concede that perhaps he had rushed things a bit. Maybe he'd shown less finesse than he might have. The moment he'd felt her in his arms, all his plans for seduction had been burned away by the simple need to have her—now. But the perspective a little distance might have given him was not yet available. In the here and now, all he knew was that she was pushing him away—again.

There was a brief moment when he considered ignoring her breathless demand to be released. He could change her mind. She wanted him. He was sure of that. Hard on the heels of that thought came another—did it really matter what she wanted? She was his. His wife, his property in the eyes of God and the law. What right did she have to deny him something that was rightfully his? Shocked by his own thoughts, Luke released Eleanor so suddenly that she had to brace one hand against the piano to regain her balance.

They stared at each other. The only sound was their breathing, lending a less than steady rhythm to the silence.

"Luke, I..." Eleanor's voice trailed off as if she couldn't find the words she wanted.

Looking at her, Luke felt all the frustration of the past weeks well up inside him. He wished Daniel had drawn the short straw that night. He wished they'd burned the damned broom before the idea of drawing straws occurred to either one of them. He wished his horse had stepped in a prairie dog hole on the way to church the day he'd first seen Eleanor. A broken neck wouldn't have been nearly the trouble getting married had been. Most of all, he wished he'd never heard of the institution of marriage.

It had taken marriage to teach him the true joys of being a bachelor. Since saying "I do," he'd had things thrown at him, been bitten for the first time since one of his cousins sank her brand-new teeth into his arm when she was a toddler, spent more time sleeping with his horse than he had with his wife and experienced more sexual frustration than he'd ever endured when he was single. He'd crawled around on the prairie picking flowers like a love-sick lunatic, paid two bits for a kitten who had dug permanent holes in his chest with her claws and showed more patience than anyone had a right to expect a man to show.

"What the hell do you want from me?"

"Luke!" It was the first time she'd heard him use profanity.

"I don't know what more you expect," he continued, oblivious to her protest. "Haven't I given you the time you asked for?"

"Yes, and I—"

"There aren't many men who would have done that."

"I know. I—"

"I've been patient."

"Yes. You've—"

"I've waited for you to come to your senses instead of trying to shake some into you, haven't I?"

Eleanor stiffened. The phrase "come to your senses" did not sit well. But She swallowed her annoyance. She didn't want to argue with him. She wanted an end to the distance between them. These past weeks had shown her that, while he might not love her with the passion she dreamed of, he cared enough to try to make her happy. That was more than many women had. She'd already decided that it was time to put their marriage on a normal footing. When he'd given her the grenadine, it had simply confirmed that decision. The thoughtfulness of the gift touched her deeply.

She wanted to be his wife again, in every sense of the word, but she'd felt as if she were drowning in the elemental force of his hunger. She'd called a halt to their embrace to give herself a chance to breathe, not because she was unwilling to be his wife in fact, as well as in name. And she'd tell him as much as soon as he gave her a chance.

"I know you've—"

"No one in their right mind would have put up with what I've put up with," Luke continued, unaware of her thoughts. "Sleeping in the barn, letting my brother make my life a living hell. It's a wonder the hands haven't quit. If I can't manage my own wife, why should I be able to manage a ranch?"

"Manage your wife?" Luke was too wrapped up in his soliloquy to heed the warning in her tone.

"I've given you flowers and that mangy cat." He threw out one hand to indicate the kitten, who continued to sleep, unconcerned with the storm brewing a few feet from her. "And now I've given you that blasted piece of cloth and you're still acting like a virgin on her wedding night." He paused to glare at her. "What the hell do you want from me?"

This time Eleanor barely noticed his language. Considering the way her pulse was drumming in her ears, it was a wonder she could hear him at all. *The fabric had been a bribe?* He actually thought he could buy his way back into her bed? That she'd sell herself like a... like a saloon girl, her price a few yards of cloth?

She turned and snatched the package up off the piano stool. Spinning back toward Luke, she shoved it into his arms, the paper wrapping crackling a protest at her roughness. His hands came up automatically to catch it.

"I'm not for sale!"

"For sale?" Luke gaped at her, caught off guard by her quick flare of temper. "What are you talking about?"

"You came in here thinking you could buy your way back into my bed with that." She gestured sharply to the crumpled length of fabric.

"I did not." Guilt added a sharp edge to his denial. Maybe he *had* thought that the gift would soften her mood but he certainly hadn't planned to *buy* her. Besides, he damn well shouldn't have to *buy* anything. The thought added new fuel to the already blazing fire of his anger. The fabric hit the floor in a sharp rustle of paper. He kicked it out of the way with a quick sideways motion of his booted foot and stepped toward her.

Finding herself trapped between the piano and her husband's tall body, Eleanor tilted her chin and glared up at him. She would die before she'd let him see that he'd succeeded in intimidating her.

"I don't have to buy my way into your bed." The soft menace of his voice was more effective than a shout. "You're my wife. It's my bed."

His hand snapped out, fingers closing around her left wrist. Eleanor gasped and instinctively tried to jerk away. But her back was against the side of the piano and she refused to sidle away from him like a frightened crab. Not that he looked much in the mood to let her go anyway, she noted uneasily.

"Let go of me." If the command was a little less forceful than she might have liked, that was hardly surprising considering the look in her husband's eyes.

Luke ignored the command, dragging her arm upward until her hand was between them. Her wedding ring gleamed dull gold in the lamplight.

"When I put that ring on your finger, I bought the rights to your bed. And to you."

Eleanor stared up at him, speechless with anger and—though she didn't want to admit it—a touch of fear. She'd never seen anyone look as coldly threatening as Luke did at this moment. She was suddenly vividly aware of the differences between them. Male and female. He was stronger than she was. There could be no physical contest between them. And, alone as they were, there was no one to whom she could turn for help. Not that anyone was likely to interfere in what happened between man and wife. Luke was right—the wedding ring on her finger made her his property, to do with as he pleased. She swallowed hard but tilted her chin up another notch, determined not to let him see her fear.

"You'll have to force me," she promised quietly.

Luke stared at her, seeing the flicker of fear in her eyes—a fear he'd put there. He'd *wanted* to frighten her, had deliberately used his superior strength to intimidate. *That's impressive, McLain. Frightening women. That would certainly make your father proud.* Shame left an acid taste on his tongue. His fingers dropped away from Eleanor's wrist as if she'd suddenly caught fire.

"I'm tired of the whole blasted mess." He spun on one heel and walked away. Eleanor swayed at the abrupt release of tension. She put out one hand to catch herself, drawing a sharp clatter of notes from the piano keyboard.

"Where are you going?" The involuntary question stopped Luke in the parlor doorway. He turned to look at her, his eyes a cool, emotionless gray.

"Enjoy your solitary bed, but don't kid yourself into thinking that I'm going to spend the rest of my life living like a monk."

He was gone before Eleanor could speak—not that she had any idea of what she might have said. The front door shut behind him with a quiet click that sounded more final than a slam.

She stood there—alone, the tangled mass of fabric and wrapping paper at her feet, and wondered if she'd just made a terrible mistake.

Two hours later Eleanor started awake. She'd dozed off curled in the rocking chair in the bedroom. Though her quilting lay in her lap, she'd barely set two stitches in place. Within minutes after their quarrel, she'd heard Luke ride out of the ranch yard. She tried to tell herself that she didn't care where he'd gone, as long as he was out of her sight. But she kept hearing his final words that he wasn't going to spend the rest of his life living like a monk. What if Luke had ridden into town to seek out more obliging companionship than his wife had been providing of late?

She kept thinking about the impure women who worked in the Golden Lady Saloon. Her aunt had refused to acknowledge the existence of such women but in a town the size of Black Dog it was impossible to avoid seeing them, at least on occasion. Though she didn't like to think about it now, Eleanor remembered that several of the women had been quite attractive, their demeanor not unladylike when their paths had crossed hers on the street or in the aisles of Andrew Webb's store.

Aside from his wife, who would blame Luke if he sought out one of those women?

Her first thought was that she'd never forgive him. But then, a small voice suggested that part of the blame might be hers. She'd refused to perform her wifely duties. And perhaps she'd overreacted a bit this evening when Luke had given her the fabric. He'd seemed genuinely shocked when she'd accused him of trying to buy her favors. As he'd pointed out, he didn't *have* to buy anything. She was his for the taking. It really was a beautiful piece of cloth. Surely, the fact that he'd bought it before he asked her to marry him absolved him of any ulterior motives. Didn't it?

Eleanor fell asleep again before she could come up with an answer, her head tilting awkwardly back against the oak rocker. She woke suddenly, her heart pounding from the remnants of a half-remembered dream. Untangling her feet from the hem of her nightgown, she rose, grimacing at the stiffness in her neck and shoulders. She bent to pick up her quilting, which had fallen to the floor, only to straighten abruptly as she heard a repeat of the sound that had awakened her—the squeal of the hinges on the barn door.

Luke! It could have been Daniel or any one of the hands but she knew it wasn't. She rushed to the window. A full moon flooded the prairie with light of palest silver. A man stepped away from the barn and started toward the house, his shadow stretching over the ground ahead of him. His features were concealed by the brim of his hat but Eleanor didn't need to see his face. His long, easy stride and the pounding of her own heart told her who it was.

He was back. And not only back but coming in!

She'd barely had time to absorb the idea when she heard the front door open and close. An instant later she heard the thud of his boots on the stairs. Good Lord, he was coming upstairs! He might even be coming here, to this very room. Considering his mood when they'd parted, that was not a reassuring thought.

She'd lock the door against him. She took a step in that direction and then hesitated. Maybe it would be better to get into bed and pretend to be asleep, as if their earlier quarrel had meant nothing at all to her. She stood in the middle of the floor, waffling between the two possibilities until she heard Luke reach the top of the stairs. If she locked the door now, he'd surely hear her. It would be like throwing down a gauntlet. She'd be making a definite statement, though at the moment she couldn't have said just what that statement would be.

Then again, it might be more in the nature of waving a red flag in front of a bull, Eleanor thought uneasily, remembering his earlier anger. A locked door might just set a match to his temper and she'd certainly be the one to get burned in the resulting conflagration.

Hardly aware of making a decision, she rushed to blow out the lamp and scurried to the bed, diving beneath the covers and pulling them up over her shoulders just as she heard Luke's footsteps stop outside the bedroom door. Squeezing her eyes shut, she struggled to control her breathing. When he knocked on the door, she wanted her response to sound as if she'd been asleep, not as if she'd just jumped into bed like a frightened child. She wanted to make it clear that his stormy departure hadn't bothered her at all. She certainly didn't want him to get the idea that she'd spent any time brooding about the possibility that he'd sought out some dance hall floozy to occupy his evening.

She'd be dignified, she promised herself. She wouldn't be too eager to forgive but she wouldn't be grudging, either. Dignity and gracious forgiveness—after an appropriate interval, of course.

Eleanor squeezed her eyes shut, as if Luke might be able to see through walls. Perhaps she'd let him knock twice to make it clear that she'd been sound asleep.

Only Luke didn't knock at all.

The sound of the doorknob turning brought Eleanor straight up in bed. She stared in disbelief as the door opened and Luke walked into the room. He carried a lantern with him, its soft, golden glow a painfully bright intrusion in the dark room. But not nearly as much of an intrusion as the man who carried it.

She opened her mouth to demand an explanation for his presence but then remembered her determination to present a dignified image. It took a considerable effort but she managed to swallow her angry words. A telling silence was her best possible response.

But, telling or not, her silence didn't seem to have much effect on Luke. Without so much as a glance in her direction, he carried the lamp across the room and set it on the dresser. He ran his fingers through his hair, eliminating the flatness left by the pressure of his hat. Eleanor felt a twinge of uneasiness as she watched him empty his pockets, setting their contents on top of the dresser. He didn't look like a man who'd come to offer humble apologies to his wife. He looked more like a man getting ready to go to bed. Her uneasiness became more than a twinge when he loosened the buttons on his cuffs and tugged his shirttail out of the waist of his pants.

"What do you think you're doing?" she demanded.

Luke turned to look at her, his expression calm. He reached for the buttons on the front of his shirt. "I'm going to bed."

"Here?" Eleanor's voice rose on a disbelieving squeak. This was a far cry from the apology she'd envisioned.

"Here," Luke said flatly. "In my house, in my bed, with my wife." He shrugged out of his shirt as he spoke, tossing the garment over the arm of the rocker as he walked toward the bed.

The sight of his bare chest stirred something in the pit of Eleanor's stomach, an emotion she preferred not to acknowledge. She was still angry with him. How dare he think he could just waltz back in here and ... and do whatever it was he thought he was going to do.

"Fine," she snapped, throwing back the covers. "You stay here. I'll sleep somewhere else."

"No, you won't." Luke set one knee on the bed and leaned across it, circling her upper arm with the fingers of one hand, effectively preventing her escape. "You're staying right here."

"I won't!" She tried to jerk away but there was no breaking the gentle implacability of his hold.

"You're going to stay here. In this bed. With me."

There was nothing in the least threatening in his tone, but neither was there an inch of give. Looking at him, Eleanor saw that he'd reached the end of his patience. The game they'd been playing was finished. She didn't have to worry anymore about how to end the stalemate between them. There would be no more nights spent alone. If there was a certain relief in the thought, she certainly wasn't going to admit it to him.

"You'll have to force me." She threw the words down between them like a duelist throwing down a glove.

"I don't think so." Luke slid his hand down her arm, the gesture caressing even as it held her prisoner. His thumb stroked lightly over the inside of her wrist, and her pulse jumped in response. Against her will Eleanor's eyes drifted to the broad muscles of his chest and shoulders. There was a fluttering sensation low in her belly, an almost painful awareness of his masculinity—a hunger she refused to acknowledge.

"I think you've missed having me in our bed," he whispered. His hand slipped back up her arm, tugging her closer as he leaned toward her, closing the distance between them. "I don't think you want to sleep alone anymore."

"I haven't missed you," she lied, trying not to notice the way his hair fell onto his forehead in a heavy black wave. "I like sleeping alone."

"I don't." Without releasing her, Luke shifted until he knelt on the bed. Taking hold of her shoulders, he dragged her up until she knelt in front of him. "I'm not going to sleep in the barn anymore, Eleanor."

"I never told you to sleep in the barn." His fingers were busy loosening the heavy braid of her hair, and she ducked her head away but it was a halfhearted effort at best. The truth was, she was tired of the distance between them, tired of fighting her own desires. "You could have slept in another room in the house."

"No, I couldn't." Luke speared his hands through her hair, spreading it over her shoulders in a thick brown cape. The way he looked at her made Eleanor feel as if her bones were dissolving. He was no longer holding her captive, but he didn't have to—the hunger in his eyes was as effective as a shackle. "I couldn't be in the same house with you and not hold you."

Eleanor felt mesmerized by the smoky gray of his eyes, by the hunger he didn't trouble to hide. There was something very seductive about being the object of his desire. She felt her determination to resist him weakening.

"Aren't you going to try and buy me with another piece of fabric or maybe a pair of shoes?" she asked, but she couldn't seem to call up her earlier outrage.

"No more presents," Luke said, refusing to rise to the bait she'd offered. He set his thumb against the pulse that beat at the base of her throat. "No more talk. No more separate beds. We're married. From now on, we're going to act like it."

"I won't—"

"Yes, you will." Luke dropped a quick kiss on her mouth, stilling her automatic protest. And that's exactly what it was, she realized when he lifted his head. She didn't really want to argue with him. They'd argued enough—more than enough. She was tired of being at odds with him, tired of pretending she didn't ache to be in his arms again.

Perhaps Luke read something of what she was thinking because his grip on her gentled subtly. His fingers shifted on her arms, his touch caressing rather than holding her captive. Eleanor felt a shiver work its way up her spine. She lifted her hands to his chest, threading her fingers through the crisp dark curls there. His skin was warm to the touch. She'd missed having his heat next to her in bed, missed the feel of his arms wrapped around her late at night.

She looked up at him, searching his eyes for answers to questions she couldn't put into words. She wanted, desperately, to know if he cared for her, if he thought of her as more than a mother for the sons who'd inherit this ranch, if he regretted drawing the short straw.

"Where did you go?" was the only question she risked.

"I rode into town and went to the Golden Lady," he admitted without hesitation. "I figured I'd get blind drunk."

"You seem sober enough," she said stiffly.

"I am." He slid one hand into her hair. The thick sable length draped over his forearm and fell to her hips. He shifted his gaze away from it, his eyes meeting hers. "I also thought about finding myself some female companionship."

Eleanor stiffened as if she'd been shot, her entire body going rigid. Pain arced through her with the speed and force of a lightning bolt. Wasn't this exactly what she'd feared? She'd thought of the possibility, but thinking of it hadn't prepared her to deal with the reality of it. She would have wrenched herself away from him but Luke anticipated her reaction. His palm suddenly flattened against the small of her back, dragging her forward until her breasts pressed against the hard wall of his chest.

"I said I thought about it," he said sharply. "After drinking one whiskey, I realized that the only woman I wanted was the one I married."

All the stiffness drained from Eleanor's spine as she registered what he was saying. He wanted her. It wasn't the same as love, but it was something. Wanting could surely turn into love. Couldn't it?

"Luke."

It was surrender and they both knew it.

"Ellie." The diminutive was a caress.

His hand slid up her back, his fingers cupping the back of her head, turning her face up for his kiss. Eleanor melted into his embrace, surrendering to her own desires, giving in to the need that was a hollow ache in the pit of her stomach.

She felt as if, in a sense, this was their real wedding night. This first time that they came together without secrets between them. Unless you wanted to count as a secret the fact that she had fallen deeply, irrevocably in love with her husband.

Chapter Sixteen

For most of the country the Fourth of July was celebrated with picnics, parades, fireworks, music and speeches. Black Dog was no exception. Though the town didn't boast anything as elegant as a village green, there was a vacant lot behind the mercantile that was shaded by a pair of ancient cottonwoods. There was room enough to set up a small stage for the benefit of those who felt it necessary to make patriotic speeches. Ned Lewis could bow a lively tune on the fiddle and Billy Lee Beaverton could make a harmonica just about sit up and do tricks. It wasn't the sort of band you might find back east but it was plenty for dancing. There was horse racing with a good bit of betting on the outcome.

And of course, there was food. The women of the town spent the days prior to the Fourth cooking in preparation for the event. Kitchens already warm with the heat of summer grew warmer still from the frenzy of cooking. Chickens were fried, cakes and pies were baked. A pit was dug near the blacksmith shop and Bar-M-Bar beef was roasted over a slow fire, the smell of it drifting through the town.

If patriotism could be measured by the fervor with which this most patriotic of holidays was celebrated, then the citizens of Black Dog deserved to be counted as a highly patriotic bunch.

"Looks like half the country decided to come watch me win the race." Daniel slanted his brother a look of friendly challenge as he spoke.

"More likely they're hoping to see a repeat of last year when you got thrown into the horse tank in front of the livery," Luke said. "Now, that was worth coming a bit of distance to see."

"It wasn't all that interesting." Daniel's tone was repressive.

"I didn't see it myself, but I heard one or two people say that it was the highlight of the race," Letty chimed in helpfully.

"I didn't see it, either," Eleanor said. "But I do recall Uncle Zeb mentioning the incident."

"That horse was dumb as a post," Daniel said defensively. He had the harried look of a man backed into a corner. "She was always trying to throw me into a wall or grab hold of the bit so she could run me off a cliff.''

"Maybe she didn't like you," Luke suggested with friendly malice.

"I understand horses can be very particular about their riders," Eleanor said, looking solemn.

"I've heard that, too," Letty agreed.

Daniel gathered his dignity about him in an almost visible cloak. "Did it occur to any of you that I landed in that horse trough deliberately, in order to provide entertainment for everyone?''

His companions considered this idea. The three of them exchanged a glance, silently confirming their agreement. Three voices spoke as one.

"No."

Daniel's eyes widened in indignation. Before he could say anything, Eleanor and Letty dissolved in laughter. Luke gave his brother a grin.

"You might as well face it, little brother. You don't have a snowball's chance of winning this race. I'm going to win it this year, same as last. About the only contest you're likely to win is the pie eating contest. Although, now that I think about it, I hear Harvey Rutherford's youngest boy has been practicing all year. You might have some real competition there.''

"We'll see who's laughing when I win the race."

"Last year your horse got the best laugh."

Luke's dry comment provoked more laughter from the two women and even drew a quick, involuntary smile from Daniel.

"We'll see," he said.

"I guess we will."

"Maybe we should change the subject," Letty suggested, and earned a grateful look from Daniel.

"Let's go see how the beef is coming along," Luke said. "I'm going to be real hungry after I win the race."

The four of them angled their steps toward the blacksmith's. Even if they hadn't known where the cooking pit had been dug, they could have followed their noses to find it. As they stepped off the boardwalk and into the street, Daniel courteously offered his hand to Letty. But Eleanor didn't think it was courtesy that made him tuck Letty's hand into the crook of his arm. She saw color tint her friend's cheeks but she didn't pull away from his hold.

The small gesture added an extra fillip of pleasure to an already nearly perfect day. It would be so wonderful if Letty married Daniel. It might be too soon to start planning a wedding but there was certainly a strong attraction between the two of them, and the fact that Letty had agreed to attend the picnic in Daniel's company was very significant. In the years since she'd moved to Black Dog she'd steadfastly refused to be seen keeping company with any man. As a widow, her reputation was too fragile to risk. Yet, here she was, in broad daylight, walking where anyone could see them, with her hand on Daniel's arm.

If Letty married Daniel, life would be practically perfect. Eleanor turned her head to look up at Luke, thinking wistfully that true perfection would be possible only if she knew that Luke loved her. As if sensing her gaze, Luke glanced down at her, his eyes meeting hers. He smiled and Eleanor's heart thumped.

She wondered how it was possible that she hadn't realized sooner that she loved him. Looking back, she thought she might have fallen in love with him that day in the churchyard when Reverend Mulligan had introduced them. Certainly she must have been in love with him when she agreed to marry him. Or maybe she'd fallen in love the first time he made love to her with such tender care. It could even have been when he'd agreed to their sleeping apart for a time. It was impossible to pinpoint the moment, Eleanor admitted. It felt as if she'd loved him forever.

This past week had served to strengthen those feelings. She didn't think it was her imagination that there was a new warmth between them, a new understanding. There had been no reference to their quarrel. The grenadine had been neatly folded and placed in the bottom of Eleanor's sewing basket. It was too heavy to wear for summer but, come fall, she planned to make it up into the most beautiful gown she ever hoped to own.

"Watch your step," Luke said as they reached the boardwalk on the opposite side of the street. He'd had one hand set against the small of her back but now he took her elbow as she stepped up onto the boardwalk.

"Thank you." Eleanor smiled up at him. One lesson life had taught her was that happiness generally came from accepting what you had, rather than wishing for the moon. If Luke didn't love her, he at least cared for her. She could be content with that.

Luke wondered if it was possible that Eleanor was growing prettier by the day. Looking at her now, it didn't seem possible that this was the same girl he'd met after church all those weeks ago. He'd thought she was a quiet little thing, almost mousy. And he'd thought she might make him a biddable bride, not prone to fits of temper. Remembering, his smile took on a rueful edge. He'd certainly gotten a surprise there. In retrospect, he could see that the kind of woman he'd thought he wanted wouldn't have suited him at all. In fact, he couldn't imagine any woman who'd suit him half as well. He liked her spirit, liked the strength that fired it. The docile bride he'd set out to find would have bored him silly. He'd enjoyed watching Eleanor whip the hands into shape. And if that spirit and strength came with a temper to match, so be it. At least life would never be dull.

Even the time spent sleeping in the barn didn't seem so bad—at least, not in retrospect. He'd certainly enjoyed making up for lost time this past week, he thought. And he didn't doubt that Eleanor had enjoyed it, too. Looking at her now, in her prim buttercup yellow gown with her hair caught up in a neat twist, it was hard to believe that a few short hours ago she'd been a more than willing participant in their lovemaking.

She glanced up at him, her eyes questioning, and Luke realized he was standing in the middle of the boardwalk, staring at her.

"I was just noticing that you look very pretty today," he said. It was a partial truth. This certainly wasn't the place to tell her exactly what he'd been thinking.

"Thank you." Eleanor flushed with pleasure. She reached up to adjust her hat in a self-conscious gesture, unwittingly drawing Luke's attention to the one false note in her appearance. She was wearing that god-awful hat again. She must like the blasted thing, since she wore it so often. If he could figure a way to get it off her head today, he was going to have to see if he could get his horse to step on it.

Luke filed the thought away for consideration as he set his hand against the small of her back, urging her down the walkway to where Daniel and Letty were waiting. He ignored the knowing look in his brother's eyes. If he read the signs right, it wouldn't be long before Daniel fell into the parson's mousetrap himself. They'd see how smug he looked then.

In years past, Eleanor had never paid much attention to the horse race. She'd never seen much appeal in a bunch of grown men riding hell-for-leather down the middle of the street. The fact that the winner received a twenty-dollar gold piece didn't really seem reason enough for all the fuss everyone made about it. But this year was different. This year Luke was riding in the race. Of course, he'd ridden in it every Fourth of July for the past six years, but this was the first year he'd been her husband. Which was why she found herself standing on the edge of the boardwalk in front of Webb's waiting to hear the opening shot that would announce the beginning of the race.

Both sides of the street were crowded with spectators. Friendly wagers were still being placed. She'd overheard more than one man comment that Luke's gray couldn't be beat, which gave her a proprietary feeling of pride.

"You don't think Daniel will get thrown again, do you?" Letty sounded worried.

"I think his horse is the only one who could answer that." Eleanor glanced sideways at her friend. "You and Daniel seem to be getting very friendly."

She didn't worry about being overheard, despite the people around them. Everyone was involved in their own conversations and there was a certain privacy in being in the middle of a crowd.

Letty flushed. "He's...rather pleasant when one gets to know him," she said primly.

"Daniel could charm the stripes off a skunk," Eleanor summed up.

"Yes." There was a rueful edge to Letty's smile. "He certainly could. I just wish I could be sure there was something a little more substantial under his charm."

"I think he's quite smitten with you. Didn't he ask to carry your handkerchief in the race?"

Letty's blush deepened to an attractive shade of rose but when she spoke her tone was firmly pragmatic. "I doubt I'm the first woman to have her hanky carried in Daniel McLain's pocket. For all I know, he's asked half a dozen other girls for the same favor this very year."

"That would make quite a lump in his pocket, don't you think?" Eleanor asked teasingly. "You might as well admit it, Letty, Daniel is courting you, whether you like it or not."

Letty's pretty features grew wistful. "What worries me is that I like it very much."

They were interrupted before Eleanor could respond. "How lovely to see you, cousin."

Eleanor stiffened at the sound of Anabel's voice. She hadn't seen her cousin since her wedding day, but her luck had apparently run out. Forcing a pleasant smile, she turned to face the girl.

"Anabel." She couldn't manage a more enthusiastic greeting than that. Really, she could have gone to her grave quite happily without ever having to see her cousin again.

"It's been such a long time. I was starting to think Luke had you chained in the kitchen, which would hardly have been a surprise, since I've always suspected that he married you for your cooking."

Letty drew in a quick, angry breath. At the sound of it, Anabel widened her big blue eyes and her mouth rounded in a pretty little moue of regret. "I certainly didn't mean to suggest that was the *only* reason," she said hastily, managing to make it clear that that was exactly what she'd meant. "I'm sure there were . . . other reasons."

Unspoken was the fact that she couldn't imagine what they might have been.

Eleanor considered her cousin in silence for a moment. It occurred to her that she'd changed a great deal since her marriage to Luke. A few weeks ago Anabel's unpleasant innuendos would have upset her. But marriage—and Luke—had given her a new confidence. Looking at the younger girl, she was surprised to realize that her strongest feeling was one of pity. Underneath the hateful words was a very unhappy person. Considering the way she'd been hopelessly indulged by her parents, how could she be anything other than what she was. In a few years, when her beauty started to fade, she was going to be forced to take a look inside herself. Eleanor doubted she would like what she saw.

"You know, Anabel, if you'd learn to converse about something other than yourself or the failings of others, you might be a happier person."

Letty gasped, but Eleanor kept her eyes on her cousin. The fact that she spoke in a not unkind tone gave the words more impact than if her intention had been to cause pain. Anabel's perfect rosebud mouth dropped slightly open in shock and her china blue eyes widened in disbelief. She stared at her cousin as if seeing her for the first time. Perhaps she read something of what Eleanor was thinking. Her mouth closed with an almost audible snap and a tide of color rose from her throat to her forehead, giving her usually lovely complexion an ugly, mottled look. Her mouth worked but, before she could speak, a gunshot sounded from the far end of the street, signaling the start of the race.

Anabel was immediately forgotten as Eleanor spun toward the street. The shouts of the spectators lining either side of the street drowned out the thunder of hoofbeats, but Eleanor could feel the pounding rhythm of their pace coming through the boardwalk beneath her feet. Her blood seemed to pulse in the same rhythm, excitement welling up inside her as she leaned as far forward as she dared, straining for a first glimpse of the horses as they came around the curve in front of the Empire Hotel.

There they were! She thought she saw Luke's gray out in front but before she could be sure, she felt someone's hands flatten against her back. She had only an instant to register the sensation before she felt herself shoved forward. Already off-balance, Eleanor struggled to regain her footing. But a second shove sent her stumbling off the boardwalk and into the street. It might have been nothing more than a nasty prank. She had only to step back onto the boardwalk and the only harm done would have been to her dignity. It might have ended there but for the fact that, in trying to regain her balance, her toe caught in the hem of her dress. She stumbled forward and went to her knees in the middle of the dusty street.

She heard someone scream—Letty, perhaps? There were shouts of warning but they were distant things. All she could hear was the thunder of hoofbeats rushing toward her. All she could see was the solid wall of horses coming directly at her. And she knew she was about to die.

Luke's attention was focused solely on the narrow ribbon of street visible between his horse's ears. As far as he was concerned, it was a waste of time to worry about what the other contestants were doing. His only concern was to get the best speed out of his own animal. Seeing someone else creeping up on him wasn't going to give his horse any more speed or stamina than it already had. He was only peripherally aware of the spectators who lined the street, shouting encouragement to the riders. They were a blur of colorful gowns and somber suits.

Out the corner of his eye he caught a glimpse of a familiar shade of buttercup yellow. Eleanor. He was too far away to see her face, but he could see the eager tilt of her head beneath that god-awful hat and he knew she was watching him, cheering him on. The thought of seeing her sweet face lit with pride added to his determination to win.

And then, too quickly for him to determine what had happened, Eleanor was no longer standing on the boardwalk. She was stumbling into the street, falling to her knees in the dirt.

Luke thought his heart would stop. She was directly in the path of the racing horses. He saw her struggling to get to her feet, but there would never be time for her to get out of the way. The rider to his right saw her and pulled back on the reins, trying in vain to stop his horse, but there was no way the animal could be halted in time. Nor was there room for all the horses to go around her. The street was too narrow and there were too many riders. All these thoughts flashed through Luke's mind in the space between one heartbeat and the next. They all distilled down to one paralyzing realization.

Eleanor was going to die.

In that instant Luke felt his entire world crash down around him. She couldn't die. Without her, he might as well be dead himself.

She finally managed to get to her feet and turned to face the oncoming riders. He didn't know whether she was paralyzed with fear or simply recognized the impossibility of getting out of the way. He only knew that he'd die himself before he'd see her go down beneath the brutal pounding of the horses' hooves.

There was one chance, one slim chance. Luke dug the spurs into the gray's sides. Startled by the rude treatment, the gelding sprang forward with a sudden burst of speed. Luke leaned low in the saddle. Just as he had earlier in the race, he blocked out all thoughts of the other riders, focusing his attention on one thing and one thing only—his wife's slender and all-too-fragile figure. He knew the exact moment Eleanor realized what he was going to attempt. He saw the blank terror drain from her face to be replaced by a look of absolute trust. If there had been time, Luke would have offered up a prayer that her trust wasn't misplaced.

Leaning out of the saddle, he caught her under the arms, jerking her off her feet. He must have hurt her, but there was no time to worry about that. The muscles in his shoulders and arms strained as he dragged her partway across the saddle. She grabbed hold of his leg, her fingers digging into his flesh through the denim of his pants. Keeping one hand flat on her back, pressing her down across his thighs, he fought to control the gray with the other.

The gelding was well trained and placid by nature, but he was not at all happy with the recent turn of events and it took all of Luke's skills as a rider to stay in the saddle while drawing the frightened animal to a halt. By the time he had the gray under control, the race had ended in wild confusion as the riders who'd seen Eleanor fall dragged their animals to a halt and those who hadn't seen her thundered on to the end of the street and the finish line, bewildered to find themselves there in such small company.

Daniel drew his horse to a plunging halt nearby. He was out of the saddle immediately, his boots sending up puffs of dust as he covered the distance between them. He was reaching for Eleanor as he spoke.

"Is she all right?"

"I don't know." Luke let her slide into his brother's hold and then swung one leg over the saddle and dropped to the ground beside them. He reached out and snatched his wife from Daniel's hold, turning her toward him. "Are you hurt?"

His eyes raked her, seeking signs of injury. But other than the fact that her hair had come down and some streaks of dirt marred the soft golden yellow skirt of her gown, he could see no damage. Yet she hadn't said a word and her eyes seemed unfocused. His hands tightened on her shoulders.

"Ellie? What's wrong? Tell me where you're injured."

"I think she's just had the wind knocked out of her," Daniel said. He put his hand on Luke's shoulder to calm him. "The saddle horn probably caught her in the diaphragm."

As if to confirm his diagnosis, Eleanor suddenly drew a shallow, wheezing breath, followed by a second, deeper gulp of air. She blinked, the frightening blankness leaving her eyes. She focused on Luke.

"I'm not dead." She seemed surprised.

"God, no." Luke caught her in his arms. Now that the danger was past, he felt fear grab hold of him like a hand around his throat, choking off his breathing. He'd almost lost her. It had been so close. So very close. If the gray had been a little slower, if he'd stumbled. The cinch strap could have snapped under the added weight. There were a hundred and one things that could have gone wrong, all of them ending in disaster. "God."

His arms tightened around her, pressing her head into his shoulder. The fear he hadn't let himself feel earlier knotted his gut and made his skin icy cold, despite the summer sun beating down on them. He didn't know what he'd do if he lost her. She was the center of his world.

"I thought I'd lost you," he whispered against her hair.

"I thought you had, too." Eleanor clung to him, her knees shaking in the aftermath of her close call. "When I saw you, I knew you wouldn't let me die."

"Never. I'll never let you go." He wrapped one hand in her tousled hair and tilted her head back, his eyes searching her face. He'd never seen anything more beautiful than her trembling smile and the love and trust shining in her eyes.

"What happened?" Daniel's question reminded Luke that they weren't alone.

"I don't know." Luke loosened his hold on Eleanor slightly but kept one arm around her waist. He looked down at her. "What happened, honey?"

"I—"

"I'll tell you what happened." Letty's voice preceded her as, in a most unladylike way, she pushed through the crowd that had gathered around the McLains. There was a murmur of surprise and a few titters of nervous laughter when she stepped into sight. One hand was wrapped firmly around a fistful of golden curls, dragging Anabel's protesting figure with her literally by the hair. "This little cat pushed her. That's what happened."

"I did no such thing!" Anabel's denial ended on a shriek of pain as Letty tightened her hold. "You're going to scalp me!"

"It's no more than you deserve," Letty said fiercely.

"I agree, but it might be best if you let her go for the moment." Daniel stepped forward and gently pried her fingers loose. Putting one arm around her shoulders, he drew her against his side. "Perhaps you'd like to explain what happened, Miss Williams?" he invited coldly.

Anabel stared at Letty and the McLains, then looked at the people crowded around as if seeking a friendly face. But in her sixteen years there was hardly a citizen of Black Dog who hadn't felt the sharp edge of her tongue, and she found no sympathy among them.

"Here, now. Let us through." Zeb Williams's deep voice cleared a path through the crowd. "What's going on here? Are you injured, niece?"

"I'm all right, Uncle Zeb," Eleanor said quietly.

"What's going on?" Dorinda repeated her husband's question. Her eyes settled on her daughter. "What on earth happened to your hair, Anabel?"

Anabel looked from her mother to where Luke and Eleanor stood. Whatever she saw in their expressions, it wasn't the reassurance she wanted. Seeing disaster staring her in the face, she responded the only way possible. She burst into noisy sobs.

"Your daughter pushed my wife into the street in front of the oncoming horses," Luke said quietly. He turned cold gray eyes on Zeb Williams. "She was almost killed."

"That's ridiculous," Dorinda said, paling with shock. "Anabel? Tell them they're wrong, sweetheart."

"I saw her do it." Letty's voice was hard and angry. "She pushed her once and, when that wasn't enough, she pushed her again. She tried to kill Eleanor."

"I just wanted to scare her a little," Anabel said through her sobs, condemning herself with her own voice.

"Eleanor could have died," Luke repeated, still looking at Zeb.

Zeb Williams looked from Luke's hard face to the condemning expressions of those in the crowd.

He was a banker. His livelihood depended on his reputation. He might own half of the only bank in town but, if they were riled enough, folks might be willing to take their business to another town, even if it meant a long drive to get to the bank. He couldn't afford to have a speck of dust mar his reputation, and his daughter's actions today threatened to put considerably more than a speck on it. There was only one possibility to salvage the situation.

"Come along, Anabel. I think it's time you learned a lesson from the flat of my hand."

"Daddy!" Anabel's voice rose on a wail of shocked disbelief.

Stepping forward, he grabbed hold of his daughter's arm and jerked her after him as he strode through the crowd. There were a few helpful offers to continue the lesson should his arm tire too soon and a remarkable lack of sympathy for Anabel's continued wails. Dorinda trailed after them, looking as if she couldn't believe any of this was happening.

"I hope he beats her until she can't sit down for a month," Letty said vengefully as the Williamses disappeared from sight.

"Poor Anabel," Eleanor said with a sigh.

"*Poor* Anabel?" Luke asked incredulously. "She tried to kill you."

"No. I think she really was just trying to scare me. I can't help but feel a little sorry for her. I think this is the first time in her life she's had to bear the consequences of her actions."

"I'd wish I could show her a few consequences myself," Luke muttered, unmoved by Anabel's plight. His arm tightened around her. "I could have lost you today."

Eleanor looked up at him, her eyes questioning his fervor, but before she could say anything a new voice intruded. "Ma'am? Miz McLain?"

She turned to see Shorty Danvers approaching. "I'm real glad you're all right, ma'am."

"Thank you, Shorty."

His lean features drew down in regretful lines. "But I'm right sorry about your hat."

"My hat?" For the first time, Eleanor noticed the object he was carrying. Only a considerable feat of imagination could turn the squashed, torn item into a hat, but she recognized one of the fat roses that trailed from the twisted brim.

"The horses run right over it, ma'am." He poked one callused finger at the end of a frayed ribbon. "Don't reckon you can salvage much of it."

Eleanor felt Luke's chest shake. She glanced up at him just as he burst out laughing.

"Luke?" She didn't see what was so funny about her hat being ruined. True, she'd hated it, but new hats were expensive and she could have gotten at least another year's wear out of it.

"Throw it away, Shorty." He grinned at the other man. "Burn it."

"Sure thing, boss." Shorty looked as puzzled as Eleanor felt.

"What's so funny?" she asked.

She brought her hands up to rest against his chest as he turned her in his arms. "That was the ugliest hat I've ever seen," he said bluntly. "It getting trampled is the second luckiest thing that's happened to me in recent months."

Eleanor decided not to take offense at his comment about the hat, especially since she agreed with him. She stroked her hands over the soft fabric of his shirt, feeling the steady beat of his heart under her fingers.

"What's the luckiest thing that's happened to you?" she asked, savoring the feel of him holding her.

"The luckiest thing?" He brushed a dusty curl back from her forehead. In his face she saw a tenderness that made her heart stop. A tenderness and . . . something more? "The luckiest thing that ever happened to me was drawing that short straw," he said softly.

"Luke?" Surely she wasn't imagining what was in his eyes. Right here, in the middle of the dusty street, she was seeing all her dreams come true. "Luke?"

"I just wish I could lose like that every time," he murmured.

And right there in front of God and the citizens of Black Dog, Luke McLain kissed his bride, thanking the Lord for the wisdom that had made him draw the short straw.

* * * * *